JOURNEY TO MACKINAC ISLAND

By

Kileen Prather

To: Judy —
Happy journeys...
Kileen Prather
Oct 2021

Journey To Mackinac Island
by Kileen Prather
©2020 by Kileen Prather
Kileenp@gmail.com

Cover Design by Summer R. Morris

Printed in the United States of America
ISBN: 9780980216738

Author's Note:

This novel is a work of fiction. All of the main characters are fictitious and any resemblance to real persons is purely coincidental. Though settings, buildings and businesses exist, liberties may have been taken as to their actual location and description. This story has no purpose other than to entertain the reader.

I would like to thank the following for their invaluable assistance:

Chief Lawrence Horn   Chief of Police, Mackinac Island
Joe Chaloka, Sarah Wisdom, Suzanne Wells,and Micki Sigmon
for their invaluable advice
Nick Spencer and Nancy Becher for final editing

Once again I would like to dedicate this book to my
granddaughter, Isabel,
and my sons and brothers
May life bless all of you.

Time goes by and slips away
Just as the sky turns from blue to grey.
We are here only for a short stay.
Don't let life pass with words you never say.
Don't live in anger, with fear and regrets.
Seek forgiveness and lay your pain to rest.
Don't judge too quickly, as you may be wrong.
Instead, choose to live life as an uplifting song.
Crystal Lewis

For More Information ON My Books: Go to
www.kileenprather.com to read sample chapters
and to order ebooks or soft cover on Amazon. You can
email me at kileenp@gmail.co,
Look for travel articles on www.The-Journey-Books.com

Books by Kileen Prather:
Journey Ahead
Journey Beckons
Journey To Port
Journey To The Tropics
Journey On The Rails

CHAPTER 1

Hardly a cloud could be seen as the sun was shining brightly against a vivid azure sky. There was a crispness to the air, signaling the approaching fall. The ferry, less than half filled with people in the lower enclosed deck, was rapidly skimming across the water towards a large bridge. On the open top deck, filled with passengers, a moderately tall woman stood near the railing. The wind was whipping her shoulder length blond hair. She was wearing white pants with a blue and white lined rain jacket that looked like perfect apparel for a boat. Her bright blue eyes could not be seen behind her sunglasses but she had a hint of a smile that made people want to smile back at her.

Olivia had come prepared since she knew Lake Huron could be cold and windy even on a nice day. The ferry traveled back and forth to Mackinac Island every hour from Mackinaw City on the Lower Michigan Peninsula and from St. Ignace on the Upper Peninsula. She also remembered something from previous sailings that the others on top probably had not. As soon as the ferry got close and rounded the curve of the Island most people up on the top would get wet.

Next to her, similarly dressed, was a woman, tall and thin under her jacket, with bright red hair tied in a ponytail. If you could get close enough to her you would notice her green eyes and freckles under the baseball cap she wore.

Although the two of them were in their early fifties they seemed to have embraced that fact giving them both an appearance of youthfulness and a feeling of well-being in their own skin. Luckily they had inherited some good genes and did not look their age. But anyone knowing them knew they wouldn't fight the aging process either.

Ginger, smiling at her friend, said, "Isn't this exciting, Olivia? It's been thirty-five years since we've been on the Island. I can hardly wait to get there. I would bet very little has changed since we left."

Although there were ferries every hour, once a day the ferry company ran a special trip that included getting up close to the bridge. So they had chosen this particular sailing for that reason. "Mighty Mac" as the bridge was called was a five mile long suspension bridge that spanned the Straits of Mackinac connecting the Upper and Lower Peninsulas of Michigan. On the West side of the bridge was Lake Michigan and the Eastern side was Lake Huron; two of the Great Lakes. There was a small section of water which was comprised of the two lakes and that part of the water was called the Straits of Mackinac.

Envisioned in the 1880's the bridge was not completed until 1957. They listened as the Captain gave all the facts and figures about the bridge as the ferry came right underneath it. Everyone on top had their cell phones out taking pictures.

The two women heard people gasp when the Captain told them about the Bridge Walk. This annual event held every Labor Day closed this portion of I-75 down while the governor led anywhere from 40,000 to 65,000 people on the walk across the bridge. "That had to be quite a sight to see," a passenger remarked.

As the boat turned and headed towards the Island, the two friends started down the steps to the enclosed section. Sitting next to each other they watched as the land got closer and closer. "Look, Olivia, there is a sight I never get tired of seeing."

As she turned towards where Ginger was pointing nestled on the top of a hill sat the imposing Grand Hotel, painted all white. Although they couldn't see it they knew the structure was known to have the longest hotel porch in the world.

"Oh, Ginger, this is almost like coming home again, even if we were so very young when we were last here. The years have gone by so quickly I don't feel that old but I know I am."

Just then the boat rounded the curve of the Island and they heard a loud ruckus up top as the waves washed over the ferry and most people up top got wet. The two women looked at each other and laughed.

"We could have told them so, Ginger, but I know they wouldn't have listened to us. Can't you just sense a magical ambiance when the boat pulls into the dock? You get the feeling you are entering a whole different world. Don't you agree?"

"You're certainly right about that. I remember when we were here previously we never saw television or looked at a newspaper the whole summer. It was like we were closed off from the real world. Of course there were no smart phones or internet back then but even so, the outside world doesn't seem important when you are on the Island."

As the crew tied the ferry lines to the wharf, the two women gathered up their belongings so they would be ready to depart when the signal was given.

CHAPTER 2

As the ferry tied up to the dock all the passengers scrambled at once to get off the boat. Then they began walking the long wooden pier towards the town. As Olivia and Ginger sauntered along following everyone else, they went under a portico and ended up at the street where the downtown was located. There were people hustling and bustling all over the place but not a single car could be seen. All they could glimpse up and down the thoroughfare were horses, carriages, and wagons.

Their luggage had been tagged at the ferry office on the mainland, and they knew the bags would be delivered to the specific hotels listed on the tags. Meanwhile they spotted a carriage that said "Grand Hotel." They went over and the driver helped them in as they sat with four other people who were already seated.

"That's the lot of you," they heard the coachman say. "Don't worry about your bags. They will be taken to the hotel on a different cart and will be delivered directly to your rooms." Olivia and Ginger smiled at each other remembering that they were now guests and most visitors didn't know how the luggage system worked.

"Since it's too early for you to check in, I am going to take you on a tour of the Island, compliments of the hotel. Then when the tour is over I'll drop you off right where you register. The tour will not include going to Fort Mackinac but you can do that on your own. They have costumed guides who do interactive historical reenactments from Colonial times."

The carriage begin to make its way down Main Street with the driver informing them about the different places they were observing. The business section ended with a park on the left. "Look up that hill," the driver said. "Fort Mackinac is right up those stairs. That is one way you can get there."

Then he continued, "Otherwise up the road from the hotel, which you can either walk or bike to, is the Carriage House Museum. That's where you get on the special thirty-five passenger carriages that will drive you through the state park and take you to the fort. There are people at the fort dressed in costume as I previously mentioned and they will tell you the history of the place. It's quite an interesting thing to do while you are on the Island. Of course, you can also bike or take your own buggy through the park on your own."

As they continued along Ginger remarked, "The only thing missing is seeing the lilacs all over the place.

Remember when we came in early June both years we could smell them all over the Island for over two weeks."

Nodding her head at the reminder, it was thirty minutes later when the carriage stopped in front of the immense white building. They were on the street level and they were dropped off in front of a door where the check-in desk was located. They saw geraniums everywhere. Meanwhile up the stairs was the porch, that overlooked Lake Huron, lined with rocking chairs running the whole length. There were also yellow and white striped awnings all along the front of the hotel with American flags waving in the breeze.

After registering and getting their keys the women went down the hallway to the Garden Terrace area where the ice cream parlor was located. Although they had worked in the gift shop and at the check-in desk when they were here previously, they had also assisted when the ice cream shop needed extra help.

They both knew they would be served drinks and appetizers as well as a five course dinner that evening. So they decided they didn't want to eat a big lunch. As they were walking down the hallway towards the ice cream parlor they were both thinking about how they had come to be here.

Six months previously notices had been sent to anyone who had previously worked at the hotel when they were in college, offering special rates if they wanted to come anytime during the second week of September. That week was a slower time at the hotel because it was after Labor Day and before the autumn foliage rush began.

Olivia was retiring that spring as a high school social studies teacher and thought a week at "The Grand" in September sounded like fun. She had looked Ginger up on Facebook and reconnected with her. Ginger, had been a loan manager at her local bank for many years. She had also recently retired since she had inherited money when her parents had died in a car accident.

There had been six girls, all from the same college dorm, who had worked together for two summers in a row on the Island. There was special housing for the workers and each room contained three beds. Harper had been Olivia and Ginger's roommate and Ginger had stayed in touch with Harper through the years.

Since she was a travel writer, Ginger had enthusiastically followed her friend's career. She had married for the first time less than a year ago. When Ginger called Harper to ask her about coming with them, her friend had quickly agreed. Her husband, Jesse, whose first wife had died a few years previously, also thought it sounded like a fun thing to do. So Harper told Ginger to count them in and get back to her with all the details.

The other three girls from their school stayed in an adjoining room. Riley and Tess had shared their room with Bree. A lot of nights after work many of the kids had gotten together in groups and had partied. Because of this, they were all pretty close. Often they were invited to gatherings at the wealthy summer homes in the East and West Bluff neighborhoods, where the rich kids lived. However, their second summer Bree had met someone and had quit socializing with the rest of them. And then two weeks before their summer work was over she had mysteriously disappeared.

Since she had kept her relationship a secret, they didn't know who her boyfriend was, and the police had no idea who to question at first. The authorities had checked with the five girls who were living with her but no one knew anything. Bree had been a stunning looking girl. She hated college and often talked about running away to New York or Hollywood to become a star. She had a terrible relationship with her parents and believed they wouldn't care if she left.

After the police talked to her parents, the officers concluded that she must have run away. Ginger had never felt that was the real story but the other girls had, and they all hoped they would soon hear she had become a famous movie star.

It was harder to find Riley and Tess. Both of them had married and divorced several times and Olivia only found them through the committee in charge of class reunions at the college. The two of them had kept in touch with that committee every time they remarried and their names changed. Since both of those women had done quite well financially through their divorces, they told Olivia they were also up for a "grand" adventure.

Ginger, too, had been divorced. She had been in love with Flynn, who had worked as assistant to a vet at the Island Carriage Company all four of his college summers. He had volunteered at a local animal shelter while in high school and discovered his love of animals. So working around the horses had been a dream job for him. He had met Ginger at one of the parties the kids went to and they had been together both summers.

Since they went to college in different states, and Ginger didn't return to the Island the third summer, they began a long distance relationship. All his life it had been expected that he would marry "the girl next door" whose father was a partner in Flynn's dad's firm. His father was constantly pressuring him and so after college, with Ginger living so far away and seeing her less and less, he yielded to his father's wishes.

Although Flynn had done what his parents expected, neither he nor his wife were ever happy together.

When Ginger heard the news of Flynn's marriage she was devastated and married the first man who looked good to her. Naturally it had not worked out but they had stayed together for the sake of their daughter. Meanwhile Flynn's wife died from cancer but with Ginger married, and Flynn thought happily, he hid himself in work and tried to forget her.

Flynn got in early into the tech and fledgling computer field. After working for years he ended up cashing out a multi-millionaire. But he would rather have had someone to love by his side instead of all his wealth.

Ginger resolved to look him up after she and Olivia decided to go to the reunion. After all, they had dated years ago and, thinking he was probably happily married, she felt they could at least be friends.

Flynn got in early into the tech and fledgling computer field. After working for years he ended up cashing out a multi-millionaire. But he would rather have had someone to love by his side instead of all his wealth.

Ginger had loved her job and found it very fulfilling so she had buried herself in work. She had been alone for almost ten years but was too busy to worry about feeling lonely. Neither of them realized it but they were definitely star-crossed lovers. After her parents died, since she was financially secure, she made a decision to start spending more time traveling. So Olivia contacting her about the reunion came at the perfect time.

It didn't take Ginger long to find Flynn on social media. She thought it would be fun if the whole gang was together again. She knew he would not hear about the reunion since he had worked at the Carriage Company and not the hotel. She wanted to invite him and his wife if they were available. She was shocked when she discovered he had been a widower for years.

How they had wasted their lives. If only they had known each of them was free sooner. Who knows what might have been. But maybe he didn't have any feelings for her any more she considered. However, when she talked to him, he told her, he would love to come. He had plenty of time for travel and would find someone else to bring as his roommate.

"It's too bad we couldn't find Dylan to see if he was coming." Shocked Olivia told Ginger, "Even if he was free I don't think he would want to come with the way things ended between us." She was happy to discover they couldn't find him on social media. He probably would have skipped the reunion anyway since he was a doctor and taking a week off might be too hard for him.

Dylan had always wanted to be a doctor. Although he had worked as a carriage driver at the hotel all through college, he had also helped the vets with the horses any chance he could get. When they met each other the two men became fast friends for the four summers they were together.

When Dylan had met Olivia they had been inseparable like Ginger and Flynn had been. But after that second summer Olivia told him, she no longer wanted to date. She got cold feet when Dylan started planning their future together. She was worried he would want to marry right after college graduation. She, however, wanted time to explore the world before getting married and having children.

So Olivia had broken up with him. This was easier to do since they went to different schools and she wasn't going back to work on the Island the following summer. She felt regretful how she had ended things with him but at the time she felt a clean break was probably the best option.

Meanwhile the three of them had this new adventure to look forward to in the fall. Who knew what exciting events might occur or people they might meet. They never dreamed some occurrences might transpire to mar their pleasure or that new friends would enter their lives.

CHAPTER 3

Harper had already told them she and her husband wouldn't arrive until later. Flynn had not been sure what time he would get there either. However, he also told them he wouldn't show up until later in the afternoon. While checking in they told the desk clerk where they would be in case Riley and Tess checked in.

As they sat eating their ice cream sundaes at a small wrought-iron table, the two of them begin talking about their accommodations. Since there would be eight of them to share the costs, and after seeing pictures online, they had decided to splurge and rent the Masco Cottage for the cost of $18,000.00 for the week!

The Cottage was a four bedroom luxury suite in a renovated two-story cottage that was as old as the hotel itself. The building was connected to the east end of the hotel by a private walkway. Inside it was beautifully decorated and designed with colors of summer flowers including the blues of the sky and the lake. There were lots of bright colors throughout the cottage similar to the rooms inside the hotel; where they claimed no two rooms were decorated alike.

Downstairs the suite featured two bedrooms with private bathrooms. There was a kitchen with fully stocked refrigerator and bar. Dishes, glassware and napkins were provided, and there was a dishwasher, stove and small refrigerator. The living and dining room areas had cathedral ceilings. Upstairs were two bedrooms but only one bathroom. There was also a media parlor with sofas and chairs, and a big plasma TV as well as a Play Station.

Outside there was a private hot tub. Off the large dining/sitting room was an outside porch with patio chairs and tables, providing enough room for up to fifty persons to congregate. They thought that area might be perfect if they decided to have a group get-together or cocktail party sometime during the week.

They came to the conclusion it was a once in a lifetime experience, and at only a little over $2,200.00 a person it didn't seem too much for the week when all meals and drinks were included. Amenities when staying multiple nights also included the option of having dinner served in the bungalow. This featured a menu created specifically for them by their own personal chef.

Cocktails and hors d'oeuvres were served in the Cottage before dinner every night. And they could eat there or have a five course dinner in the 200-foot-long Salle a Manger main dining room in the hotel while listening to the orchestra play.

Since you had to dress to go into the hotel public areas after 6:30 p.m., and with everyone arriving later in the afternoon, they had pre-ordered dinner to be cooked by their private chef. That way everyone could sit at the dining room table together and catch up with each other while not worrying about dressing up and going out for dinner.

"We still have some time, Olivia, before we can get into the cottage. Why don't you tell me about your life since college?"

"I still can't believe it's been thirty-five years since we've seen each other. I'll be honest with you, Olivia. Since I found out about Flynn, I've been thinking how much our lives were wasted and messed up."

"How so?"

"The two of us really loved each other, as you know. And even though we went to different colleges after I stopped working up here we wrote letters to each other every week and got together every two to three months. But Flynn was under tremendous pressure to marry 'the girl next door'. Nancy's dad was a partner in Flynn's dad's law office. Even though neither of them were really in love with each other, it was a different time back then. And because of that they acceded to their parents' wishes. When I got ahold of him about he and his wife coming to this reunion he told me she had died from cancer years ago."

"That is really sad."

"I know. And I was devastated when I heard he got married. I was dating a new guy practically every week. Finally my mother told me I needed to settle down. I was so distressed about losing Flynn, I married the first man who seemed nice to me. Boy was that a mistake! We were so different and discovered we had nothing in common. By then we had our daughter, Amber, and decided to stay together for the sake of our child."

"It seems like your life got worse and worse."

"Yes, it did. Harry was seeing other women by that point and I buried myself in my work. I was a bank loan manager and loved the work. Meanwhile Harry found a woman he loved and practically moved in with her. However we did come together for all the important milestones in Amber's life. But the day after our daughter left for college, I was served with divorce papers. It was pretty amicable. We just split everything equally and as soon as the divorce was final he married his girlfriend.

"Didn't that bother you?"

"Not really. We had been living separate lives for so long I hardly felt I was married. And, like I said, I really loved my job. But last year my parents died in a car accident. I inherited some money, and since I had almost thirty years in at the bank at that time, I decided to retire. Besides my IRAs, the bank gave me a nice retirement package. I have put off vacations for so long I was determined to travel before I was too old to enjoy it. And now you are caught up to my life so far."

"Maybe since you are both free now, you and Flynn will get a second chance."

"I'm not sure, Olivia. Maybe it's too late for the two of us. I keep thinking we might have lost our chance. But who knows what fate has in store for anyone. But what about you? How did your life turn out?"

"I guess I'll never know if breaking up with Dylan was the right choice or not. I thought it was at the time. He was so intense and I knew he would want to get married as soon as we graduated. I also realized he'd be tied up for years in school becoming a doctor and I was scared I would feel trapped.

I really didn't want to be tied down, especially with children, and I also wanted to see the world. After I graduated, I got a job as a high school social studies teacher. I really liked it and then I got my Master's in classical history while I was working."

"It sounds like you were happy."

"I was. And every summer I would travel to Greece, Rome, Turkey, Egypt and anywhere else I was studying about. It was what I wanted at the time and I don't regret my choice. There were six of us teachers who bummed around together. Ben, the only other single one, was also a social studies teacher. We were often paired together since our other friends were couples. We had a lot in common and would travel together to save money. We eventually drifted into marriage. It was not a great passion like I had with Dylan but we were very compatible and I thought happy. But nine years after we got married Ben died in a boating accident."

"Oh, my gosh! That is so tragic!"

"It was. But like you, I loved my work and the years just seemed to fly by. My only regret is we never had children; but that obviously was not meant to be."

The two women sat silently finishing their ice cream after their revelations.

CHAPTER 4

Meanwhile as the women were finishing their ice cream, Flynn, who had decided to look up his old pal, Dylan, was driving on I-75 North towards Mackinaw City. It had turned into a beautiful Indian summer day with temperatures in the low 80's.

The two men were traveling in Flynn's convertible with the top down enjoying the beautiful weather as the north woods zipped by.

"I'm so glad you looked me up, Flynn. But since I'm not on social media how did you find me? I had gotten the invitation to the reunion but since I don't really go anywhere, I threw it away."

"I had a friend who was a doctor and he sent me a link about a doctor with your name. When I read the bio I knew immediately it was you. After that, it was easy to contact you. I worried you might not want to come to the reunion with the way things ended between you and Olivia. You never had a serious girlfriend after her, those last two years we worked on the Island. But you were so much a part of our group that it didn't seem right if you didn't come to the Island with the rest of us this week."

"Tell me, Flynn, what have you been up to all of these years?"

"Sometimes I think my life is like a Greek tragedy in a way. You know how much I loved Ginger. I am here to tell you that long distance relationships don't work! We wrote each other every week and saw each other five or six times a year the last two years we were in college. But since I lived in Ann Arbor and Ginger was in Madison it became harder and harder to visit. Eventually we saw less and less of each other."

"Yes, that makes for a tough relationship."

"And besides that my father kept pushing me to get together with Nancy, the girl who lived next door to us. My dad and her dad were law partners in the same firm and we were constantly paired together at the same parties and gatherings. My father incessantly berated me about Ginger. He said what we had was just an adolescent fling I would get over. I finally gave in thinking maybe he was right and married Nancy."

"That had to be so difficult for you."

"It was. Nancy just wanted to be married. She had no desire to work. She had been raised that her husband would take care of her the rest of her life. It was not long before we both discovered we really had nothing in common. She wanted to go to the Country Club several times a week. Meanwhile I was really getting engrossed with the whole new tech field that was opening up. The only good that came out of the marriage was our son, Peter. I never realized children could bring you such joy. And my son and I seemed to have an even greater bond since Nancy died when Peter was seven."

"Having children was something I never had a chance to experience."

"I feel sorry for you for that loss. My son and I are extremely close. And I haven't pushed him in any direction like my dad did to me. Don't get me wrong. I love my mom and dad but they are now retired and living in Florida which makes me happy. They were starting to coerce Peter and expecting him to become a lawyer. I let him know from the time he was old enough to understand that whatever he did with his life, if he was happy, I was happy. When my parents moved away he no longer had to put up with that pressure."

"You are very lucky you have such a good relationship with your son."

"I know I am. And the ironic thing is even though I never tried to influence him he ended up in the same career field as me. I had a software company I ended up selling for a lot of money. I would have let Peter take it over but he is more involved with the technical side of the industry so we both agreed I should get rid of it. But what about you? I know as a doctor your life has to have become so much better with computers."

"You're sure right about that, especially with the ability to research almost anything instantly. Sometimes I marvel at how much easier living is because of them. My life is like yours as far as finding any kind of true love. At first, I was devastated when Olivia broke up with me. But as I got older I began to understand. I think if we had married back then we would probably be divorced by now. Everyone needs a chance to grow, and I would have probably stifled her, especially with those old fashioned ideas of men and women's roles back then."

"That is undoubtedly true even if you hate to admit it to yourself."

"Yes, you are right. Anyway I worked hard to become an oncologist. There was a history of cancer in my family, and so I went into that field. Then a couple of years later I married my nurse. I thought I loved her but I know now I never really got over Olivia. Meanwhile Jane was having affairs with practically anyone she met. She was also big into the Country Club scene like your wife. It took me almost ten years before I realized what Jane was doing. I guess I was the only one who didn't know. My best friend made a comment about it thinking I knew. But I was shocked. We were divorced within six months."

"And you have been alone ever since?"

"Yes. I even changed the direction of my career. I decided to get into research. I guess it was my way of closing myself off to the world."

"Wow, we are both kind of messed up when it comes to women."

"You're right about that."

As they looked at the road ahead they saw a sign that said, Mackinaw City ten miles ahead.

"You know it seems weird how there is a Mackinaw City and a Mackinac Island, Flynn. And even stranger that the City is spelled and pronounced with a "w" and the Island is spelled with a 'c' but pronounced like a 'w'. I know that was due to both the French and British influences."

"Yes, most people who come here for the first time pronounce the Island wrong."

Meanwhile, as they were talking the convertible pulled into the ferry lot. The two men got their bags out of the trunk and walked towards the ferry office. They were both worried and excited about meeting the girls they had loved during their college lives.

It was often said that you never forgot your first love. In reality, it was possible to get past that and have a wonderful relationship with another person. However that was not the case for either of these two men.

CHAPTER 5

As Olivia and Ginger glanced back down the
hallway towards the check-in desk, they saw two very
overweight women, dressed in sweaters and jeans, coming
towards them.

"Hi you two. Ice cream sounds like a good idea.
Hang on while we go get some, and then we can sit and
chat with you. Riley and I have been so excited ever since
you called, and have been really looking forward to seeing
everyone again."

Both women, bleached blonds, looked tacky and out
of place in their surroundings. As they went for the ice
cream Olivia remarked, "I would never had recognized
them. Would you?" Ginger shook her head "no" at her
friend.

As they sat down with their ice cream, it was
obvious they had become very loud obnoxious women over
the years. Olivia knew having eight people to split the cost
of their accommodations was why they had rented the
house in the first place. But she wondered if it was going
to be a very long week with these two offensive women
sharing the place with the rest of them.

"It's good to see you two again," Ginger said as Olivia nodded in agreement. "As soon as you finish your ice cream, why don't we go check out our home for the week? They said it would be ready by 3:30 p.m. which it is now."

"I saw the pictures online and I hope we don't have to stay in one of those upstairs rooms. I hate climbing stairs. Tess and I feel with the money we are paying we should get a room on the first floor."

Thinking that climbing stairs in their obese condition was not a good idea anyway, Ginger said, "Don't worry ladies. We thought the four of us would take the two downstairs bedrooms and the men and Harper and her husband could take the two upstairs ones. Why don't we go check the place out and see what it looks like? Are you two ready?"

Going outside the two women complained non-stop about how long the walk was to the house from the hotel, even though they were right next door. Olivia and Ginger just looked at each other with trepidation. But that was all forgotten when they went inside the cottage and saw how amazing it appeared.

The first room when they entered was a large sitting room with a white wicker couch and chairs with cushions done in blue and white stripes. The room looked so fresh and clean and had a huge cathedral ceiling. There was a light oak table that seated four with two vases on top filled with blue hydrangeas. "That table would be perfect for playing cards," Ginger interjected.

Next they walked into the dining room which was connected to the living room. From a large opened ceiling hung a beautiful glass and blue chandelier. Below was a table that sat eight people comfortably. From there the kitchen could be seen and a library with wall to ceiling shelves filled with books.

There was a bright yellow bedroom that Olivia and Ginger said they would take. Next to that was a light blue room with checkered floors. Tess and Riley agreed they wanted that one. Geraniums were the hotel symbol and could be found everywhere. When they checked out the bathrooms they saw bars of geranium soap and geranium hand lotion which they knew could also be purchased in the hotel gift shop.

Upstairs was a red bedroom. Although one would think it would look tacky since the walls and carpet were done in red as well as the chairs in a dormer sitting area, it wasn't. There was a king sized bed with a red canopy and red bedspread. To top it off the seating in the dormer area overlooked the lake.

"If we didn't need two beds, I would have loved staying in this room. But it will be perfect for Harper and her husband," Ginger remarked.

Olivia noticed the two women snicker at each other when they heard what Ginger said. From there they moved on to the media room. The walls were a pretty lime green and the furniture was white wicker with light green and white cushions. There was a large built in plasma TV in the wall.

Finally the last bedroom had green carpet and multi-colored flowers for the wallpaper. The bedspreads were a peach and white color. "I guess the two men can stay here," Olivia said.

Meanwhile Riley and Tess were whispering back and forth. Then Olivia and Ginger heard, "Wait a minute. Tess and I want this room."

"But I thought you wanted to be downstairs," Olivia exclaimed.

"No, we changed our minds. We like this green room better. Besides the two of us watch a lot of television and we want to be closer to the media room. That way we don't have to go up and down stairs just to watch something."

Actually, Olivia and Ginger were very much relieved about the situation. This meant the two women would not be constantly hanging around the main part of the house. The more TV they watched, the better, the two of them were thinking. Little did they know they would soon regret thinking like that.

"That's fine. The bellman should be here with our luggage soon and we will make sure he gets your bags upstairs," Ginger answered.

Just then they heard noise below and thinking it was the bellman they went rapidly down the stairs. Much to their surprise two older men were standing there.

Ginger gasped and her eyes got wide when a man about 5'10" with salt and pepper hair and brown eyes turned and looked their way. Her stomach gave a lurch when she realized it was Flynn. He looked very dashing in his brown khakis and white dress shirt. He had slung a tied by the arms navy blue sweater over his shoulders.

She was speechless until Olivia standing behind her gave her a shove from the rear. That brought her back to reality. Starting down the stairs she and Flynn could hardly take their eyes off each other as Ginger heard herself say, "Hi, Flynn."

Meanwhile the other man who was over six feet tall also with salt and pepper hair, a mustache, and piercing blue eyes that seemed to look right through you, also turned towards them. He was dressed similar to Flynn but had navy pants and a beige sweater.

Oh, my gosh, no! Olivia thought as she stopped on the steps. It can't be Dylan. How in the world will I ever get through this week with him here? As the two women stared at the men they heard Tess in a loud repugnant voice behind them say, "Are you two going to move down the stairs or not?"

Just as they reached the bottom they heard a knock and the bellman came in. "I have all your luggage outside on a cart. Can someone direct me to which rooms the suitcases go into?"

That seemed to break the tension, and saying hello to Flynn and Dylan, Olivia told the man, "I will show you."

Meanwhile Ginger said to the men, "Let me show you to your room and after you get settled if you don't mind you can fix us all a drink. We have a fully stocked bar."

Ginger showed them the room that Riley and Tess were originally going to take. I have to try and act normal she told herself as she walked back to the living room. It was hard not to come back to reality when she heard the other two women complaining about being hungry.

"Why don't you go check out the kitchen? I'm sure you will find snacks in there."

Olivia was just finishing up showing the bellman the room the last bags went to when the women came out of the kitchen carrying cheese and large bags of crackers and pretzels. Tess had a small tray with two cans of Coke and a glass with ice. Riley had gotten two cans of beer out of the fridge by the wet bar and was carrying them one on top of the other.

"Thank goodness they had some decent snacks in there. That ice cream would never had held me until dinner."

Well we do have appetizers coming soon," Ginger said. And without looking at the two women she turned and walked into her bedroom.

"What am I going to do?" she half cried as Ginger entered the room. Without waiting for a reply she continued, "I can't believe Dylan is here. This is so awkward. My stomach is in knots and I know he probably just wants to go home now that he's seen I'm here. I am sure he hates me for what I did to him."

"You have to let that go, Olivia. Flynn told me before he went into his bedroom that he let Dylan know ahead of time you would be here. They are friends and he didn't want to put him in an uncomfortable position. Your break up was thirty five years ago and Dylan told him he was over it a long time ago. He also told Flynn he hoped you might be friends."

"Really? He really said that? I guess if he can let go of what happened in the past I can, too."

"Exactly. Now go wash your face and let's go have a drink and see what these men have been up to these last thirty five years."

The men came out of their room at the same time as Olivia and Ginger. Heading towards the bar they heard Flynn say, "And who are you two lovely ladies?"

Tess stopped shoving potato chips in her mouth long enough to say, "Flynn, don't you remember us? It's Riley and Tess. I know we have all changed a little bit but then we have all gotten older."

Olivia turned her head to keep from laughing in front of them and met Dylan's eyes. He too had a grin on his face.

Then she heard Flynn say, "Of course, how stupid of me. I should have guessed it was you two."

She noticed Riley saying something to her friend and then Tess continued. "I know we haven't changed much over the years but since we both used to be brunettes I'm sure the blond hair made us look different." As Flynn nodded his head in agreement she continued, "If you don't mind, Riley and I are going upstairs to unpack and see what's on TV."

Leaving their empty cans on the table they grabbed another Coke and beer and taking their snacks waddled up the stairs. It wasn't long before they heard the TV playing.

CHAPTER 6

"What can we get you two ladies to drink," Dylan asked with a twinkle in his eye.

"At this point surprise us," Ginger said. "Since the weather is still nice outside, why don't we take our drinks and sit out on the patio? I can help you carry them out. Olivia why don't you and Dylan go outside and organize the table and chairs and we'll bring the drinks?"

Following their advice Dylan held the door opened as Olivia went outside. They saw two small tables with chairs down on the grass and they moved them up onto their porch facing the water.

As they sat Dylan said, "Wow those two are really something, aren't they? They said they had not changed much except for their hair color. But I think it is obvious people look different when they put on over one hundred pounds."

Knowing he was referring to Riley and Tess, she said, "Ginger and I didn't recognize them when we first saw them either. I know it's been thirty five years but they came right up to our table and started talking, so they must have known it was us. We were worried about them when we saw them. They complained they wanted a bedroom on the first floor and whined about the walk over here. Then when the only TV was upstairs they wanted a room on the second floor. On top of that, we all had ice cream before we could get into the cottage and then you heard them just now grumbling about being hungry."

"I felt a little embarrassed when Flynn and I didn't know them. But how can you recognize someone who has bleached their hair and added at least a hundred pounds as I mentioned previously?"

"I told Ginger we got really lucky. I was worried they would be constantly around interrupting us if they were in a downstairs bedroom. Then just before you got here they said they wanted to be upstairs so they could watch television, which made us happy. I can put up with a little TV noise as long as they are not whining around us continuously about other things."

"You're right about that. And maybe we can convince them to keep the media room door closed when they are in there."

Nodding in agreement he continued, "Look Olivia. I know I took you by surprise when I showed up here. I don't want to make you uncomfortable. I took our break up hard at first but I came to peace with it. I finally understood that I was rushing things. You needed your space and I realized much later I would probably have smothered you." He looked towards the water as he finished speaking.

"Thank you for saying that. I am glad you accepted why I did what I did. I was sad for a long time after we parted but I knew it was for the best at the time."

Just at that moment Flynn and Ginger walked outside with a pitcher of martinis and glasses. "I know I don't drink a lot anymore. But a martini now and some wine with our meal sounds perfect tonight. We should take advantage of the fact that it is free. Not only that but it is Tanqueray gin," he said, sounding pleased.

"Why don't we catch each other up on our lives these past years?" Flynn asked.

As they sat sipping their drinks they each described a shortened version of their lives since they had last seen each other. As they were finishing up, they saw a couple walking towards them,

Jumping up Ginger said, "It's Harper. I would recognize her anywhere."

They watched as a man and a woman came walking towards them. The man was of medium stature, very muscular, wearing glasses and with short cropped brown hair. The two of them were about the same height. He had on gray pants and a white dress shirt similar to the other two men. He was also wearing a navy blue blazer. Next to him the woman had on a headband holding back her long jet black hair. She was wearing white pants like the other two women and a red sweater.

Running towards the woman, Olivia and Ginger embraced her. As they walked back to where the men were sitting, Harper introduced her husband to the group. Jesse had thoughtful brown eyes that matched his hair. He seemed like a nice man. He told them all that he was an accountant.

Harper's grey eyes lit up as she watched her husband talking. The two women knew she was a travel writer and had met her future husband while he was auditing the books at a hotel she visited often. Jesse had inherited money from his first wife but still liked working. He was now an independent auditor which allowed him to go along on some of Harper's work trips. They seemed like a good match.

Since the weather was cooling down they decided to take their cocktails in doors. They wanted to show Harper and her husband to their room. All four traipsed upstairs behind the couple because the men wanted to see what the bedroom looked like before the couple settled in. Riley and Tess were sitting in the media room and barely paid attention to the newcomers.

"Our show is on," Tess said. "We'll see you at 6:00 p.m. for appetizers and dinner." And with that she shut the door to the media room.

The six of them realized they were all very compatible and were relieved to know the other two women would not spend much time around them.

"As soon as you two get organized why don't you join us for drinks? We are having martinis or you can have whatever else you might want," Olivia said as the four of them turned and went back down the stairs.

CHAPTER 7

As they came down the steps they heard the bellman coming with the last set of bags. Directing him up to the second floor, he took the bags to Harper and Jesse's room. The door was now opened to the Media room. He saw soda and beer cans and empty snack bags all over the room. He knew the turn-down maid would have her work cut out for here around these guests. He wondered if some people were messier when they stayed at a place with a "No tipping policy." Probably not he thought to himself. He'd bet their houses were just as messy.

Meanwhile the four of them went into the living room, which felt more like a sunroom. As Dylan was refreshing their drinks, Harper and Jesse joined them.

"I will have one of those," Jesse said as Harper nodded in agreement. "It's so good to finally be here. We had to make a stop on the way up. The last one hundred and fifty miles seemed to take forever with nothing but forests."

"Where do you live?" Flynn asked.

"We live in a suburb just north of Milwaukee and we came up through Green Bay and across the Upper Peninsula. We took the ferry from St. Ignace. But I have to say Harper said it would be worth the trip, and it certainly seems to be so far."

"And you haven't even seen the inside of the hotel yet, darling."

"How about all of you," Jesse asked. "Where do you all live?"

"It is kind of ironic," Olivia said. "The four of us discovered, as we were talking on the patio just now, that we all live in the Chicago area. Here we've been living close to each other all these years and didn't even know it."

"That is pretty weird," Jesse replied. Then he continued, "As we were driving I wondered what it would be like to be on an Island with no cars. The year round residents must be used to it. I read there are only six hundred people who live here year round. And there are five hundred horses brought to the Island in the summer. Looking at the hotel's website it seems like there are a lot of activities here so I don't think any of us will get bored."

"There is a lot to do but naturally it's at a much slower pace," Dylan reassured him. Tomorrow Flynn and I have a tee time at 10:00 a.m. to play eighteen holes of golf. Do you want to join us, Jesse?"

Looking at Harper who was nodding her head in agreement he said, "I would love to. I know you have all worked here before so you know the Island well but I want to experience everything. And, Harper told me she wanted to spend some time tomorrow morning catching up with her friends if they are agreeable."

"We would love that, too," Ginger interjected. "We'll have plenty of time to ride bikes, swim, and play tennis. We also want to visit Fort Mackinac and naturally do a little shopping. I'm not sure what you read about the hotel?"

"I read about the butterfly conservatory and definitely want to visit the place. It is called Wings of Mackinac. It is the first of its kind in Michigan and the third oldest live butterfly exhibit in the United States. It is a world renowned facility with eighteen hundred square feet filled with hundreds of live butterflies from four continents. In case you haven't guessed, I have always been fascinated by butterflies," Jesse told them.

"And don't forget there is Afternoon Tea, although with all the food that is included I don't think we will have room for that. Lunch is a buffet and we would probably be better off skipping that, too. Maybe we could get something light at one of the restaurants outside the hotel. We have lots of choices like The Gate House or the Sushi House which is adjacent to the other. There is also The

Jockey Club at the Grand Stand which is located at the first hole of the golf course. And it might be fun some night to take a carriage ride down to the Woods Restaurant. They serve Bavarian style dishes in a relaxed atmosphere. And there is a duckpin bowling alley located there, too."

"All of that sounds like a lot of fun but if we want to try those places we'll probably need to stay here another week," Harper said with a laugh.

"If we go to breakfast together every morning we can go over the daily activities in the TODAY paper. There is croquet or bocce and if we are out at the pool in the afternoon there are free snow cones. It is only about a fifteen minute walk to downtown and I'm sure everyone will want to get T-shirts and other souvenirs at some point," Ginger continued.

"And don't forget Dylan and I talked about doing the eight mile bike ride around the Island. We will take Lake Shore Drive which is an actual highway called M-185. It's strange to have a highway when there aren't any cars here," Flynn said.

"Are there a lot of hills on the bike ride?" Harper asked. "I guess I was too busy working to ever bike around the Island."

"No. Amazingly the perimeter of the Island is pretty flat. You only get the hills as you travel inland."

Time passed very quickly as they sipped their drinks and chatted. Before they knew it Riley and Tess came down the stairs and greeted Jesse pleasantly. They barely looked at Harper. Both Ginger and Olivia wondered what that was all about.

"Where are the appetizers?" the two women asked loudly.

Just then they heard a knock and the waiter came in with a tray filled with food. They couldn't believe their eyes when their server arrived. Usually the wait staff was from Montego Bay but instead they immediately recognized Neal.

He had lived on the Island his entire life and worked as a supervisor in the carriage shop helping with the brushing, feeding, washing and taking the harnesses on and off the horses. It was just in the last few years he had moved to working with the horse stables for the hotel. He was not comfortable working around a lot of people and much preferred the smaller work environment "The Grand" afforded him.

Neal was a short, beefy man with a tanned weather beaten face from spending so much time out in the sun. He had big, strong hands hardened from his work with enormous callouses. He had been an athlete when he was younger but was not spectacularly built. He had a full strong neck and looked every bit of his age, if not more, especially with his black hair mostly streaked with gray. Nevertheless the women had recognized him immediately.

"Neal it's good to see you again but how did you happen to be our waiter," Harper inquired? "I thought only the men from Montego Bay were the waiters."

"I heard you had registered for the reunion and when I saw you were renting the Mateo Cottage, I asked if I could be your waiter for old times' sake. I thought it would be fun to see you all again."

Because Neal was their age he had partied with them when they had worked on the Island. As they moved to the dining room table, Tess and Riley fawned all over him. The other five just looked at each other with their eyebrows raised.

CHAPTER 8

Since they had already had appetizers with their drinks, the first course served was salad. And it was delicious. It was made from romaine lettuce with lots of fresh vegetables that looked and tasted like they had come out of a garden.

Neal, coming out with a tray of glasses filled with wine, told them there now was a special garden behind the hotel where the grounds men grew herbs and vegetables for the chefs to use when cooking. He then went around the table placing a glass of white wine by each setting.

"I don't like wine," Riley said. "I want a beer."

"And I want a Coke, chilled with ice," Tess added.

Harper rolled her eyes at Neal as he took their wine glasses away and hurried to the kitchen area to satisfy their demands.

They had chosen a fish dinner of northern pike and they all felt the chef had outdone himself. They especially enjoyed the tiramisu they had for dessert. As they were finishing up Olivia brought up the subject of breakfast.

When asked if they wanted to join the others for breakfast, Riley told them that she and Tess were going to eat as soon as the restaurant opened at 7:30 a.m. At that point the women got up from the table telling everyone they had a show on television they wanted to see. On their way out they asked Neal to bring them up some soda, beer and snacks for the evening as soon as he had time.

"They didn't even say goodnight," Ginger observed.

"Well, it's a good thing we don't want to watch TV because they probably wouldn't let us in that room. I noticed the place had cans and snack bags all over when we came down before dinner. That poor maid who was turning down our beds, as we were eating, probably had a mess dealing with that."

"Let's forget about them," Dylan said.

"Harper, I meant to ask you, is that a penguin pin you are wearing on your sweater? It's small but colorful with just a touch of red mixed with the black and white."

"It is, Ginger. For our honeymoon we went on a cruise to South America. It started in Buenos Aires and went south to the tip and then back around on the Pacific Ocean side north to Santiago, Chili."

"Sweetheart can I tell them about our journey?"

"Oh, dear. I think you're in for it now. Jesse just loves talking about our trips, especially regarding geography and animals."

At that point Jesse began telling his story. "First of all, I don't know if you are aware of the geography in that area. At the bottom of the continent is Tierra del Fuego,

meaning 'Land of Fire.' Both Argentina and Chile share
the territory. It is an archipelago, and if you remember
from science that means a few islands. It sits across the
Strait of Magellan, naturally named after the explorer who
was there in 1519. A Strait, just like up here at Mackinac,
means a narrow passage of water connecting two other
large areas of water. In South America it is a navigable
waterway which separates the archipelago from the
continental mainland and actually connects the Atlantic
Ocean to the Pacific Ocean. I hope that makes sense."

Just as Harper was about to say something Flynn
jumped in. "I don't know about the rest of you but I find
what Jesse is talking about fascinating. I always wanted to
travel to that area."

"The land down there is very unique. The Tierra
del Fuego is part of Patagonia. In that region, there are
national parks, lakes, rivers and immense untouched
corners of the world. And at the very tip is the quaint town
of Ushuaia, the capital and biggest city of the archipelago.
The city is the jumping off point for expeditions to
Antarctica and there are signs when you visit calling the
city 'The End of the World.'"

"That's amazing, Jesse. Now I really want to visit
there."

Nodding his head he continued, "When we cruised
that area we both agreed we weren't as impressed with the

Eastern side of South America that borders the Atlantic Ocean. It was pretty flat and not a lot of vegetation but that is where we saw the Magellan penguins. We went to a national park and walked across sand dunes and suddenly they were everywhere. They would go back and forth to the sea and some would peek out of their burrows. It was obvious that humans didn't bother them. Since they are protected they must have felt safe. I could go on and on since there are several different penguin species but I'll save that talk for another day."

Laughing, Harper nodded in agreement.

"As I said, Flynn, the Atlantic Ocean side is pretty ordinary. But if you visit that part of South America make sure you travel up through Chile along the Pacific Ocean. That area of the continent is spectacular. We went into fjords and saw glaciers moving right into the sea. Then we visited an area known as 'the lakes region.' And although very dangerous since it is part of the 'Ring of Fire' the volcanoes there are an awesome sight. Different sources put the number of volcanoes between ninety and one hundred and five and most of them are active. I hope the rest of you didn't mind my narrative. I really loved going there as well as talking about the experience."

"We can tell you loved that area and didn't mind listening to you at all. Actually I think we all found it enlightening. Thank you for sharing that with us, Jesse," Dylan replied.

After his account of their South American travels, since Harper and Jesse were tired from their journey to the Island, they decided to go to their bedroom to read. They just hoped the TV wouldn't be too loud.

After saying goodnight to everyone, Olivia reminded them, "Don't forget to check your room." The maid was here to turn down our beds and she should have left a copy of the TODAY newspaper. They leave one in the rooms each night and the most important thing to look for is the list of daily activities for tomorrow."

"Thanks, Olivia, we'll be sure and do that," the couple said as they went up the stairs.

They all agreed to meet in the morning at 8:30 a.m. to walk to breakfast together. Since breakfast ended at 9:30 a.m. that would give them enough time to eat and then the men could make their tee time. After Harper and Jesse left, the four of them went into the living room. Sitting down at the smaller table that was placed there they began to play cards.

As they finished their first round of cards, Neal was finishing up cleaning in the dining room. He put all the dishes into the dishwasher and started it. Then he made some microwave popcorn. Next, he put two cans of soda and two cans of beer with some glasses and an ice bucket on a tray and added a couple of bags of chips and pretzels. He then made his way up the stairs to deliver the snacks to the two women who were sitting in the Media room watching television. After he served them, on his way out the door he told everyone to have a good night.

CHAPTER 9

It was 8:30 a.m. when the six of them met in the sitting room and started on the walkway to the hotel for breakfast. The breakfast menu included a wide selection of entrees including omelets, eggs any style, hot and cold cereals, pancakes and French toast with real Michigan maple syrup, hot oatmeal, breakfast meats, salmon, steak, fresh breads and pastries, fresh juices, fruits and more.

You could also choose a full buffet if you didn't want to order off the menu. For non-paying guests the price was $27.00 so they knew it would be quite extensive.

On their way out the door Ginger noticed that Harper didn't look too well and asked her about it. "I think either that wine or something I ate last evening didn't agree with me. I was up sick most of the night. I almost had Jesse call the doctor when my heart started beating rapidly. But then it slowed down. My hand was even trembling but after I threw up I felt a little better. However my fingers were a little numb for a while. I definitely ate something that didn't agree with me."

"I wanted to call the doctor," Jesse told them, "but she kept saying she would be okay. And you never told me about those other symptoms or I would have called immediately."

"I didn't want to worry you. As you can see I am much better this morning. I am feeling like I will live again. I thought some tea and toast would help me feel a lot better. I really wanted to walk with you girls after breakfast while the men go golfing. With all the travel writing I do and places I visit I can't believe I have never stayed at this hotel for my job. My boss agreed to pay some of my expenses if I write an article about the hotel and the Island. Essentially he is paying for my part of the hotel so we only have to pay Jesse's share ourselves."

"That is a really good deal," Ginger agreed.

As they walked through the hallway into the parlor Jesse gave a low whistle and they realized he had never seen the inside of the hotel. There was a long narrow walkway through the parlor to get to the dining room. The walls and ceilings were painted a light lime green with white pillars throughout. The carpet was a checkered red, black and white. There were loveseats and chairs spread all over the area in red and green. Hanging from the ceiling were several chandeliers.

When they entered the dining room Jesse looked around in amazement. It stretched back two hundred feet and he noticed a side extension about half way down as they were taken to their table. There was also an alcove by the extension and Jesse thought that was probably where the orchestra played during dinner.

The waiters were all from Montego Bay in Jamaica and many of them came with their wives who worked in housekeeping. The hotel was only opened from late April through October and these people had been coming to work at the hotel, in some cases, for generations. Then they went back to their country in the winter and were able to live a wealthy lifestyle from the money they made in Michigan each summer.

All the tables had white tablecloths and all the chairs were either a solid green or white and green striped. The walls were a pale apricot and the carpet had some kind of green and orange running through it. There were lights hanging from the ceiling with the lampshades a flowery fabric orange pattern. With the sun shining in from the windows it gave the room a light cheerful feeling.

Olivia remarked to the group how she loved the way they mixed pastels that a person wouldn't normally think would go together. But somehow here at "The Grand" each room seemed perfect.

After a leisurely breakfast the men left for their golf game and the women walked to the east end of the porch near their cottage and sat in the rockers.

"I know we all worked here," Harper began, "but I have done some extensive research on the history of the hotel for my article and I thought you would be interested to hear about it before we go find the Secret Garden."

"What and where is the Secret Garden?" the other two women asked simultaneously.

"The garden has only been around for a couple of years but has become an instant sensation. I know the general vicinity so we'll go look for it after we sit here awhile."

Both Ginger and Olivia were worried about their friend. She had not looked too bad during breakfast but now just walking to the end of the porch had seemed to tire her out.

"As to the history you probably won't remember all the facts and dates I tell you but it will give you a great feel for the place. Tomorrow I am supposed to go on a tour of the hotel for my article so maybe you will want to tag along. It will be a great way to see some of the special suites we might not normally get a chance to see. And I have always been interested in seeing some of the behind the scenes places, like the kitchen, that we never saw when we worked here. Remember how we had our own little dining area in the back."

Little did they know that tour of the hotel would not be happening as Harper continued giving them her history lesson.

She began, "Some of the basic facts we probably all know about like the six hundred sixty foot front porch - the longest in the world - where we are now sitting. There are three hundred ninety seven individually decorated rooms. I'm looking forward to seeing some of those tomorrow because many were renovated since we were here. Then down the lawn from us is the two hundred twenty foot swimming pool, four tennis courts and a full-service spa. And the historic 18-hole golf course across the street where the men are now."

Then she continued, "We talked about all the dining options last night but in addition there is afternoon tea in the parlor, dressing up for dinner, nightly dancing to the sounds of the Grand Hotel Orchestra, and sitting in a rocking chair. Since we are doing that right now we can cross that off our bucket list of things to do here. Also new since we were here is the Cupola Bar which is up a flight of stairs only accessed from the 4th floor. A friend told me if we go up there and take in the view before dinner, at this time of the year, we should see the sunset over the strait with the bridge in the foreground."

"Maybe we should go find the Cupola Bar after we go to the Secret Garden so we know where it is," Olivia remarked.

Nodding her head in agreement Harper continued. "Let's start at the beginning. Back in the late 1880s railroad men like J.J. Hill from the Great Northern Railroad began building hotels and lodges all over the West because people would have to ride their trains to get to those places. It was no different here. A couple of railroad businesses and a steamship company got together in 1886 and formed the Mackinac Island Hotel Company. The next year the hotel opened and vacationers arrived by lake steamer from Chicago, Erie, Montreal, Detroit, and by rail from across the continent. Can you imagine rates were only $3.00 to $5.00 a night?"

Pausing for a couple of seconds, she continued, "In the 1890s the Front Porch became a promenade and meeting place for the elderly as well as the Island romantics. In 1895 Mark Twain gave a lecture here. By the early 1900s the automobile came to the Island but visitors thought they were too noisy and they passed a law to prohibit them. But that law was not strictly enforced until the 1930s."

"I am impressed. You really did your research," Olivia told her.

"As I walk around, it benefits me to have the history in my head. I am better able to picture the order of my story and that's why I'm telling you all this. Anyway by 1919 rates were up to $6 a day. That was the year W. Stewart Woodfill, was hired as a desk clerk. He then bought the hotel in 1933 and there is now a suite dedicated to him. In 1960 he appointed R.D. (Dan) Musser as president and then sold him the hotel in 1979. The Musser's have owned the hotel over eighty five years but just sold it this last fall to KSL Capital Partners. The Davidson Hotels & Resorts will manage the hotel from now on. I hope I am not boring you with too many facts."

"No, not at all," Olivia replied. "I love history and I think it's interesting that this hotel has not had very many owners over its lifetime.

"Well now for some fun facts. In 1947 Esther Williams, the movie star who had won Olympic Gold for swimming, made a movie here. You probably know they named the swimming pool after her. There was also some other films done here. But I think everyone is most aware that in 1979 the movie *Somewhere In Time* was filmed at the hotel starring Christopher Reeve, Jane Seymour and Christopher Plummer. It was released a few years before we started working here. And now every year the last weekend in October before the hotel closes they have a

Somewhere in Time weekend and everyone comes dressed in Victorian outfits and relive those early days."

"You know, I always wanted to come sometime for that event. Maybe we should think about doing it next fall. There are some beautiful rooms and suites inside the hotel. As much as I love staying in the Cottage, it would also be fun to stay in the hotel, too," Olivia added.

"Yes, that does sound like a great idea," Ginger replied.

Continuing with her history Harper said, "The 1980s and 1990s saw several developments. In 1987 the Cupola Bar was added and The Jewel golf course was renovated. By 1994 nine holes were added and the golf course became 18 holes."

Taking a breath she continued, "In 1998 five new 'Named Rooms' in honor of former First Ladies Lady Bird Johnson, Betty Ford, Rosalynn Carter, Nancy Reagan and Barbara Bush were included in the west end of the hotel. Later they added the Jacqueline Kennedy Suite in 2002, the Jane Seymour Suite in 2005, and finally in 2011 the Laura Bush suite became the seventh First Lady Named Room."

As they continued rocking and looking out at the water, Harper continued. "Some note-worthy events were in 2003, the Masco Cottage where we are staying was opened. And, in 2006, The Gate House, a casual bar and restaurant was added to the Hotel's offsite dining options.

That's the white building just down the hill from us. Also that year the hotel welcomed its 5,000,000th overnight guest. In 2016 the fifth off-site restaurant, Sushi Grand, was added adjacent to The Gate House."

Concluding, she said, "To me the most impressive thing is that the hotel has been certified as a Green Lodging Michigan Leader. In 2016 they installed a state-of-the-art air-conditioning system that uses water for cooling guest rooms which is then used to heat the swimming pool. The last major change, which we have already talked about, was in 2018 when work began on the Secret Garden. But I'll tell you about that when we walk down and find it. That's it for the history and I hope you weren't bored with my narrative. I have been trying to put all the facts together in my head for my article, and sometimes it helps to talk out loud about what I plan to write."

Reassuring her they had enjoyed her narration they sat in peaceful contemplation for a little while.

CHAPTER 10

As the three of them got up from their rockers, Ginger announced, "I could sit here half the afternoon reading my book."

"I know what you mean," Harper added. "But let's go find the Secret Garden." Pointing to the yard down the hill to the left, "It's over there somewhere," she said.

They went down the large staircase to the street where the bellman's desk was located. From there they crossed the street and continued down another long staircase. When they reached the grass they went left towards some tall bushes.

They stopped for a minute because Harper was winded and tired. Then they continued on and saw a break in the shrubs. "Maybe it's in there," Olivia stated.

As they continued on the narrow path between the vegetation all of a sudden a large area opened up. Flowers were everywhere and a wide area with grape hyacinths and a bridge over them had been planted to look like a flowing river. A bench was there and a winded Harper sat down. "There are over 22,000 hyacinths that make up that river of flowers," she told them.

"A couple of years ago the head gardener kept walking by this cedar grove. For years it was a brush pile for garden debris. He knew the compost pile had made the soil very rich underneath and he decided to work on the area in his off time.

Eventually the ground workers helped him take out one hundred trailer loads of landscaping debris before he started planting. He decided to separate it into perennial and annual sides. He wanted the spring bulbs to be handpicked as their blooms faded and then replaced by summer annuals that would last through the fall. And this was the result."

"It's so beautiful and peaceful here. I can see why this place became a media sensation.

When she was finished speaking, they looked around and took some pictures which gave Harper a chance to rest.

Finally, Ginger asked with concern in her voice for her friend, "Are you ready to find the Cupola Bar?"

"I don't know what's wrong with me. I feel so winded and even my muscles hurt," she said as she got up from the bench. "I'm also getting a little sick to my stomach again."

"Maybe Jesse is right and you should call the doctor."

"No, I'll be fine. I just need to get back up the hill and go take a nap. You know I hate to say it but if I didn't know better. I would almost think Riley or Tess put something in my food to make me sick."

"Why in the world would you say something like that?" Olivia asked.

"I don't know why but for some reason Riley has never liked me. Tess was not so bad but she would go along with everything Riley wanted. One time when we were working here I saw the two of them come out of our room. That night, when I went to go to sleep, I discovered my bed had been short sheeted. The next day they were giggling a lot whenever they looked at me."

"That's terrible, Harper. Why didn't you say anything to me when I told you about the reunion? I wouldn't have invited them to be with us. Thank goodness they spend most of their time watching TV so we don't have to deal with them," Ginger added.

"Honestly I have been so happy with my marriage I didn't really give it a thought at first. I was planning on telling you two when I got here but Jesse and I ran a little late. He thought it was a good idea if we took out life insurance policies on the two of us; in that way the other person would be protected in case something happened to one of us. I really didn't think it was necessary but he insisted. And I just wanted to please him. Anyway when we got here I saw what slobs those two had turned into. It was obvious they didn't want to spend much time with any of us, so I just forget to mention it."

"That seems weird with you married less than a year needing life insurance policies. If you don't mind me asking how much did you buy?" Ginger asked.

"We each got million dollar policies."

"Wow! That seems like a lot."

"I know but it makes Jesse happy." She started to get up from the bench and felt very dizzy.

"I don't think I can make it up the stairs and back to the cottage."

"Can you walk over there to the street? I'll help you and Olivia will flag down a carriage to get you back up to the hotel."

Just at that moment a grounds keeper came into the garden on a golf cart. When he saw one of the women was not feeling well he immediately agreed to take them back up to the cottage. When they got there Ginger wanted to call the doctor but Harper was insistent they not phone.

"If you just make me cup of tea and help me to my room I just really need to rest. Why don't the two of you go check out the Cupola Bar and then when Jesse gets back if I still don't feel good I will have him ring the doctor?"

"I really don't want you to stay alone," Ginger said as they were helping her up the stairs.

As they passed the media room they saw Tess and Riley watching the television with several bags of chips and soda cans strewed all over the room. As Ginger helped Harper into bed Olivia started pushing a chair closer to her friend.

"No, don't bring that chair over here. Please go over to the hotel and let me rest. I think I'll skip the tea for now. If I need something those two are next door and can help me."

Feeling bad about leaving her they stopped in the media room and asked the two women to keep an eye on Harper because she wasn't feeling well.

The women nodded "yes" as they continued to watch the television. As they were going down the stairs they didn't hear Riley say to Tess "as if I would help that woman."

A few minutes later Harper realized she was in trouble. She tried to move to let Riley and Tess know she needed help, even though it would not have mattered at that point. It was then she became very afraid because her mind was still working but she couldn't move her body. She tried to yell out, but even if they had heard her over the sound of the television, she couldn't hear her voice. It was then, although in no pain, she slipped into a coma. She no longer knew her heart would soon stop.

CHAPTER 11

As they followed the path back to the hotel Ginger said, "I am really worried about her. Let's go find the Cupola Bar and then go back and insist she call the doctor right away."

Having no idea it wouldn't have made any difference Olivia said, "I totally agree. I don't want something to happen to her that could have been prevented if she saw a doctor."

As they entered the long hallway into the parlor they saw an elevator to their left. They took it up to the 4th floor. They knew they had to walk from there but luckily there were signs directing them. Along the way the maids were cleaning the suites on that floor and they were able to see a few rooms.

"Just look in there. These rooms overlooking the lake are awesome, Ginger."

"They really are. It would be a lot of fun to come back here next year and stay in one of these rooms or maybe in one of The First Lady Suites."

Walking along the hallway they saw a narrow staircase with a sign and arrow pointing up to the Cupola Bar. It was an amazing place. It was not real large but the whole area was windows looking out over the town, the lakes and the bridge. There were several tables lined up against the walls with chairs that looked out over the water. The walls were a dark blue and black striped and there was a black and white checkered floor. There was also a bar with more chairs and a small square area that looked up into a large square hole.

They discovered there was actually another area up above the first floor bar that opened up into a window-to-window room with chairs and tables. What they thought was a cathedral ceiling was actually just an opening with a large chandelier hanging and coming down through the hole between the two floors. They spied a piano and realized the bar probably turned into a very lively and fun place after dark.

"This is incredible, Olivia. I can see how watching the sunsets from up here would be astonishing."

"We definitely have to bring the others up here. Maybe we could do it tonight?"

"That would be enjoyable. But let's go back now. We have been gone almost a half hour and I'm really worried about Harper."

They walked back down the stairs, took the elevator to the first floor, and then went down the hallway and outside following the path back to the Cottage. When they arrived, they could hear the TV blaring.

"Don't those women ever do anything besides watch television and snack? What a waste of money for them to come here."

"I agree with you, Ginger. But at least we don't have to socialize with them. I can barely look at them after Harper told us what they did to her years ago."

Getting off the couch Riley walked over and closed the door when she saw them go by. They walked past, ignoring the closed door, and knocked at Harper's bedroom. When they didn't get an answer, looking and nodding at each other, they entered the room.

They saw Harper lying on the bed and they immediately knew something was wrong. She had a faint pulse and her body seemed stiff. As Ginger tried to wake her, Olivia picked up the phone and called 911.

Luckily the doctor was at the hotel on business so he was notified right away. Olivia went back downstairs to wait for him just as the men returned from their golf outing.

"Olivia, Olivia come up here quick," she heard Ginger's panicked voice.

Telling Jesse that Harper was sick, Olivia, the doctor, who had recently arrived, and all three men raced up the stairs to her bedroom.

Ginger was standing there crying, "I think she just died!"

"What? This can't be happening," Jesse said as he rushed to his wife's side and tried to shake her awake.

"Get back," the doctor said. "Let me see if there is anything I can do."

As the doctor tried to give her CPR it was obvious she was gone and nothing would bring her back. "I need all of you to go back downstairs. I am going to call the police and you need to sit there and wait for them."

"But I want to stay with my wife," Jesse cried.

"No one can be in here until the police check the scene out."

"But she was sick and died. You're acting like she was murdered or something."

"She is not that old of a woman, and since she wasn't sick before she came here, that makes this a suspicious death. The police need to check out this bedroom first and then I will take blood samples to send to the lab. The body needs to go to the county facilities on the mainland for an autopsy."

"Why does she need an autopsy?"

"That is standard procedure in these cases. Even though I am a doctor, I'm not the coroner and we need to go through proper channels. Who's in that room next door blaring that television? They need to go downstairs and wait for the police, too."

On their way downstairs, Ginger and Olivia knocked at the media room's door. When the door was opened Ginger told the women what had happened and that they needed to follow them downstairs.

"I'm not going to miss my show just because Harper died. That's her problem. I'm not leaving this movie unless the police come and force me to."

"Come on, Ginger, let's go downstairs. Obviously those two have no feelings about the pain that's surrounding them."

With eyes filled with tears the two women descended the stairs.

CHAPTER 12

Coming down the stairs they could see Dylan pacing while Flynn tried to comfort Jesse who was sitting on the couch, sobbing. The five of them sat and waited for the police to arrive.

Looking at her smart phone, Ginger told them, "I was looking up information about the Island's police department. They have five officers in addition to the Chief. But in the summer they add four more officers, usually fresh out of the academy. Summer patrol is on foot and bicycle naturally, but there is a motorized police vehicle available for emergencies. I would think that's what they will drive up here to get Harper."

"Do they even have a jail on the Island?" Dylan asked.

"Yes, but it's small with only a couple of holding cells for detention. Serious criminals are transported to the county jail on the mainland for arraignment in court. They take them to Mackinac City. I suppose St. Ignace being a part of the Upper Peninsula is in a different county."

"What do they do in the winter with the year round people?"

"Winter police work requires a smaller force, and a core department of six officers who patrol, often on snowmobile. Also, sometimes the police vehicle is used to transport seniors to church, the medical center, the airport or any shops that are opened downtown during those months."

Ginger realized this was a lot of extraneous information but it felt good to be busy talking and not thinking about what happened to Harper while they were waiting for the police.

It wasn't long before they heard a vehicle approaching. It was obvious to all of them because it was a sound you didn't normally hear on the Island. They heard the engine turn off and shortly afterwards three men came into the cottage just as the doctor came down the stairs.

"Chief Logan, I have been guarding the deceased's room. There are two women up in the media room and they won't come downstairs. They are watching something on the television."

Dispatching the two younger men to go get the women, they surmised the older man the doctor had been talking to must be the Chief.

Introducing himself as Chief Logan he said, "As soon as I talk to the doctor, I need to speak to everyone, one at a time. Are you the deceased's husband?" he asked, looking at the man openly crying on the couch.

Jesse shook his head "yes."

At that moment they heard Riley and Tess arguing with the policeman and complaining about being made to go downstairs. Each officer had taken a woman by the arm and was forcibly bringing her down to where the others were sitting.

"Why do we have to go to the living room? We didn't see or hear anything. Unless it's time to eat, we don't like using the stairs."

As they glanced in that direction the two couples were amused by the sight of the officers coercing them down to the first floor.

"This is an outrage. I am missing my show," Riley continued.

"Just sit down and be quiet," the Chief said quite loudly. "Don't you have any respect for the fact that someone has died here?"

"I never liked her when she was alive so why should I care that she's dead?"

Everyone in the room gasped at that and Jesse got up from the couch and ran over and began choking Riley.

"Quick get him off of her," the Chief told his officers.

As they got his arms away from her neck, choking she sputtered, "I am going to sue you for assault."

"Listen, lady, this man just lost his wife. Don't you have any empathy for him? And if you say 'no', I don't think there is a single person in this room who will corroborate what just happened."

Turning to his deputies he said, "Take that man into the library area and also bring a couple of chairs there."

One of the officers escorted Jesse out of the room while the other one went to get the chairs

The Chief pointing his finger at Riley muttered, "Now sit down there and don't say another word. As soon as I have questioned you, it will be okay for you to go back to your show."

"Turning to Dylan and Flynn he continued, "Do you two men mind helping my officer and the doctor get the stretcher down the stairs and into our vehicle? I need my other officer to help me keep the husband calmed down."

"No problem," the two men said together, relieved to have something constructive to do.

As the men went upstairs with the officer, the four women sat in the living room not saying a word to each other. It wasn't too long before they looked up and saw the stretcher being brought down the stairs. The officer was leading the way going down the steps backwards with the doctor in front of him in case he started falling. Flynn and Dylan were in the rear, one on each side.

Once they got to the bottom the doctor went ahead and opened the door while they carried the stretcher out to the emergency vehicle.

Dylan asked the doctor what would happen next and he said, "She will be going to the county morgue for the autopsy. I'm sure that the Chief will be sending everything to the State Police Crime Lab. There is a post in St. Ignace if the Chief needs more police help here on the Island. But usually he has all the lab work sent to the State Police detachment in Grayling for testing."

They watched with a sigh as the vehicle took off with the police officer driving and the doctor sitting beside him. The officer had told them there was a special freight ferry that was used for emergency vehicles, snowplows, garbage trucks, and the like. The boat landing was on the other side of the Island so most people weren't even aware of its existence.

Cars did come to the Island on occasion. One had been shipped over for the *Somewhere In Time* movie, and the previous summer there had been an outcry when Vice President Pence had insisted that an eight car motorcade be used during his visit. It definitely seemed like overkill since only one car was smuggled over, but never used, when President Ford had visited the Island.

Knowing that Harper would be taken off the Island safely, the two men turned back towards the cottage ready for their questioning. Neither of them were looking forward to being back around Riley and Tess. They felt bad they had been given a break while Olivia and Ginger had to sit inside and endure those two women.

"I can't believe this has happened, Dylan. I know we are getting older being in our early fifties but you still don't think about someone our age just dying when they weren't previously sick from some disease."

"It does happen occasionally and being a doctor, I have seen it. But, you're right. She seemed so healthy and strong last night and to die so quickly does seem strange. But they will know more when they have the preliminary autopsy results."

With that they opened the cottage door and walked inside.

CHAPTER 13

Walking into the living room they heard dead silence. All four women were looking at their phones or at least pretending to. Ginger was sitting on the couch and Flynn went and sat next to her; picking up her hand and holding it. There were tears in her eyes but her stomach did a flip flop when he touched her. As she looked at him it seemed like the years disappeared and they were young and in love once again.

Even though I haven't seen her in years, Ginger thought, Harper was once one of my best friends. How can I be reacting this way towards Flynn when Harper has just died? And I get the sense Flynn is having a similar response towards me. I thought I was too old to be experiencing these kinds of feelings again.

Meanwhile Dylan went to a chair near where Olivia was sitting. He sat down close to her but didn't touch her. None of them spoke. They had no interest in starting a conversation where they might have to interact with Riley or Tess.

Tess got up and went over and got a beer and a can of soda from the refrigerator. She also took a bag of pretzels that was sitting on the wet bar.

"Don't look at me like that," she yelled at Olivia. "They have a very nice lunch buffet in the hotel but it certainly isn't enough to hold a person until dinner."

Olivia just shook her head thinking there was no way she could eat a lunch buffet after breakfast and if by some chance she did, there would be no way she would be hungry for dinner, much less munchies in between. She wondered if the hotel would run out of snacks the way those two loud-mouthed women were constantly going through bag after bag.

Meanwhile the Chief was questioning Jesse. It had been difficult talking to the man because he broke down in tears after every question. He asked him about their trip up to the Island and what they had to eat and drink the previous day. When Jesse mentioned his wife had been sick throughout the night the Chief immediately wondered if she had been poisoned. The doctor had done a cursory search of the body and had found no signs of physical injury.

Thinking he would make more progress questioning the others first, he said, "Look! Why don't you go lie down in bed for a while and we can talk at another time. Do you mind going back to the room where your wife died? Or we could find you another room that you could move to."

"No, I don't mind going to our bedroom. I will feel closer to Harper laying down on the bed she and I shared. And it should still smell like her, too."

Of course, that brought a new set of tears and the Chief nodded at his man to take Jesse upstairs. It was too bad he was okay with going back to that bedroom. I would have had the hotel bring a bed into the media room if necessary. That would have driven those two women nuts if they couldn't watch television, he thought with a smirk.

Returning back to the living room the Chief started to interview everyone separately. As long as their stories were similar he would know no one was trying to hide something from him. He decided to interview the two loud mouths at the end. They had come down last and that would give Jesse some time to perhaps fall asleep before the television started blasting. The doctor had left a couple of sedatives for the man and he had told his deputy to make sure Jesse took one as soon as he went upstairs.

He called Olivia into the library area first and asked her to take him through what had happened from the moment she had arrived on the Island. He broke into her narrative from time to time with some specific questions about what had happened when they had been drinking and having dinner the evening before. Satisfied with her narrative he asked her to send Ginger in next to talk to him.

Once again he took the same approach with Ginger and asked the same questions about dinnertime the previous evening. The two women told him almost the same things and he didn't get the feeling they were holding anything back.

He then asked the same questions of the two men. Since they had arrived later than the women and had been able to come to the cottage directly on checking in, their narratives were a little different. However, they said the same thing about dinner and what had happened the rest of the evening that the women had told him.

It was now almost 4:00 p.m. and the Chief knew the two couples would probably welcome a drink. He decided he would interview the last two women upstairs to give the other four a little peace and privacy.

Returning to the living room he told the two women to follow him up the stairs.

"What! You made us come all the way downstairs for nothing? We could have been watching TV," Riley said.

"There will be no television watching until I am finished conducting my interviews."

"But that's not fair," Tess chimed in.

"If you two are not quiet my officer and I will walk both of you down to the police station and interview you there. And, by the way, I don't have TV there."

When Riley started to say something the Chief gave her a look that said he meant what he said. She decided she better cooperate. The sooner they got the questioning over the sooner they could get back to their shows.

Directing Riley into her bedroom, he took Tess into the media room. Tess told him how they had met Olivia and Ginger at the ice cream parlor. From there they had walked to the cottage and checked out the rooms. As soon as they decided they wanted the room upstairs close to the TV, they had gotten snacks and retreated to that area. Since they had gone back upstairs right after dessert, Tess didn't know what had happened after dinner.

"This morning," as she continued her straight-forward narrative, "Riley and I left for breakfast early before the others were up. We did see them come into the dining room for breakfast but we didn't speak to any of them. Then we came back to the cottage and have been watching television all morning until the lunch buffet started. We walked to the hotel to eat and we got back here a few minutes before they brought Harper back to her room. They told us to keep an eye on her because she was resting."

"And that's the extent of what you saw? Did you keep an eye on her?"

"Not really. We were watching our program and I thought she would call us if she needed something. And that's all I know," she told him. "I never heard another thing until Ginger came pounding on our door that we were supposed to go downstairs. Since she is not the boss of our lives, we ignored her."

"But don't you even feel a little bad that Harper is dead?"

"Yes, I am sorry it happened. I hate to see anyone die, especially under those circumstances. I guess she was sick all night. But Riley and I didn't like her when we worked here so it is hard to feel a lot of sympathy now."

"But why didn't you like her before?"

"Well, I guess I really didn't mind her so much. It was Riley who hated her and since the two of us were so tight I decided to dislike her, too."

"But why?"

"She always did things so perfectly and she was so beautiful. Boys were always swarming around her but she just wanted to hang out with the gang. 'Little Miss Perfect' is what Riley used to call her. I guessed we wished the boys would hover around us like that. But it just goes to show you."

"What does it show you?"

"She has been alone all these years and only recently married. Meanwhile Riley and I have been married twice and Riley has been divorced three times."

"And why is that a good thing?"

"We both have gotten some serious cash from our exes and are set for the rest of our lives. Life doesn't get much better than that. We can do whatever we want and we don't have to fix meals or cater to anyone else but ourselves."

After her last answer, Chief Logan had a strong distaste for the woman. I guess love didn't fit into their scenarios. He was pretty sure she was not guilty of harming Harper. But he wondered if he would think the same thing when he interviewed Riley. Telling her to go back to her bedroom and wait, he told her to send Riley in.

The woman walked in with such an attitude he decided to put her in her place immediately.

"Listen I'm not going to take any of your guff. So far your distaste of the victim seems to be the biggest motive I have encountered up to this point. If you continue to be hostile I am going to lock you up overnight and you can say good-bye to any television or decent food. My jail is pretty bare bones. Now just answer my questions. The sooner we get through this interview, the quicker you'll get rid of me,"

Mollified while looking with real distaste at the man she said, "Tell me what you want to know? I never hurt Harper and the sooner you leave here, the better off I will feel. Besides it's almost time for appetizers and dinner."

Food! Is that all you think about, he thought to himself. I guess it must be from the looks of you two.

She pretty much told the Chief what Tess told him had happened the evening before. She seemed really surprised he thought of her as a suspect but there was no way he was ruling her out yet. Although she was not forthright about her distaste for Harper, like Tess had been, he decided he had questioned her enough for the present. He knew tomorrow he would be talking to all of them again as soon as he got the preliminary reports back from the pathologist.

CHAPTER 14

The room was very somber, compared to the day before, as Flynn went about mixing martinis for everyone.

"I think I have had more to drink in the last two days than I have had the last six months," Ginger commented.

"I know what you mean," Olivia added. "I sometimes have wine with my meal but not on a regular basis."

"Personally, I think we are all in shock," Flynn chimed in. "Maybe the doctor should have left sedatives for all of us. Meanwhile the alcohol will have to do."

"I know it's not a great time to think about food but Ginger and I never had lunch today. What about you men?"

"No, we didn't either. In fact when we came back from our golf game we were planning on asking you ladies if you wanted to go get a salad or sandwich at The Gate House," Flynn replied. "Why are you asking?"

"I just don't feel any of us will want to dress up and go to dinner tonight. Maybe instead we should call over to the kitchen and see if they can send us over something to eat. I don't believe we need to have the chef make us anything special. Either Neal, if he is available, or one of the waiters could just bring us something from the menu tonight."

Just then Ginger interjected, "But what about the two women upstairs?"

"Knowing them, and I feel I'm starting to now, it doesn't seem likely that they could care less that Harper is dead. All they seem to think about is eating and watching television. I am sure they will go over to the restaurant tonight. They won't settle for just having some food being sent from the hotel. Personally, I hope they don't want to be around us. I have a hard time saying a civil word to either one of them."

"I'll tell you what I think," Ginger said. "I pretty much agree with you Olivia. But I'm willing to go upstairs right now and ask them if they want to join us for dinner or see if they prefer to go to the hotel restaurant. I'm sure, like you, that they will want to go to the hotel but we are living with a lot of stress right now. Since we have to live here in the same place with the two of them it seems better if we don't have an all-out war."

"I think that's a very good idea," Flynn responded.

"I am going to go right now and get it over with."

A few minutes later they all heard Ginger knocking on the door upstairs. They couldn't hear what she was saying but she returned to them a few minutes later.

"We were right. They want to go over to the hotel for dinner. They said to let them know when the appetizers arrive and they will have some of those before they go eat. So at least we only have to put up with them for a little while and we'll still be able to keep the peace."

Going over to the table by the library, Olivia picked up the phone and called the hotel kitchen. When she explained why they were calling, the person she was talking to said the restaurant would be happy to take care of them. She listened a few minutes more and then hung up the phone.

"Rather than ordering individually they'll put together an assortment of dishes from things on the menu tonight. Then they'll send it over with whomever the waiter will be when he brings the appetizers. That way we can serve ourselves buffet style whenever we're ready. They will also send over some soup for Jesse."

With the dinner taken care of they began to talk about Harper. The two men pointed out how much Jesse seemed to gush about his wife while they were golfing.

"I know if she was murdered," Dylan said, "the husband is always the logical suspect."

"Do you really think she was murdered?"

"I'm in total agreement with the Chief as far as it being a suspicious death, Olivia. As a doctor her symptoms, that I was aware of, whether accidental or on purpose, definitely point to poison."

"She did tell us the reason they came so late yesterday was because they stopped at their insurance office to sign papers. They took out million dollar policies on each other in case of death."

"As far as insurance money one of three things will happen. If Jesse killed her, he will inherit nothing. If it was an accident, he will be a rich man. And if she was murdered by someone other than him and there is a double indemnity clause, he will become a very rich man."

"I can't believe he would try and kill her the same day they took out the insurance policies. That would seem pretty stupid."

"You're right, Olivia. But criminals are not always smart. I guess only time will tell. I would think the Chief will have a preliminary report from the pathologist by sometime tomorrow."

"Will they be able to figure out the poison, if that's what it was, that fast?"

"No, chances are they won't know right away. They will be able to tell if it was poison but it will probably take a while to know the exact poison."

"Why don't we do something? Take a walk or something," Ginger said.

"We could take a walk down to The Gate House. I think they have their menu posted somewhere so we can check that out. Then maybe we could go sit in the rockers on the porch for a while."

"As long as we don't sit in the same area as we sat with Harper this morning, it would probably do us good to get a little fresh air."

The four of them left the cottage walking as couples and went down the hill to the Gate House Restaurant. After checking the menu they returned to the porch sitting on the side by the hotel's restaurant. No one said anything as they silently looked at the water in the distance.

CHAPTER 15

As they headed back to the cottage they ran into Riley and Tess walking to dinner. The two women were dressed almost identically wearing black pants and short black shirts. It was not very formal but they were dressed well enough to get into dinner.

"We ate some of the appetizers," Tess told them.

Nodding, they went into the cottage where Neal was waiting for them with a disturbed look on his face.

"I am afraid those two women made a mess of your food. I was trying to clean up a little before you returned. I showed them the appetizers and told them the rest of the food was your dinner. They ate most of the appetizers and when my back was turned they dished up big plates from your food. I'm really sorry. I'll go back to the kitchen and get you some more things to eat."

"Did they eat Jesse's soup?" Ginger asked.

Nodding his head "yes" Dylan told the man, "I think we have all lost our appetite. Do you think you could bring us some cheese and crackers and soup for all five of us? Then we will just eat what's left here. Is that okay with everyone? I think that would be plenty for tonight."

They all nodded their head in agreement and Neal took off to bring them their new provisions.

"Those two women are total slobs," Olivia remarked. "They knew we were not going to the hotel for dinner and they deliberately ate our food. What's worse is they ate Jesse's soup. They have no empathy for anyone. I don't think I have ever seen such self-centered women in my whole life."

"Trust me there are others just like them out there," Dylan told her. "It's just that we aren't usually around people like that.

It didn't take long for Neal to come back with a large tray filled with cheese, crackers, some more appetizers, and soup.

"That's a neat little cart you have outside to bring the tray over to us."

"It is, Ginger. That way I don't have to carry a heavy tray or spill the soup. I just want to tell all of you how sorry I am for your loss. I always liked Harper. She was nice to everyone she met."

Ginger agreeing with him asked, "I was wondering Neal, didn't you used to work for Island Carriage Tours Company?"

"I did but I had a falling out with one of the other stable men who was friends with the owner. I worked there for over twenty-five years but they took the other guy's side in our argument. That really made me mad after working there for so long. So that autumn before "The Grand" closed for the year I came over here and talked to the man in charge of the stables. He knew I had always been a reliable worker so he told me I could work for him the following spring."

"Wasn't it hard leaving a place you had worked at for so long?" Olivia questioned.

"Not really. In my type of job you don't really socialize with the other workers that much. I liked the idea of coming to a place that only had a few horses. It gave me a chance to get to know the animals better. And, in addition, I know the grounds keepers here and I have always liked working with herbs and plants, so they let me help out from time to time in the gardens."

"Was your boss at the Carriage Tours upset you left?"

"I never even told him. I just didn't show up for work that following spring. I was one of their best workers but when they sided with that other guy I didn't feel I owed them anything. By the time my boss realized I wasn't coming back he called me and offered me a 20% raise. But I figured if they did it once they could do it again. So I came here and never looked back."

"Well it sounds like it turned out to be a good move for you."

"It was, Olivia. Now do you want me to wait here while you eat or should I come back to clean up later?"

"No you can go for the night. Don't worry about coming back. We will probably just eat the food at our leisure and Ginger and I will clean everything up. All we have to do is put the left-overs in the refrigerator and the plates and things in the dishwasher."

"Thanks, Olivia. Like Harper, you are also one of the good ones. I have to tell you there are a lot of people who tend to treat us 'townies' as if we are beneath them. Most of the kids were really nice to me when we were young but every once in a while I would run into someone who treated me like dirt. I feel I am just as important to this world, in my own way, as anyone else."

"I agree, Neal. Hopefully you are finished working now and can go have a relaxing evening. See you tomorrow."

After saying goodnight to the others, he left.

"He sure was talkative tonight," Ginger said. "I just went up and checked on Jesse while you were talking to Neal, and he was sleeping. I left him a note on the nightstand he will easily see when he wakes up. I wanted him to know there was soup in the fridge if he wanted it."

"Thanks for doing that, Ginger. Are you men up for some cards tonight after we eat? It almost doesn't seem right to play anything with Harper dying today but I don't feel like reading and, there is no way we could get any TV time even if we wanted to."

"That sounds like a good idea," both men said at the same time.

"I'm hungry after no lunch," Dylan said. "Let's see what kind of food Neal brought us.

And, so despite the terrible circumstances surrounding Harper's death, the night passed pleasantly. Ginger noticed Flynn looking at her quite a bit throughout the evening and wondered what he was thinking. At the same time, she kept wondering what their lives would have been like if they had married years ago. But that was water over the dam. Never one to dwell on what was past, she decided she needed to look positively towards the future while enjoying what the present offered her.

CHAPTER 16

The next morning they met once again at 8:30 a.m. to go to breakfast. Ginger had taken some coffee up to Jesse mainly so she could check on him. She had noticed the soup dish soaking in the sink so she knew he had eaten sometime during the night.

Flynn had come into the kitchen while she was making the coffee. The air seemed charged with an electric current the minute he walked into the room. I should not feel so happy as soon as he comes near me, especially with Harper's death. But all I keep wishing is that he would kiss me, she was thinking.

Pretending not to notice the charged atmosphere when they were together she poured a cup of coffee for him and put a cup and small carafe filled with coffee on a tray. She then took the tray upstairs and knocked on the bedroom door. When she heard him say come in, she entered and saw him sitting by the window.

"Thanks, Ginger, for looking out for me," Jesse said as she handed him the coffee cup.

"We are all concerned about you, Jesse. I wasn't sure if you wanted cream or sugar. Are you sure you don't want to go to breakfast with us?"

"I drink my coffee black, thanks. I just want to sit here in my room this morning. I was up most of the night trying to figure out what could have possibly happened to Harper. I can't believe she is gone. One minute everything was fine and she was happy and we were laughing together and the next, she was dead. I never even got to say good-bye to her."

"I know when my mother died there were things left unsaid and it's so hard because you can never have a redo when that happens. How about I bring you something for breakfast from the dining room?"

"I'm fine, really. I noticed there was some bread and cereal in the cupboards when I was in the kitchen last night. I might go get some toast and maybe some cereal later. Right now I just want to sit here. But I really appreciate you bringing me coffee. It probably seems silly but Harper and I had such a short time with each other so I just want to sit here and reminisce about all the fun times we shared when we were together."

At that moment they heard the television blaring so they knew Tess and Riley were back from breakfast.

"I wrote down my cell phone number and left it on the nightstand. The four of us are going to breakfast and then we'll probably take a walk downtown. But if you need anything at all, just call. Don't even think twice about it. On my way out, I'll tell those two to keep the media room door closed while they are watching television. Hopefully that will lower the noise level a little bit."

"Thanks, Ginger. And, thank you again for watching out for me."

"I know I haven't seen her in a long time but Harper was always my friend and I know she would want me to look out for you. And even though I didn't have much contact with her, I did read all the travel articles she published. Someday I'm hoping to visit many of the places she wrote about."

As she left the room she stopped to see Riley and Tess. If you two don't mind can you keep the door to this room closed while you are watching TV, please. Jesse is resting."

"I don't see what the big deal is," Riley said in a nasty voice. Even Tess stared at her and gasped.

"Look, I know you didn't like Harper and apparently could care less that she's dead, but at least you could have some respect for her husband. He is grieving for the loss of his wife."

"Don't worry, Ginger. I'll make sure we keep the door closed when the TV is on," Tess said.

Nodding her head in thanks Ginger continued down the stairs and motioned for the others to follow her outside.

"I just can't believe how nasty Riley is." And, with that, she told them what had just taken place.

"That is so offensive," Olivia said.

"Come on ladies. Let's forget it and go have breakfast. Ginger and I talked about taking a walk downtown after we eat. Do you two want to go with us? Flynn asked.

"Definitely," Olivia and Dylan said together.

As they were having breakfast Ginger brought up the subject of their evening. "I know there have been extenuating circumstances but we really should try to go to the dining room tonight for dinner. It is quite a spectacular meal. We probably don't need to eat the appetizers at the cottage. We could just have Neal skip bringing them to the house tonight."

Laughing at her Olivia said, "Do you know what those two women would do if their appetizers didn't show up as expected?"

"Well besides the appetizers, which those two can get here in the restaurant, there is soup, salad, entrée, and dessert. I asked the waiter this morning and he said they were having crème brulee for dessert tonight. That is my favorite. I will tape a note to their bedroom door telling them we are not getting appetizers and they can order their own if they want them. "

"Also, Ginger, why don't we show the men the Cupola Bar before we walk downtown? We do not need to go for a drink, especially since we have cocktails at the cottage before dinner, but perhaps we could go up there tonight before we eat and watch the sunset. It's supposed to be one of the top things to do here this time of the year."

"I think all of us are definitely up for that," Flynn said while looking at Dylan who was agreeing.

When they finished eating they went back into the parlor area. On their way to the elevator Ginger pointed to the right. "Do you see that room back there? That is the Terrace Room and that is where they have dancing every night. Then they took the elevator up to the fourth floor and finding the staircase walked up to the two level Cupola Bar.

"This place is amazing," Dylan remarked after checking out both floors.

With tears in her eyes Ginger said, "The last time we were here, Harper was dying and we had no idea that was happening."

"Come on. Let's go take that walk downtown," Flynn replied as he took Ginger's hand and led her downstairs to the elevator.

CHAPTER 17

The four of them took the elevator down to the lobby level where The Garden Terrace area was located. As they walked down the hallway and passed the ice cream parlor to get to the exit they heard people talking about going to the history lecture.

"I forgot about that," Ginger said. "Every morning at the West end of the porch, unless it is raining, Bob Tagatz, the hotel historian, gives a lecture relating to the history of 'The Grand'. I once heard him give a fascinating speech about the history of filmmaking at the hotel and the stars who came here during filming."

"What happens when it rains?"

"The lecture is moved inside to the Terrace Room, Dylan."

Outside the sun was shining brightly and the temperature was in the low 70's. Because they were so close to the water, with the sun reflecting off the lake, the temperature felt much warmer.

As they started walking down the hill to town a carriage went by. "I wonder what it costs to ride in one of those buggies."

"I checked at the bellman's stand yesterday. It's $5.50 one way per person," Olivia answered. "I think it would be worth it if you were coming from downtown and had a lot of packages you were trying to carry up this hill, Flynn. You can also rent private ones. Maybe we should rent one to take us to Fort Mackinac one of these days. That would be fun."

As they continued along, they passed a little church on their left. "Look," Olivia pointed towards the building. "There is The Little Stone Church. I think the real name is Union Congregational Church. There are about one hundred members but most of those are summer people. It is a very popular venue for weddings and vow renewals during the season. I went there a couple of times when I worked on the Island."

As they continued walking another carriage went by. "It's a good thing they don't have cars on this Island," Dylan remarked. "It's busy enough with all the carriage traffic. Do you remember the old saying?"

"Yes," they all said together.

Dylan continued, "There are two smells on the Island. One, of course is fudge. There are thirteen fudge shops that make ten thousand pounds or five tons every day. The Island imports ten tons of sugar each week. I looked this up because I think it is our duty to sample all thirteen shops this morning."

"Not right after breakfast," Olivia groaned.

"Well, if it gets to be too much we can just go outside and check the other smell—horse manure! I know most cities who have horses and carriages put bags on their animals. But not here," Dylan continued. "Just imagine how many men would lose their job if they put bags on the horses. Besides they pile the muck up on their small carts and it makes great fertilizer for all the flowers growing everywhere."

Continuing on down the hill they came to a dead end. To the right was the lake. They turned to the left and continued down past some shops and the police station. They eventually made another right to get to the heart of downtown.

They spent the next couple of hours roaming in and out of stores, including the fudge shops. They watched as a couple of the ferries landed and dropped off numerous tourists who came to explore the Island for the day or overnight.

"Why don't we stop at The Gate House Restaurant on the way back to the cottage and pick up some salad and sandwiches to take back with us. It's such a beautiful day and we could eat outside on our deck."

They all agreed that would be a good idea. Since all meals came with the cottage rental all they had to do was charge the food to their lodging. They also decided to get a couple take out containers of soup. They wanted to bring food back for Jesse and they knew whatever they didn't eat, the other two women would finish.

CHAPTER 18

"I guess you came back to question us again," Ginger said as they returned from their walk and saw the Chief sitting on the patio apparently waiting for them.

"Yes. That's why I'm here. I have a few more questions for all of you.

"Do you want to join us for some lunch," Dylan asked?

"Don't mind if I do," The Chief answered.

As they laid out the food and got plates and silverwear from inside, Dylan continued, "Do you know how Harper died yet?"

"Why do you ask, sir?"

"I am a doctor and although I specialize in the cancer field, it's obvious from her symptoms that she was probably poisoned. So the question becomes, was it deliberate or accidental?"

Ginger went upstairs to ask Jesse to join them since he would need to answer some questions, too. As she left she heard the Chief explain, "On television crime shows the results of toxicology tests are quickly released sometimes before the autopsy is even complete. But as you know that's not the way it happens in real life."

Dylan nodded in agreement as the Chief continued. "Test results take a lot longer. Some of these tests can take days, weeks, or even months. Blood, urine, and tissue samples are taken before the tests begin but just as important is the field investigation. It is crucial that I check and see what other drugs she might have been taking whether prescription, over-the-counter or illicit drugs."

"I'm positive she wasn't taking any illicit drugs," Ginger chimed in.

"How do you know that?"

"Well, I don't know for sure but I had a nephew who was married and he and his wife were heavy drug users. I spent a lot of time with my sister helping her cope with the situation. So I can usually recognize when a person is on drugs. Harper showed no sign of drug use when she arrived. I'm positive of that."

"That's why I'm here. As I said previously, a thorough field investigation is very essential in helping to write a good autopsy. As the doctor will attest, the first thing a forensic pathologist will do is a basic screening for drugs. Then more sophisticated tests will be run and if she was poisoned, the experts will then be able to tell the exact concentration. This will lead them to whether or not it was a toxic, therapeutic, or a lethal dose."

He checked his watch and then continued, "Looking for other drugs this helps them ascertain whether the poison would have contributed to her death or caused it. It also helps them to know what symptoms she had before her death. So I wanted to go over that again; especially with you two ladies, since you spent the whole morning with her. I can tell you we have a very preliminary toxicology screen and it appears she may have been poisoned by hemlock."

Before he could say anything else Ginger returned with Jesse in tow. The man looked terrible as he sat down and pulled out one of the take-out containers of soup from a bag and placed it in front of him.

While he was doing that, with everyone sitting there, the policeman asked, "Before I go into anything else can you tell me, Jesse, why you took out a million dollar life insurance policy on your wife the day you came up here?"

With the spoon filled with soup half way to his mouth, flustered and turning red he sputtered, "How did you know about that?"

"Apparently your wife mentioned it to her friends the morning she died."

"Oh. It wasn't a big deal. Since we love traveling, we decided to take out the policies in case something happened to one of us on one of our trips. That way the other person would have protection, especially if for some reason they were hurt and unable to work anymore. You can't possibly think I did something to Harper?"

"We need to look at all the possibilities and you have to admit the fact you took out policies and your wife died almost immediately afterwards does look pretty suspicious."

"I can't believe you're accusing me."

As Jesse started to stand up the Chief said, "Sit down. I have some more questions for you."

Jesse sat back down and pushed the soup away. "What do you want to know?"

"I need to know what kind of drugs your wife took."

"My wife didn't take drugs."

"I wasn't necessarily talking about illegal drugs. What about prescription or over-the-counter drugs?"

"Harper was very healthy. She just had her yearly health exam a month ago. You can check with her doctor but she didn't take any prescription drugs. We kept some Tylenol around in case of a headache but I never even saw her take those pills."

"Tell me what happened during the night before your wife died."

"We went to sleep about 10:00 p.m. We both usually get up in the middle of the night to go to the bathroom. I guess it is a getting old thing you probably don't understand."

The other four looked at each other with a smile when Jesse said that.

"It was sometime after 2:00 a.m. when Harper woke me up. She left our bedroom door open when she went to the bathroom and I heard her vomiting. I went down the hall to see her but she told me she was feeling better since she had just been sick. She felt she had eaten something that had disagreed with her. When she first woke up she had a rapid heartbeat but that finally slowed. I helped her back to the bedroom and she got back into bed. I noticed her hands were trembling. I then went and got a cool compress and put it on her head since she had a slight fever. I wanted to call the doctor but she insisted she would be fine. I told her we would call the doctor in the morning if she wasn't any better."

The Chief was writing down what Jesse was telling him.

Continuing, "It wasn't much longer after that she fell back to sleep. So I thought she would probably feel okay in the morning like she said. Looking back now I think she hid from me how bad she felt in the morning. I told her I would cancel the golf game but she said 'absolutely not' because she wanted to spend the morning with her friends. And that's all I can tell you."

He is either telling the truth or is the most consummate actor I have ever encountered, the Chief was thinking to himself. Looking at the man the policeman said, "Thank you, Jesse. That's all I need for now. You can either sit here while I question the others or you can take your soup back to your room."

"I'm not really hungry anymore. I think I'll just go back to my room and lie down. I just wish there was some way to get those women to turn the television down or even off altogether."

At that Jesse stood up and went into the house.

CHAPTER 19

As they sat there eating the restaurant food Dylan said, "Chief Logan, why did you say it could be hemlock poisoning? Do you think it might have been accidental?"

"There is no way of knowing at this point. I don't need to go over everything that everyone told me yesterday. I took extensive notes. But I'm interested in any symptoms you didn't mention and any place Harper went where she might have come in contact with poison hemlock."

"I don't know anything about poison hemlock," Ginger said as Olivia nodded in agreement. "Can you tell us something about it?"

"I just read up on hemlock this morning when I got the preliminary findings. It seems many of her symptoms you described seem to fit her profile. It grows on the Island and can grow up to nine feet tall. The roots of poison hemlock can easily be mistaken for wild parsnips, while the leaves can be mistaken for parsley. That is the primary culprit for accidental poisoning."

"I have never heard of it," Olivia said.

Then he continued, "All parts of the poison hemlock plant contain poison alkaloids. If ingested it will cause paralysis of various body systems. Paralysis of the respiratory system is the usual cause of death. Meanwhile, a victim cannot move but is aware of what is happening since the mind is unaffected until death is imminent."

"Except for being sick to her stomach and looking bad, she didn't seem to be in any pain," Olivia said.

"I don't think people poisoned by hemlock suffer pain. The entire plant, however, is toxic to animals and humans," he told them. "Touching it will produce a rash and it is deadly if swallowed. We don't think she touched it since she had no rash but that's why I wanted to ask you again about what you did and noticed. Don't worry about you all going to the Secret Garden. I checked with a gardener and there is no hemlock growing in there."

"Well, that's reassuring," Ginger added.

"Just to finish up. The initial symptoms may include a burning sensation in the mouth, nausea, vomiting and confusion and my notes indicated you or her husband had mentioned all those symptoms."

"She didn't really seem confused about anything but I wish we had ignored her and called the doctor immediately when we knew she was sick," Olivia proclaimed.

"Don't beat yourself up over that," Dylan told them. "She wouldn't have been in pain, as the Chief just said, although she would have realized at the end that she was dying. And, she probably wasn't capable of even moving to summon help. But since there is no antidote for that poison there was nothing anyone could have done for her at that point anyway."

"The doctor is correct," Chief Logan concurred.

Knowing they had been in shock, he doubted they had lied to him in the initial interviews. Since he had interviewed them separately and their stories had matched pretty closely he felt confident they had told him the truth. But given the nature of the poison, he was pretty certain someone had given it to her.

The Chief had come to the Island only a few years previously after working homicide in Lansing, the capital of Michigan. He had extensive experience in these kind of matters and tended to trust his gut. Most folks just thought he was some local yokel cop. That worked in his favor when they got too cocky and blurted out the wrong things or assumed he was too stupid to know any better.

The detective had no idea that the people he was questioning had looked him up and knew his background. However, after not seeing each other for over thirty-five years, there did not seem to be a reason why any of them would want to kill Harper. Neither of the men had been in a romantic relationship with the deceased in their youth. And he just couldn't fathom what other motive could be involved.

"One last time, I just want to ask again, since it has been almost twenty-four hours since Harper died, is there anything any of you remember, maybe a little out of the ordinary, you forgot to mention yesterday?"

I can't believe it's been almost a whole day, Ginger was thinking after the Chief's question. It seems like only a few hours had passed since they found her.

Both women told him there was nothing else they could add. Harper had not appeared well, and she was so short winded she sat down to rest a lot. But now it seemed obvious she had definitely tried to hide how sick she really was. Jesse had made note of that when talking to the Chief and thinking back, the two women agreed. They couldn't believe she had any idea she was dying. They really felt she would have had someone call for a doctor or tried to get some kind of help if that were the case.

"I really don't want any of you leaving the Island right now until we can look into this whole situation a little deeper."

"We're actually staying here through this next weekend. Our time is up on Sunday morning but since the others here for the reunion were given discounted room rates, and the cottage was not booked next week, we were given an extra day free. So we're not planning on leaving until next Monday morning," Ginger told the Chief.

"That's great. Thanks for letting me know." And, with that, he got up and left.

They watched the man walk back towards the hotel and then back down the hill towards town.

"I don't mean to be taking over but I think we should decide what we want to do these next couple of days. We are paying a lot of money to stay here and since we can't bring Harper back to life we should probably avail ourselves of the facilities. I think we should try and stay busy rather than sitting around moping."

"I agree, Ginger," Olivia added.

"Why don't we go down by the pool and play croquet," Flynn suggested. "I used to love watching the guests do that whenever I walked by there and hoped someday I could play on that lawn just like they did."

"That's a great idea," Dylan added. And tomorrow morning why don't we take in the history lecture? I overheard some people talking about yesterday's talk while we were eating breakfast and we also heard them on our way downtown."

"And then after lunch we could rent bikes and circle the Island. And I would also like to go up by the butterfly pavilion. I don't know if Jesse wants to tag along but the stables for the Carriage Tour Company are up near there. I'll call this afternoon and see if it is all right for me to stop by."

"Why do you want to go there?" Ginger asked. "The veterinarians who used to work there are probably long retired."

"Yes, I have kept in touch with some of them and they all are retired. One is even dead. But when I got home after my last summer here on the Island, I realized I had left my trunk with my riding clothes and boots in the rafters at the stable. That is where they had us store our things. I kept thinking I would come back and get the trunk but eventually I totally forgot it was here. Since we have a car on the mainland it would be easy enough for me to haul it back on the ferry with our suitcases when we leave."

"Do you think those clothes will still be wearable?" Ginger asked him.

"If they aren't, I'll throw them away. But the boots should be fine and I can always use an extra trunk."

Laughing, Ginger said, "I'm sure glad I took over and planned out all our activities for today and tomorrow."

Watching her with an enigmatic smile Flynn said, "I'm glad you did, too."

Looking in his direction she couldn't take her eyes off of him as her stomach did flip flops.

CHAPTER 20

Cleaning up after their lunch on the deck, they went down by the pool to where the croquet court was set up. Before they started, Dylan got out his smart phone and looked up the rules and read them to everyone. "I just want to make sure we play the game properly," he told them.

Amused by his words, Olivia said, "I guess Dylan wants us to take this game seriously."

"I think it's very important to play by the rules, too," Flynn added.

The others laughed but it wasn't long before they tried to knock Flynn's ball out every chance they had, since he was almost always in the lead. Despite their effort he won the game easily. They were planning on playing a second round but another group of people had come to play so they turned the mallets over to them.

It was just as well. At one point Ginger and Flynn had reached for their balls, which were right next to each other, at the same time. Ginger had planned to hold her ball until Flynn had played. But while reaching their hands touched. A jolt similar to static electricity passed between the two of them.

Although they never said a word they both felt the adrenaline rush and slightly elevated heartbeats. They knew the feelings they had for each other in college had not lessened. It didn't matter that they were older now. They realized these sensations would have to be addressed soon.

After they finished playing they sat by the pool eating snow cones and discussing how Harper died.

"Dylan, do you think Harper was deliberately poisoned?" Olivia enquired of him?

"As we talked about this before, if she had accidentally touched the poison hemlock she would have had a rash. So I don't believe it was an accident. From what I observed that morning at breakfast, and what you women told us about her symptoms, I believe someone poisoned her."

"It's so hard to believe Jesse is guilty the way he has behaved," Ginger protested.

"I agree with you, but he's the only one with a motive that I am aware of."

"You're right, Dylan. A million dollar life insurance policy is a pretty big motive."

"Well, what about Riley? I just don't understand her deep hatred of Harper."

"Yes, that's true, Olivia. But when would she have had the opportunity? And that means she would have almost had to bring the hemlock up here with her. In that case, it would definitely be premeditated and the best lawyer in the country couldn't get her off that rap."

"Did you notice Chief Logan never said anything to Jesse about poison hemlock? And he questioned us but never asked to see Riley or Tess."

"He did tell Jesse he could stay while he questioned us. Don't you remember Ginger? And I asked if we should go get the women while you went to get Jesse, but he said he had run into them going to lunch at the hotel. So he had questioned them before coming to the cottage."

"That definitely clears up that mystery. At this point speculation is probably not going to get us anywhere," Olivia continued. "I think I'll return to the cottage and read. I started a good book last night and I'd like to get back to it."

"That's a great idea. I brought some medical journals with me I haven't had a chance to read. Now seems like the perfect time."

The four of them walked through the grass, up the hill to the staircase, and returned to the cottage. They could hear the television but it wasn't as loud as usual. Maybe Jesse had said something to the women.

They spent a peaceful afternoon reading. They then dressed for dinner and arrived at the same time in the living room when Neal came with the appetizers.

"What can I get you to drink?" the man asked them.

"Never mind, Neal. That has been my job the last couple of nights so I'll take care of the cocktails." And with that, Flynn went over to the bar and begin mixing martinis while Dylan got the glasses out.

At that point, the two women came down the stairs dressed in the same outfits as the previous night.

"Are the appetizers here?" Riley demanded as she looked right at Neal?

"Yes, ma'am. Let me get you your drinks."

Neal went into the kitchen and came back with a can of beer, a can of soda and a glass filled with ice.

"Thank you, Neal. We won't need you any more tonight. I know you work hard at your day job and the maid can pick up the dirty dishes when she comes for the turndown."

"I appreciate that, Ginger. I hope everyone has a good night. I'll see you all tomorrow."

With that, the man left just as Tess asked if the others were going to dinner with them.

"We want to go up to the Cupola Bar and watch the sunset before dinner. Do you two want to come with us?"

"That is just plain stupid, Olivia. Why would you go spend money for drinks at that bar when they are free here?

"We aren't going for drinks. We are going to see the sunset. But you just gave me a great idea. Everyone, why don't we carry a glass of wine with us when we go? That way we'll have something to drink while we watch the sun go down."

They all nodded in agreement as Ginger was wondering how she could spend another minute in the company of these two insufferable women.

"Where's Jesse?" Tess asked.

"I'll go check on him," Ginger replied as she went up the stairs. Knocking on his door she went in when she heard him say, "Come in."

Jesse was sitting in bed with his pajamas on. It was obvious he had been crying.

"I just came to see if everything is okay with you. I wondered if you wanted to go to dinner with us."

"No, I don't, Ginger. As you can see I am not dressed. If that policeman would let me, I would just go home. I just hate being here without Harper. This Island has definitely lost its luster for me. I got some soup and made a sandwich while you were all resting this afternoon. So I'll be fine. I took a sedative and will probably fall asleep soon."

"Tomorrow afternoon we plan to rent bikes and circle the Island. Then we're going to the butterfly conservatory. Would you like to join us?"

"Thank you for asking. I'll see how I feel. I might just walk up there in the morning. Thank you again for caring, Ginger. I'll see you tomorrow."

Realizing she was being dismissed from the room she turned and left. When she got downstairs she told everyone Jesse was not up for going out. She didn't want to say anything else in front of the two women.

It was almost 6:30 p.m. when the six of them left for the hotel. Riley and Tess liked being one of the first people in line for dinner which didn't surprise any of them.

Carrying their wine glasses across the path and into the hotel, the other women were farther back huffing and puffing from the exertion. They finally passed them as the four were waiting at the elevator to go upstairs.

CHAPTER 21

When they were in the bar they ran into two other couples who they remembered from the past.

Even though they were all sad from the recent happenings, surprisingly it turned out to be a fun night.

"I see you four did get together with each other. It's kind of amazing how many kids fell in love while working on the Island and ended up getting married."

"Oh, we're not married to each other," Ginger told the others. "We have all been married to other people and have just recently found each other on social media. But it's ironic that none of us have spouses anymore."

The way they act around each other I would have sworn they were married. Well, maybe something will develop this week, the woman named Julie thought to herself.

"We haven't seen you up here in the bar previously. Did you just get here?"

"No," Olivia answered. "We've all been here since Sunday afternoon. But do you remember Harper? She used to be our roommate when we worked here."

When Julie nodded in the affirmative, Olivia told everyone about Harper dying and that murder was suspected.

"That's just terrible. But that reminds me," Julie said. "Did anyone ever find out what happened to Bree? I always liked her and really thought she would be famous someday."

"Unfortunately that's another mystery that has never been solved. I know something bad had to have happened to her. There is no way her family wouldn't have heard from her by this time."

"Hopefully someday we will find out what occurred. I know she wanted to become a famous star but she was also so in love with George. I just assumed they ran off together and got married. But if that happened I would think their families would have heard from them by now."

"George disappeared, too? I never knew that. I just thought he didn't come back that following year." Flynn seemed shocked by that statement since they had worked together.

"Was George, Bree's boyfriend?" Olivia interjected. "We never knew the name of the boy she was dating. I think I remember him from the first summer that I was here. Thinking about it, I can see why they got together. They were perfect for each other."

"I knew he was seeing someone but he would never tell me who it was for some reason. As I said previously, I just assumed he didn't come back my third summer. I knew someone was missing from the previous summer and I heard it was Bree but I never heard about George also going missing."

"You ladies didn't come back for a third season but it was all anyone talked about that next summer. And Flynn you never socialized with any of us after Ginger left so that's why you probably never heard anything about his disappearance. Anyway let's get back to the present. Are you coming to the special talk they are having for us tomorrow morning?"

"We don't know anything about it," Olivia told the woman.

"You must not have gotten your turn down information yet. Along with the TODAY sheet there was an additional paper with reunion news. Tomorrow morning the historian is giving a special talk about the hotel in the 80's and 90's when most of us were working here. It will be held in the Grand Pavilion Meeting Room at the north end of the Main Dining room at 10:00 a.m. They didn't want to hold it on the porch because the other hotel guests would probably crowd the area, and they wanted it to be a special talk just for all of us."

"Thanks for letting us know, although we would have read about it when we got back to our rooms."

Then Julie continued, "Saturday night we'll be having a special banquet. There aren't too many other activities going on this week. Besides letting us enjoy the hotel and the Island, I guess there are a lot more people coming for the reunion but only for the weekend."

"Well, even with the discount, it is pricey to stay here. But definitely worth it. We are going to ride bikes around the Island tomorrow afternoon. Do you four want to join us?"

"Thanks, Olivia. But we did that today," Julie replied.

"Since there are eight of us we rented the Macao Cottage. I am wondering if we should ask the hotel if we could host a cocktail party at our place either Friday night or before dinner on Saturday. We have plenty of room and it is such a nice setting."

"What a great idea! They listed a Welcome Reception with a cocktail party on Friday night since everyone will have arrived by then. It said place 'to be announced.' Why don't you ask the people in charge of our event if you could host it at your cottage? You mentioned eight of you. I know you said Harper's husband was here but who are the other two?"

"Do you remember Riley and Tess?"

"Sure they were Bree's roommates. We ran into them going into dinner last night. They sure have changed. We never would have recognized them, although they knew us."

"Yes, the same thing happened to us when we first saw them. They have changed a lot. And trust me, not for the better."

As they were talking the sun began setting and every one watched quietly as the amazing sight took place. Even after the sun went down, the colors that appeared were spectacular.

Then Olivia asked the others, "Do you want to join us for dinner tonight?"

"That would be fun," Julie replied. "That dining room is so big that asking for a table for eight is no big deal."

As soon as it was dark outside the four couples left the Cupola Bar and departed for dinner. The conversation was very lively while they ate with everyone catching up on each other's lives. As they were finishing dessert they decided to go to the Terrace Room and listen to the orchestra and dance.

"I haven't done anything like this in ages," Olivia whispered to Ginger. "I just hope the men are not uncomfortable having to pair up with us."

Ginger didn't hear what Olivia said. She was contemplating, and could hardly wait, for Flynn to hold her in his arms. Recently she had read a saying that had struck a chord within her, especially since she realized what a lonely life she had led for years even while being married.

The quote said: "Every day given to you is a gift. That is why it is called the present." The saying continued, "Relish it and enjoy today since it will be over before you know it." Now that she had reached over fifty years of age as she looked back she couldn't believe how quickly the years had flown by. I know I don't feel that old, she reflected.

Continuing with her musings, she supposed all little girls believed in fairy tales and finding their one true love. I thought I had found mine, however it wasn't to be. But maybe fairy tales can come true. Maybe we reach a point in our lives where we deserve it. I guess I need to acknowledge and accept what is occurring between Flynn and me. I need to let go of all the hurt from the past and enjoy what is happening now.

There were several people already in the Terrace Room when they arrived. The orchestra was warming up and had not started performing yet. Looking to the right, they found two tables they pushed together and it wasn't long before the orchestra began playing.

Olivia was thinking how much fun and how compatible all four couples were. As she sat down next to Dylan, she whispered, "I'm not trying to foist myself on you. I guess everyone has just paired up which leaves us together."

"Don't worry about it, Olivia. I didn't realize it before we met again but I have missed you and I think I still have feelings for you."

"I know. We have been over for so long I didn't believe we could feel what we had together previously."

"Let's just enjoy the moment. We can figure the rest of it out later. Shall we dance?" And the two got up and proceeded to the dance area.

Meanwhile Ginger and Flynn were moving very slowly around the dance floor. Neither one of them could stop the feelings they were experiencing. Looking deeply into her eyes Flynn said, "We have to talk about this."

Looking at him she nodded her head in agreement before moving back close to him.

They continued dancing for about an hour and as they walked back to the cottage the two couples could be seen holding hands.

None of them could believe that fate had brought them back together one more time. Knowing how precarious life could be, they wanted to cherish the new sensations they were once again feeling for each other.

Maybe things would work out for them this time around and maybe they wouldn't. But they all realized a second chance to be together was worth striving towards. Que sera, sera—what would be, would be.

CHAPTER 22

The next morning they all woke up early. Not wanting to go to breakfast so soon and since the weather was especially warm for that time of the year, they took a carafe of coffee and their coffee cups and sat outside on their patio. They were soon joined by Jesse.

Carrying an empty coffee cup, he said, "I came in search of coffee. Do you mind if I join you?"

"Not at all. We would love to have you," Ginger told him. "Do you want to go to breakfast with us?"

"Yes, I think I would like that. Previously I was so shocked about Harper I could hardly talk. Now I just feel numb and feel perhaps I should be around people rather than just sitting in that room listening to the television blaring next door."

"I'm sorry we can't do something about that situation," Flynn said. "Those are two of the most rude, selfish, and uncaring women I have ever met."

"Riley is the mean one. I just don't understand why she hated Harper so much. Tess follows her lead a lot but she does try to be a little bit nicer to me. Yesterday she kept turning the TV down. However, Riley kept putting it back up again. I swear there is something wrong with her hearing."

"I believe there's something wrong with her period."

"This morning they will have a talk about the history of the hotel when we were working here. Do you want to come with us," Ginger asked him?

"I don't think so. I think I'll go to breakfast with you and then come back here and read. But I would like to go bike riding with all of you this afternoon and stop at the butterfly conservatory after that. Let me just run upstairs and get my jacket before we go eat."

As he left and went inside Olivia said, "It's almost impossible to believe he killed Harper. It's obvious he is grieving and he doesn't look very well. He seems to have lost all the joy he had when he first came here and was telling us about their travels."

"I agree with you," Dylan added.

It was only a couple of minutes later that Jesse arrived back with a jacket over his arm. As the five of them walked over to the hotel for breakfast they ran into Riley and Tess returning to the cottage. After they passed each other they overheard Riley say, "Thank goodness that man left his room. I'm sick and tired of listening to him complain about the volume on the TV."

Walking behind him Ginger put her hand on Jesse's shoulder and murmured, "Ignore that woman."

"You know I keep trying to think of some positive things to say about those two. That usually helps reduce the tension between people. But I can't think of a single thing," Olivia said. "But, like the others I'm glad you joined us for breakfast, Jesse."

They were able to get a table by the window overlooking the lake. Breakfast was awesome as usual.

"I would like to order off the menu but the buffet has so many choices, especially the fruit, that I guess I'll stick to that again this morning," Dylan said.

Everyone agreed with him and they enjoyed another fantastic dining experience. Jesse didn't eat a lot but they could tell he just liked being around them and felt very comfortable. They saw their friends from the previous night and introduced them to Jesse as they were leaving the dining room. As he left them to go back to the cottage, they agreed to meet him to go to lunch together at 12:30 p.m.

"Let's go back to The Gate House for lunch. They have a good variety and the restaurant is close to the pool where we have to go to rent our bikes. I did reserve five bicycles for 1:15 p.m. They probably wouldn't have run out but I wanted to make sure we all got one."

"That was a good idea. I'm glad you did that, Flynn. We have about a half hour before the lecture. Why don't we check out the hotel? It has been ages since we have been here and I like looking at the pictures on the walls and the different rooms that our tucked in all over the place," Ginger said to the group. "But first let's go down to the office and see if we can host the Welcome Reception and cocktail party Friday night."

Getting a positive response to their request it wasn't long before they went to hear the lecture. When they arrived in the room there were several people they remembered working with and told them about the party on Friday night. Everyone was looking forward to being together again. They also made plans to meet Julie and her friends in the Cupola Bar in the evening again before dinner.

As they were walking back to the hotel, Olivia told the group, "I really loved that talk this morning. I guess being a history teacher brought back many memories of those times. I also forgot we were called 'yuppies.' But we were definitely part of that "yuppie" generation since we were baby boomers, had earned a college education, a well-paying job, and without doubt had expensive tastes. And we all tended to live in or near a large urban area. And the curious thing is we all tended to stay near Chicago throughout our lives."

"Yes," Flynn added. "We were graduating from college right after the worst recession since the Great Depression hit. I remember how businesses closed and families I knew lost their homes. I even had some relatives who were farmers who lost their land. But it never really affected my family. Since my dad was a lawyer, and you always need them, we never realized the extent of the problems at the time. Many people thought we were self-centered and materialistic and they were right. We were more concerned about buying consumer goods and making money than anything else. I know my parents drilled that into me."

"And even though I always wanted to be a doctor," Dylan added, "Making a lot of money in that field was always in the back of my mind."

"I didn't have to worry about that," Olivia said. "Being a social studies teacher didn't provide a huge income level."

Returning to the cottage Ginger said, "Well, enough of that. I think I'll go read since we have about an hour before lunch. I'll see you all then," she said as she went into her bedroom.

CHAPTER 23

The time passed swiftly and soon they were all walking down the hill to The Gate House for lunch. After ordering, they decided to take their food to some tables outside.

"After our ride and the butterfly house I'm going to stop by the stables where I worked. Does anyone want to come with me?"

"Olivia and I talked about coming back to the hotel. We thought we would go sit down by the pool and enjoy the rest of the afternoon," Dylan told the group.

"I wouldn't mind seeing the stables but I'll probably spend more of my time at the Butterfly Conservatory than all of you would want to," Jesse added.

"I guess that leaves me," Ginger said. "Actually, I think I would enjoy seeing the stables with you. I don't really know too much about the place."

"It has a very interesting history. Are any of you interested in hearing about the company?"

Every one nodded their head in agreement as Flynn continued.

"The Mackinac Island Tours Company has a very noteworthy story. Carriage men officially began providing tours of the Island in 1869 when the first city carriage license was issued.   However, it wasn't until 1948 that the company was incorporated. It also had a very prominent role in making the   Island Michigan's most popular tourist attraction. It all started when the carriage men petitioned the village to ban automobiles because the "horseless carriages" startled the horses."

It's amazing the company is that old," Ginger remarked."

"Yes it is. And to think there are descendants who still actively manage the company after over one hundred years is also surprising. There are other horse companies on the Island but just this one enterprise has approximately one hundred freight and passenger carriages operated by over four hundred horses. It is a very labor intensive job and not a lot of money is made. These people work here because they love it. And they obviously have the biggest horse presence on the Island."

"I read after World War II the owner of 'The Grand' started a promotion called 'Horse is King' and it has continued right up to the present day," Dylan told them. "Having worked with the horses at the hotel everyone connected with the stables was very proud of that fact."

"I remember when I worked as a vet's assistant he told me it took years to assemble the herd. They had to constantly weed out the old horses and make sure the new ones could function safely. Most people don't realize how fragile this venture is. I think the business thrives because of the multi- generations who have worked here with such passion for what they're doing."

Then Flynn continued. "When I had a job here there was a sort of class system on the Island. I remember many of the boys, myself included, were invited to the parties at the mansions of the rich kids. You know we all went to those gatherings. But the fathers' of the Island boys who worked at my company used to tell their sons 'Don't get too uppity. Coachmen use the back door.' Although times were somewhat changing, there was definitely a division between rich and poor. I would hear several of the Island boys talk about resenting that fact. Unlike their fathers, they felt they were just as good as the summer residents."

"It was definitely a different era back then," Ginger added. "And even with changes I would bet there is still a little resentment of the rich people by the Island boys."

"Yes," Flynn agreed. "This is definitely a closed world onto itself. From the moment we arrived, I don't think any of us have known what is going on out in the real world. And, it doesn't even seem important to catch up on what is happening or watch the news while we are here either."

"As interesting as this talk has been," Ginger said, "I think we're all finished eating. How about we go get our bikes and start exercising off some of this food we've been consuming."

Agreeing, they all stood up and walked to the Pool House to get their bicycles. Since there were over seventy miles of natural and paved trails on the Island they thought they might rent bikes on another day to explore the interior. Some of the highlights on the Island included Fort Mackinac, Arch Rock, British Landing, Brown's Brook, Devil's Kitchen as well as great views of the Straits of Mackinac and the Mackinac Bridge, which they had already seen from the Cupola Bar.

Today they were taking the eight-mile perimeter ride. Since it was fairly flat, they had been told it would probably take about an hour and a half. Dylan had gotten a trail map from the Concierge Desk to map out their inland journey on another day.

It was just about an hour and a half later when they returned to the hotel. But instead of turning their bikes in, they continued up the road to the Tour Company's Museum. They spent a few minutes looking around and using the bathrooms before walking down some steps to get to the butterfly house. They spent about twenty minutes at the facility before deciding to leave. They left Jesse there cheerfully asking many questions of the staff.

"He almost looks happy," Olivia remarked as she and Dylan started back to the hotel.

Meanwhile Ginger and Flynn headed to the stables. Introducing the two of them to the employees who were working there, Flynn took Ginger's hand and helped her up the narrow stairs that led to the rafters.

When they got to the top Ginger gasped. "There must be at least twelve to fifteen trunks all over this place. Since they mostly look alike, do you know which one is yours?"

"No, but all of these old trunks use the same key. They gave me two keys downstairs when we arrived so I guess we better start. Who knows what treasures we might find up here?"

CHAPTER 24

Flynn started on one side and Ginger the other. When they opened the trunks they would find a small drawer across the top. Lifting that up they could see what was stored inside. Not finding what they were looking for, they finally got to the last two trunks.

"I'm almost ready to give up, Ginger, Flynn said to her from across the room. There is no reason why one of these last two trunks shouldn't be mine. I guess it makes sense my trunk would be pushed to the back of this area since it has been almost thirty-five years since I left it up here."

Lifting the top of his trunk up, he was relieved to find his belongings. Meanwhile, turning towards Ginger to let her know the good news, he heard her scream. Running towards where she was standing he heard a couple of the workers come racing up the stairs.

"Flynn. Flynn. They're dead!"

As Ginger sat down on the floor crying he looked in the trunk. He saw two bodies entwined wrapped in heavy plastic in the foot locker. Since they had been wrapped in plastic the bodies had been highly preserved since there was no insect activity or bacteria that could get to them. In addition, the trunk had prevented scavenging from rodents so the bones remained intact. Inside the wrapping they looked like classic mummies- shriveled, dried out corpses, but blackened in color.

Turning to the two men who had just arrived, Flynn said, "Call the police." With that he sat down next to Ginger, and to comfort her, he put his arms around her.

Within ten minutes they heard the sound of a vehicle and very quickly Chief Logan came up the stairs. Looking in the trunk he then turning towards Ginger and said, "Do you make a practice out of finding dead bodies?"

Since she appeared shell-shocked, Flynn realized the Chief was trying to add a little levity to the situation hoping she would come back around.

"Looking at the policeman with tears in her eyes she snapped at him, "I am over fifty years old and I have never ever seen a dead body before. Now I have seen two in a matter of days."

Looking back towards the trunk the Chief turned to her and said, "Three bodies, not two. Let's go back downstairs while we wait for the doctor," he said kindly.

Flynn helped her down to the ground level with the Chief right behind them. The officer who came with him stayed to take pictures. Knowing the bodies had been there a long time, the detective knew he wouldn't find any forensic evidence around the area. Too many people had been up there over the years.

One of his other men was bringing the doctor. He wanted the physician to take a cursory look in the original setting. But then he planned to have his men bring the trunk down and send it over to the mainland as quickly as possible for preliminary testing. He had a feeling this time the state lab would probably get involved. And to think I moved to this Island for a relatively quiet lifestyle he thought to himself.

Pulling Flynn aside he asked him what he was doing at the stables. Ginger was finally coming back to reality and watched closely as the Chief questioned her friend.

Flynn explained they had been bike riding and how he had gotten permission to check and see if the trunk he left in the stable almost thirty five years ago was still in the rafters. He then asked if it would be okay for him to take his trunk back to the hotel.

"Let's go back upstairs and show me which one is yours."

As Ginger stayed where she was, Flynn led the way back upstairs and went to an opened trunk on the other side of the room. He told the Chief since there were so many trunks, he had taken one side and Ginger the other looking for his belongings.

The officer was still standing guard where the bodies had been discovered and he called the man over to where they were standing.

"We still need to examine the crime scene." But pointing at Flynn's trunk he told his deputy to bring it downstairs after they took care of the bodies.

"Don't worry. One of my men will deliver this to the cottage as soon as we finish up here. Even though this is a crime that obviously took place a long time ago, remember none of your party should leave the Island."

When they came back down from the loft, Flynn went over to Ginger and asked her if she was okay riding her bike back to the cottage. "The Chief said he could drive us back there if you would like that," he told her.

"No. I'm fine. I think some fresh air will help."

Riding back down the hill they returned the bikes to The Pool House. They noticed Olivia and Dylan sitting at the pool quietly talking together.

As they walked towards their friends, Ginger said, "They aren't going to believe what just happened."

CHAPTER 25

Olivia and Dylan had returned their bikes while Ginger and Flynn were opening trunks at the stable. They decided to sit down by the pool since the weather was so nice and that was where they had to return their bicycles. The area was unoccupied so they knew no one would be listening in on their conversation.

"I want to tell you right off that I am very conflicted about us. I really cared for you Dylan—perhaps even loved you. But we were kids and I thought what we shared was not necessarily a forever thing. People change as they grow up and we were so young."

"I know what you're saying. And obviously we have both changed since then. But I do have feelings for you. Probably not that extremely passionate thing we had back when we were younger but that's not necessarily a bad thing. We liked each other and we were friends. Maybe that gives us a good basis to start a new relationship and see where it leads. At least we have the getting-to-know-you-thing out of the way."

"Do you really think that's possible?"

"You are the only woman I ever felt 'in love' with. As I look back I now realize I married my nurse more out of loneliness than anything else. I was hoping to have children one day but that wasn't to be. And, I really believe Jane married me for the way of life I could provide for her. She immediately fell into the country club and parties' lifestyle I have never cared about."

"That is really heart-breaking, Dylan."

"Yes, I know it was. And instead of trying to work on our marriage we quit communicating. I just worked more and more and she started partying more and more. She drifted from one affair to the next and I was oblivious. Finally, my best friend asked me why I stayed married to someone like her. I didn't know it at the time but later he told me she had made several plays for him. He ignored her since he was happily married but he was also the type of man who would never cheat with his best friend's wife."

"That's terrible. You know I keep thinking that Ginger and Flynn are star-crossed lovers but maybe we are a little like that, too. I certainly wasn't in love with Ben. I married him for the companionship we shared with each other. He was a history teacher like me and we traveled every summer. We liked many of the same things and since we were always paired together we just kind of drifted into marriage. I also wanted children but that never happened for us either. I was sad when he died in a boating accident. But I have never had any interest in dating; much less marrying anyone after he died."

"I felt the same way. It just seemed like too much hard work looking for someone to date who you might not end up being compatible with. But since I have been around you again, I kind of long for a chance to perhaps have someone to share my life with. I'm not talking about a lifelong commitment necessarily. I don't ever want to put that kind of pressure on you again. But since we live close to each other, I would like to try dating if you would like that, too."

"I think we need to take it slow and easy. We could try going out with each other and see what develops."

"I work a lot but I can take time out to explore our relationship and see if it leads anywhere this time around. I realize I've become very tired of being alone. However, at the same time I won't settle for just anyone. I already went down that road. As the song says, 'Love's more comfortable the second time around,' and maybe it can be for us, too."

"Well now that we have that settled do you think Ginger and Flynn stand a chance to get back together? They always seemed like the perfect couple and I couldn't believe it when Flynn married that other woman."

"Long distance relationships are tough. They had two years of long-distance dating and from what Flynn told me, the constant pressure his dad put on him to marry Nancy finally got to him. In a way he just drifted into marriage like we both did. It's a shame because I thought those two would easily weather a forever-after marriage."

"I agree with you, Dylan. I felt so unhappy for the two of them when they drifted apart. They are two people who should have been together forever right from the start. I also wish that I hadn't wasted so many years not contacting her. Now that we know all four of us live so close together I hope we can all be close friends again."

"I guess we'll have to see how things develop with their relationship but I also want that for us, too."

At that moment they looked up and saw Ginger and Flynn coming towards them.

"Oh, oh. Something is wrong. I can see it in Ginger's demeanor."

CHAPTER 26

Standing up Olivia said, "What's wrong?"

"Does it look that obvious?" Ginger replied.

"Are you two okay?"

"We are," Flynn answered.

"Did you find your trunk with clothes?" Dylan asked his friend.

"Yes. And we also found two bodies."

"Bodies? As in dead murdered bodies?" Olivia questioned in disbelief.

Flynn told them how they had been searching on different sides of the loft since there were several trunks that had been left up there.

"We were down to the last couple of trunks when I found my things. Unfortunately Ginger opened her chest and found two mummified bodies entwined with each other. They had to have been murdered because otherwise why were they hidden in a trunk up in the loft?"

"The Chief said they had been there a long time," Ginger told them.

"You had to deal with the Chief again?" Olivia asked.

"Yes, and the man thinks all I do is go around this Island looking for dead bodies."

"That's not true, Ginger. He only said that because you were in shock."

"Well, I have never seen a dead person in my life. And, now three in three days."

"Come on. Let's go up to the cottage. You two need a drink," Dylan said.

"Who do you think they are?" Olivia asked.

"It seems pretty obvious to me. It's not like they have a lot of murders on this Island. I would bet anything that it has to be Bree and her boyfriend, George."

"Ginger, I would love to say you are wrong but that's probably the obvious answer as you suggested," Olivia told her friend.

"As terrible as that sounds I think everyone would be relieved to know what finally happened to them, Dylan told the others. "I don't think you women ever knew but I actually dated Bree a couple of times."

"Really?" Olivia said in a shocked voice.

"Yes, really. But we both realized we were not right for each other and the following weekend I met you for the first time and never looked back."

They soon arrived at the cottage and Flynn immediately went behind the wet bar while the others sat down. Ginger sat down on the couch and waited for him as he mixed up a pitcher of martinis.

"I have not had a martini in years and now this is the fourth day in a row I am having one. I need to break this habit, especially when I go home," Olivia bemoaned.

The rest of them laughed and they started to relax after that.

As they were sipping their cocktails, Ginger said, "I don't really feel up for going to the Cupola Bar and dinner at the hotel tonight. It won't take long for the word to spread about the bodies being discovered. And I'm not really ready to answer a bunch of questions about what we found this afternoon. Do any of you mind if we go eat somewhere else?"

"I'm all for that," Flynn replied. How about you two? Do you two want to join us and go somewhere else for dinner?"

"I know I would," Olivia answered as Dylan nodded in agreement. "Why don't we go to the Woods Restaurant? I think some Bavarian food sounds good. And it might be fun to take a carriage ride there."

"That sounds like a great idea and we can dress more casually. Since we just had a drink I think I'll skip the appetizers tonight."

"Good thought. Let those two women have them all for all I care. And how about if we two men team up against you two ladies for a couple of rounds of duckpin bowling after dinner."

"I think we're in trouble, Olivia. It's like croquet all over again except this time in teams. I'm going to take a long soak in the hot tub to prepare myself for tonight's competition. Flynn, why don't you call for a dinner reservation for about 7:30 p.m. and order a carriage to take us? I don't know if we have to reserve a time for bowling or not."

"Don't worry. I'll take care of it. What about Jesse? Should we invite him?"

"I asked him about going to dinner with us tonight when we were at the butterfly house," Ginger answered him. He said he would just eat some of the appetizers or find something in the cupboards. I think he really felt Harper's loss today doing the activities he did with us without her."

Olivia, who had also decided to get in the hot tub, left with Ginger for their room to get their swimming suits.

As they were departing Flynn said, "After the calls, I think I'll take a shower and read a little before we go to dinner."

"That's a good idea. I like that our room has some nice chairs for reading. That way we can avoid those two women when they come down for their appetizers. I guess we're lucky they don't spend more time downstairs where we would constantly have to interact with them."

"Yes. That is a blessing."

CHAPTER 27

They could hear Riley and Tess talking to Neal since their rooms were right next to the living room. It was 6:25 p.m. on the dot when they heard them say good-bye to the waiter.

Coming out of their rooms at the same time the four of them saw plates of food and cans all over the end tables.

"I don't know how anyone can drink all those sodas and beers," Ginger said.

"Don't worry about a thing. I'll take care of this mess. Can I get you anything?" Neal asked.

"No, we don't want anything else. And, we aren't worried about this mess. We know you'll do an excellent job of cleaning up. We had drinks earlier and we decided to go to The Woods Restaurant tonight so we didn't want any appetizers. Our carriage will be here soon."

"Did you hear that they found some bodies at the Carriage Company stables?" the man asked them.

"Actually, Ginger found them," Olivia answered.

"Really? How did that happen?"

"We were looking for a foot locker of clothes that Flynn left here many years ago. When I opened up one of the trunks, there they were."

"Everyone in the hotel is talking about it."

"And that's why we aren't going to the hotel for dinner tonight. I just wasn't up for answering a lot of questions."

"I'm sorry, Ginger, I didn't mean to pry."

"I wasn't talking about you, Neal. I meant our friends who are staying in the hotel. That will be the main topic of conversation tonight. And, when they find out I discovered the bodies they'll want to interrogate me, if you know what I mean."

"You're probably right about that. Do the police know who the bodies were?"

"Not really. But the Chief thinks they have been dead a long time. So since there is not a lot of crime on the Island, speculation seems to point to Bree and George."

"Really? Is that what the police think?"

"I don't know for sure. Did you know them, Neal?"

"I only knew Bree, mostly in passing, since I went to some of the same parties you all went to. Of course, I knew George. He worked at the stables where Flynn and I did."

"Probably after all this time there will be no way for them to find out who killed them but at least their families will have closure."

"It's so distressing though," Olivia remarked. "Not just their deaths but also the fact that Bree might have become a big movie star and all her potential was lost at such a young age."

"That's very true. Do any of you know if Jesse is coming down tonight?"

"He will be down later. He said he would just eat some appetizers or something in the cupboards. Can you wrap up the leftovers and put them in the fridge? I think he wanted to avoid those two women and will probably be down when the maid comes for the turn down."

Just then they heard a knock at the door and realized their carriage had arrived to take them to dinner.

"Time to go ladies," Dylan said.

They all said goodnight to Neal as they left the cottage.

It was a beautiful ride to the restaurant. Since the sun was setting, the air was crisper and everyone had brought a sweater or light jacket for the ride since the carriage was uncovered.

"Just think. Everyone is up in the Cupola Bar watching another beautiful sunset," Ginger mused.

"We can go back up there tomorrow night," Flynn said. Maybe by then some of the hoopla over the murders will have lessened a little bit."

When they arrived at the restaurant they saw an opulent looking Tudor Mansion. As they descended from the carriage, their driver gave them a number to call when they were ready to go home. "Just give me fifteen minutes to get here," he told them.

"We will be bowling after dinner. What time do you quit for the night?" Flynn asked the man.

"I am at your disposal. I usually don't work past midnight. I know the bowling alley closes at 10:00 p.m. so you'll probably be ready about then."

"Yes, I'm sure that's right. How about we'll call you if it's going to be later than that but otherwise why don't you plan to be here at 10:00 p.m.?"

Entering the restaurant they discovered a room with a beautiful Bavarian atmosphere. The dining area had a lot of charm as well as a unique casual feeling. They were all happy they had decided to come here.

As they were eating dinner, Olivia said, "I can't remember the last time I went bowling. I know it's been a long time. But I have always liked to bowl. However, I have no idea what in the world is duckpin bowling?"

Laughing, Dylan said, "The pins are arranged in a triangle just like ten-pin bowling. But the pins are shorter and slightly thinner and lighter. Because of that it makes it more difficult to get a strike. So everyone gets three rolls per frame."

Giggling Ginger asked, "Does that mean gutter balls don't count as a roll?"

Dylan raised his eyes towards the sky and sighed at her question which made her giggle all the more.

Dinner was delicious as usual. They supposed it would be very difficult to find a bad meal at any restaurant connected to the hotel. The men ended up winning the first round of bowling. But the women got used to the feel and with the lighter balls beat the men the second round. They would have gone for the rubber game of the match but the bowling alley was closing for the night. Because of that, they decided they would have to come back again before they left the Island to determine which team won the competition.

As they walked outside they saw their carriage arriving to take them back to the cottage. Although cooler than on the way to the restaurant, the night was still pleasant. They enjoyed the ride back and except for the clip clop of the horses, the peacefulness that surrounded them.

As the carriage pulled up to the cottage, they were not aware of Jesse watching from above. He was sitting in the alcove by the window and observed them as they alighted from the landau.

He had waited until everyone had left for dinner before he went downstairs. As he was preparing his food, Riley and Tess had come back from their meal. They immediately told him about the murders and how supposedly Ginger had found the bodies.

Remembering that conversation, he watched as Ginger descended from the carriage. At least she couldn't accuse him of those long-ago murders he was thinking to himself. He still couldn't believe that his beloved Harper had been taken from him so early in their marriage.

CHAPTER 28

It was another beautiful fall day which was definitely not a given. This time of the year could be rainy and cold. Jesse went with them at 8:30 a.m. to breakfast. They had read in their TODAY paper that the history lecture would be on the porch. The topic was the movies that were made on the Island.

"That should be interesting," Olivia commented. "I remember hearing a similar lecture years ago."

Just as Ginger suspected, several of their friends came to the table asking about her discovering the bodies. She knew there was no way around it, so she just told those asking that she would be in the parlor after she ate, and before the lecture, to answer their questions. She didn't want to ruin breakfast for her friends by constantly talking about the subject while they were eating.

"I know you have to do this, Ginger. People love to hear the details, especially about murder," Flynn told her.

They finished eating about 9:30 a.m. which gave her about twenty minutes to answer their queries before going to the lecture. She wasn't really excited about talking about the situation but she knew if she didn't, she would be asked all day long about what had happened, whenever anyone saw her.

Ginger could hardly wait to get the matter over with so she sat patiently and gave them her version of what had happened.

"The thing is," she told the group while she was sitting in the parlor, "I don't really know anything other than finding them in the trunk. They were wrapped around each other as if holding on for dear life."

However the questions still continued as to why and how and when the situation happened. At 9:45 a.m. her friends went out to get chairs for the lecture letting her know they would save one for her. Finally, just before 10:00 a.m. everyone, seeming to be satisfied with her answers, drifted out to the porch to hear the talk or went to ride bikes or horses.

It was a very interesting lecture and even Jesse seemed to enjoy it. As they continued sitting and rocking on the porch after the talk was over, Flynn said, "Ladies, we have a great plan for this afternoon."

As the women looked at him, he continued, "Dylan and I want to rent a horse and buggy for part of today. We made a reservation at Jack's Livery Stable for a four passenger rig. We can cancel if you don't want to do it. But we thought we could take a ride through the state park and stop and hear the interpretations at the fort. After that, we can just go wherever the mood strikes us. How does that sound to you two?"

"I like it," Ginger said. "Once again I just want to say I am so glad I planned everything out for everyone."

"We are, too," Flynn said, laughing at her.

"Why don't we go over to The Jockey Club and get some sandwiches for lunch," Olivia suggested. "I'm not really a golfer but I would like to check out the restaurant. We could do take-out and eat on our patio again like we did the other day?"

"That would be nice," Ginger said. "Then we could take our buggy ride through the park. And I would love to have some time to read later this afternoon. And, now that I have everyone's questions out of the way about the bodies we found, we can enjoy our time in the Cupola Bar before dinner tonight, without anyone bothering us."

The two men took off for a little while and when they returned they all walked over to The Jockey Club. Jesse walked with them to get lunch but earlier had passed on the idea of riding a horse beside their carriage.

"I'll probably come back to the porch and sit in a rocking chair and read. It'll feel good to get out of my room. And that way I won't have to listen to that television blaring through the house."

"I can't believe all those two women do is eat and watch TV. As a doctor it pains me to see such an unhealthy practice," Dylan remarked.

"And it's also a shame about Tess. She seems to have no thoughts of her own. She just follows blindly and does whatever Riley tells her to do. Sometimes I get the feeling she doesn't like some of the things Riley says or does but she just keeps quiet," Ginger observed.

"Well at least we are all having a good time despite their behavior," Olivia replied.

After lunch it was a short leisurely stroll to Jack's Stables. As they walked Flynn gave the women a brief history of the stables.

"In 1953 Jack's was started by the Gough family. Before that you could only rent a couple of horse and buggies around the island. When the two brothers died in the 1970's their children took over the business. Dylan and I actually knew those men when we worked here. They are now into their fourth generation of Goughs in the horse business here on the Island. It is amazing to think they had three horses in 1952 and today they have over seventy-five carriages and riding horses."

"They also have a pretty strict horse and buggy policy," Dylan added. "We walked over here earlier and filled out the driving questionnaire while you were rocking on the porch. We knew that would save us some time now.

The questionnaire is their way to assess our driving experience."

Flynn continued, "As soon as they knew we had worked with the horses on the island previously, they realized we didn't need any further training. However, when we get there they want everyone to read and agree to the rules of the road. They want to make sure our experience is as safe as possible. And they gave us a road map and suggested the route we plan to take."

And, just as Flynn said, when the four of them arrived at the stables they were given a sheet with the following information: Keep the horse and buggy at a walk when going uphill and downhill. Steer wide around corners. Absolutely no U-turns. The horse is to be driven only by the designated driver. Trot or walk, but never gallop the horse. Rest the horse by walking it between periods of trotting. Do not tie the horse or leave the horse unattended at any time. If driving along Lake Shore Drive, do not stop the horse until British Landing. If a stop is made, have an adult hold the horse by the bridle. All passengers remain seated while the buggy is in motion. Finally, stay out of the downtown area.

When they finally got into the buggy and on their way, Ginger said, "That was a lot of rules. But the only one Olivia and I need to worry about is staying seated while we are moving. Since this was your idea, and a good one at that, you two men are the designated drivers and you both can worry about those other rules."

CHAPTER 29

Flynn took the reins as they started out with Ginger sitting beside him. Olivia and Dylan sat in the back. While they were trotting along, Dylan told them, "When I used to drive the carriages for the hotel, people would ask me a lot of questions about the Island. And amazingly, even after all these years, I remember a lot of what I used to tell them."

"Where are we going first," Olivia inquired?

"Flynn will drive us into the State Park and we'll make our way over to Fort Mackinac. After that I'll take over and will take all of us over to Arch Rock."

"I know that is one of the must see places on the Island," Ginger said to him. "For some reason I never got over to the rock when I worked here.

"Yes, it's definitely an Island must see," Dylan continued. "It stands one hundred forty six feet over the Lake Huron shoreline, and is nearly fifteen stories high. It is made from a rare limestone for the Great Lakes and took thousands of years by wind, water and receding glaciers to be created. And it's over fifty feet wide which can take your breath away at such a beautiful sight. The sweeping views of Lake Huron and even up to Canada are amazing on a clear day."

"It sounds fantastic," Olivia remarked.

"It is. But let me give you an overview of the State Park since that's where we're headed first."

As Dylan was talking they saw a sign that read: "Entering Mackinac Island State Park."

"Talk about good timing," Ginger declared.

Back into teaching mode he continued, "This is Michigan's first state park and 82% of the Island is contained in this park. And it's free to the public. Since automobiles are banned you can definitely feel a quieter way of life when you're here on the island as I am sure you all know. Other things you'll notice in the park are limestone bluffs, beautiful vistas of sparkling water, vibrant forests, and mystical geological formations. I never get tired of looking at those sites when I drive through this place."

"What kind of animals live here in the park?"

"Not a lot, Olivia. Since this island only has about an eight mile circumference very few mammals inhabit this place. There are a few that come over on the ice in the winter months and coyotes have become a problem for local wildlife. Bats are the most common mammal because of all the caves that are found here and there are a lot of birds. Blue Jays, woodpeckers and cardinals live here year round but eagles, hawks, herons, loons and seagulls are mostly summer visitors. And there are lots of fish like whitefish, trout, walleye, and perch."

It was so peaceful and quiet as they drove along in the buggy and the forest seemed to surround them. Just like the previous evening, as they cantered along, the only noise they heard was the clip clop of the horses. After listening to Dylan's talk everyone sat back and enjoyed the ride in a peaceful silence. It was about twenty minutes later that the forest gave way and they entered a large field where Fort Mackinac was located high on a bluff overlooking the lake.

Just before they got to the fort, Dylan started talking again. "As you look out over the Straits of Mackinac you can see the bridge that divides Lake Huron from Lake Michigan. This was a very strategic area in the late 18th to late 19th centuries and was especially important for controlling the fur trade. Because of that fact, the British did not relinquish ownership of this area until fifteen years after American Independence."

As they pulled the buggy over to park, a teenager came walking towards them.

"I already purchased our tickets online. And I took care of paying this boy you see coming over here to take care of the horse and buggy while we're inside. That way we can all go in together since we aren't allowed to leave the horse and carriage unattended."

Then he continued, "There are fourteen restored building that are furnished with period settings related to each building's particular function. And there's a movie that repeats every twenty minutes. You'll also notice costumed interpreters everywhere to answer questions and at some point while we're here we'll see a drill, tactics and firearms program. It's pretty interesting to see the cannon blasts, rifles fire and soldiers march."

"This is so exciting, Dylan. Even though I worked on the Island for two summers, I never got up here to the fort or to see the program," Ginger explained.

They spent an hour roaming around the grounds and watching the program. They went in to see the movie last because by then they were ready to sit down for a few minutes. Everything about the fort had been so interesting and they had all learned a lot.

"I just hope I remember all this information I heard today," Ginger told the others.

"It's amazing that there can be that much to absorb when you visit an Island as small as this one."

"You're right, Dylan," she agreed with him.

Ginger observed Flynn getting on his phone just as they were getting ready to leave. By the time they exited the grounds they saw their buggy come towards them. She then noticed Flynn give the boy some money. As they walked over to the carriage he directed her to the backseat of the buggy while Dylan and Olivia sat in front.

"That is enough history and talking," Dylan told the others. "Let's just enjoy the ride over to Arch Rock. It's not very far from here."

As they sat relaxed in the buggy Flynn took Ginger's hand. With a sigh she looked at him and smiled. It was turning out to be a perfect afternoon as they continued through the park.

When they arrived at Arch Rock, the two women followed the path with Flynn over to the bridge. As they climbed to the middle they could look all the way down to the beach. Dylan stayed back and held the horse. After he took a couple of pictures Flynn went back to the horse and buggy and Dylan joined the women. Everything was so peaceful and all thoughts of murders were forgotten as they serenely made their way back to the stables.

CHAPTER 30

"Let's go for a walk down by the water," Flynn suggested as he took Ginger's hand after they had returned the horse and buggy.

Olivia and Dylan started back up to hotel. "I want to show Dylan the Secret Garden on the way to the cottage."

"That's a great idea. Flynn and I will also plan to stop there on our way back."

Saying good-bye to their friends they began walking towards the lake. On their way to the water Flynn took her hand. She immediately felt a bolt like electricity surge through her. This is crazy she thought to herself. How can he possibly affect me like this? We haven't seen each other in years and yet it seems like yesterday. Even her stomach clenched up in anticipation of what she was feeling.

She didn't realize it but Flynn was having similar feelings towards her. They found a bench close to the water's edge and sat down. They had no idea Olivia and Dylan had already addressed their new developing relationship.

As they looked out at the water, Flynn said, "We have to talk about this. You can't deny something is happening between us. I didn't think I would ever feel this way again. I know you're probably worrying that I will hurt you like before but I'll never do that to you."

"I know you wouldn't hurt me. But we have evolved and we're different people now Flynn."

"I don't believe we are that different from before. We have grown up and we have gotten older and our hopes and wishes may have changed. But we are still the same people we were back then. I have been thinking about 'us' a lot the last few days. Being honest with myself, I know I never got over you. When we finished college we had just drifted apart mainly because of distance. And my dad kept hammering at me to be with Nancy. I know now he was brainwashing me into living a way of life he was brought up with. Nancy was nice enough but I never loved her; not like I loved you. And, that was a terrible way to base a marriage on."

"I couldn't believe you had married someone else. I kept waiting for you to call and ask me to come be with you. After I heard of your marriage, I was devastated."

"I knew what I had done to you was unforgiveable. I know I owed you some kind of explanation but I ignored what my heart was telling me. It was only a few hours after we were married that I realized I had made a terrible mistake. Nancy kept telling me how happy she was that someone would take care of her the rest of her life, and now she would never have to work. She went on and on about the 'Country Club' style of living we would enjoy."

Ginger could hear the anguish in his voice as he continued.

"I knew I had 'made my bed' so to speak. My parents would have been humiliated if I had the marriage annulled. Although all I thought about those first few days was running away to be with you. But I realized it was my own stupid fault for agreeing to marry her, and I had to take responsibility for my actions. The only thing good about my marriage was our son, Peter."

"Surely Nancy realized something was not right...didn't she?

"No, not really. I don't think she really knew how to love. She had this romanticized vision of how her life should be and she was living it. She never really bonded with Peter. And after she produced our 'heir', she eliminated sex from our life. She felt she had done her duty. I shouldn't speak ill of the dead because I really felt sorry for the empty life we were living."

"I feel so bad for you, Flynn. I had no idea you were suffering like that."

"Because of our circumstances I buried myself in work. I became extremely wealthy but if it wasn't for my son I don't know if I would still be alive today. I really didn't wish her any evil. I knew I was partly to blame since I didn't want to live the kind of lifestyle she wanted. When she got cancer, I scaled back on my work and took care of her. I felt it was the only right thing to do. But I have to tell you it was like a huge burden was lifted off my shoulders when she died."

"I can understand that."

"Ironically, I had several single women who chased after me when Nancy passed. But I wasn't interested in any of them. I looked you up and saw you were married and realized our being together could never be. So I took care of Peter and my work and eventually the women quit pursuing me. They thought I had lost the love of my life. The paradox was it was not who they thought."

Laying her head on his shoulder she said, "Maybe we can have a second chance, Flynn. It's so strange how empty our lives have been. After I heard about your marriage I married the first eligible man I met. We were definitely not compatible. My husband had affairs right from the beginning of our marriage. I was too naïve to know but he was probably having them before we married, too. I got pregnant almost right after the wedding. By the time I realized what he was doing I didn't think I would have enough money to support myself and my daughter."

"Surely you would have gotten alimony?"

"Probably, but times were different back then for a woman. He agreed to support Amber and me so we had an amiable separation. There was no need to divorce. I certainly wasn't interested in having another man in my life. And I was busy raising my daughter and working. It was also perfect for him. He continued having affairs. But telling the women he was married kept them from pressuring him into a more lasting relationship."

"I just feel terrible about what you went through. I blame myself for your horrible marriage."

"It wasn't your fault. I had no blinders on when I married. Back then being married was what was expected of women. If it had been today I would have stayed single. So it really had nothing to do with you. It was just the way it was in those days."

"I suppose you're right about that."

"We always said we would stay together for Amber's sake. And he was not a bad father. It was like being divorced because he would take her to his place every other weekend. He was very involved in her after school activities and always spent Christmas and Thanksgiving with us. I know it seems like a strange situation but it worked. And then when our daughter was in high school he fell in love with a woman he met. We decided we would divorce when Amber left for college."

With a sigh she continued, "He helped with Amber's schooling when she went to college. We divorced as soon as she departed. I got the house free and clear. I had my job and made pretty good money and had been saving for years. So he kept his money. I didn't want anything else from him. It just felt good to be finally clear of him. And my life has continued that way for the last ten years. There was one man at the bank who was interested in me but I told him I had no desire to date so he found someone else to go out with."

"I really felt bad when I heard about your parents. That was a terrible way to die, although I know they were very close and at least they went together."

"It was devastating. Amber and I were extremely close to them. They never said a word or reproached me for my lifestyle. I think they knew about my husband's affairs. But they were nice to him because of how involved he was with Amber throughout the years. But I have to tell you, if it wasn't for them, I would have never believed there could be such a thing as a happy loving relationship. It seemed like everyone I knew got divorced."

"I often wondered about my own parents. They were so caught up in the 'Country Club' scene and with keeping up appearances. I question whether they really love each other. Their life together seems like an empty shell."

"I think in their own way they are happy together, Flynn. They wouldn't have stayed together otherwise. People were raised so differently in those days. Like your wife, they did what was expected of them. Their parents drilled into them on how they should lead their lives and they tried to do the same with you. In a way, we were like a misplaced generation. We didn't want to live the old lifestyle of our parents but we weren't sure what the new way should be like either."

"I can tell you have really thought this through, Ginger."

"Yes. I truly believe, as C.S. Lewis said, 'You can't go back and change the beginning but you can start where you are and change the ending.' Now that we have gotten our little talk over I'll tell you what I want right now."

Worrying about what she would say, he turned towards her.

Unexpectedly, he heard her say, "I want to have fun! I am retired and I have enough money to travel and I want to see the world. I want to be there for my daughter but she has taken her own path which is the way it should be. I know we will always be close but I don't want to cling to her. So I am looking for adventure and hopefully no more murders."

"Definitely no more murders," he said, laughing. "Besides, we haven't solved these three yet."

"You don't think they are related do you? Even though it's hard to believe the way Jesse is acting that he could have killed Harper, inheriting a million dollars is a big motive. And don't they say it's usually not the most obvious person?"

"That's only in books, Ginger. In real life criminals can be stupid and give themselves away. I looked Jesse up online. Do you know he was married previously? He was only married for three years when his wife died under mysterious circumstances. He cashed in a big life insurance policy on her, too. It just seems kind of suspicious something like that would happen twice to the same person. I know the Chief is looking into him as a very serious suspect. He told me it's hard to believe in coincidences."

"I didn't know that. It always amazes me that you can look people up on the internet today and find pretty much everything about their life. It's pretty hard to hide your past nowadays. I keep wondering if Riley is somehow involved. Maybe it's because I don't like the woman. She and Tess came back here another summer after we left. Maybe she was also somehow involved in the missing case of Bree and George."

"It probably wouldn't hurt us to question some of our friends when we go for drinks tonight. Several of them were here after the disappearance and maybe we can learn something from one of them. But right now it's getting late. I would really like you to show me the garden and then get back to the cottage to get cleaned up for the evening."

Getting up from the bench, Flynn once again took her hand as they cut through the pool area and over to where the Secret Garden was located. He was astounded, as most people were, when the little path opened up to the sea of flowers.

"Those blue flowers are amazing. They look like a river."

"They are grape hyacinths and that's exactly what they are supposed to be; a flowing river of flowers."

With tears in her eyes on their way out Ginger showed him a bench. "That was where Harper sat before we took her back to her room on the golf cart. She was so winded from walking in here. But she seemed so happy with her life. I just can't believe she's gone."

CHAPTER 31

They walked back to the cottage holding hands, and when they arrived they could hear the sounds coming from the upstairs television. Otherwise all was quiet and there was no one in sight.

"I'll see you at 5:30 p.m. for drinks," she told him.

Leaning over he kissed her lightly on the lips. Then smiling at her, he went into his bedroom.

"Obviously something good has happened to you," Olivia said as Ginger entered their room.

"Why would you say that?" she asked her friend.

"You're grinning like a Cheshire cat."

Sitting on her bed she told Olivia what had happened between her and Flynn. "I can't believe we may get a second chance at love."

"You two are perfect for each other and have always been. I'm so glad you are getting the possibility to work things out again. You both deserve happiness. The two of you have been alone for such a long time. You know it's important to grab happiness when the opportunity comes along. You don't always get a chance for a do over. You know they say that without risk there is no reward. It was obvious something had to give between the two of you. There was such a palpable tension between you both ever since you laid eyes on each other on Sunday."

"But what about you and Dylan? I can sense something is different with you two, also."

"We had a talk."

"Why didn't you tell me?"

"We just finished talking when you came up and told us about the bodies you found. All thoughts other than that flew out the window, or into the pool, as the situation dictated."

"So what did you decide?"

"We told each other about our past lives. I think we are both a little gun shy but we realize there is a definite spark between us, also. We decided to take it slow and easy and see where the relationship leads. We are hoping when we get back home all four of us can see more of each other."

"That would be so much fun. I know I would enjoy that and I think Flynn would, too. The four of us seem so compatible when we're together. Sometimes it feels surreal that this reunion even came up and we all got a chance to be with each other again."

"That's true. But you could also call it fate."

"Yes, I guess you could. I still find it hard to believe that Dylan dated Bree."

"They were definitely not suited for each other. I know she met George right at the end of our first summer on the Island. Even though we didn't know his name, do you remember that second summer how happy she was? And, since they were so wrapped up in each other we barely saw her."

"They were definitely in love. That's why everyone thought they had run away together to New York or Hollywood. Bree always wanted to be a star and George definitely supported her dream."

Standing up from the bed, Ginger said, "I need to take a shower and clean up. The time for appetizers and drinks will be here soon."

At 5:30 p.m. the women came out of their room. Flynn was fixing the martinis with Dylan's help and Neal was just coming into the cottage.

"What took you so long?" Riley shouted at him from the chair where she was seated. "We have been sitting here waiting for you to bring the food and get our drinks.

"I am so sorry, ladies. They were backed up in the kitchen preparing the food for tonight, and I came as fast as I could."

"Don't worry, Neal," Ginger told him. "It's just 5:30 p.m. right now anyway."

"You mind your own business," Riley said as she turned towards Ginger.

That is odd, Olivia was thinking. If looks could kill Riley just got one from Neal. I'll have to talk to Ginger about that.

Meanwhile Flynn barely able to contain himself said, "If you can't say anything nice to people, then why don't you two leave and go back upstairs to the media room?"

"I am paying just as much for this dump as you all are. Whoever heard of a hotel with no television sets in the bedrooms? I have to go up and down those stairs all day long and I'm getting sick and tired of it."

Hearing a gasp from the stairs they all turned as Jesse said, "What in the world is going on down here?"

"You keep out of this," Riley continued as she looked at him. "For all we know you're a murderer and one of us could be next."

In a very low voice they heard Flynn say, "Get out. Get out right now. You two go upstairs and pack your things right this minute. I will call the front desk and get you a room in the hotel. I will also have a bellman come get your luggage. I want you out of here as soon as possible. And as far as I am concerned, I don't want either of you talking to any of us ever again."

"You can't make us leave here. And besides, I don't want to be in a small room with Tess. We have more room here. You can't..."

"Stop! Not another word. I will get you both your own rooms over there. But you better be quiet right this minute. If you say one more word, negative or otherwise, I will have you kicked out of this hotel. And don't for a second think that I can't do it. So are you going upstairs to pack or am I having you thrown out of the hotel altogether?"

No one said a word as the two women got off the couch and went up the stairs. Once again glancing towards Neal, Olivia saw a smirk on his face. That's interesting, she thought.

"I am really sorry about that," Flynn said apologetically. "I couldn't take another minute of those two women. I am sick of the television blaring constantly and how sloppy they are. But when they started putting us down, they went too far. If you'll excuse me for a minute, I need to call the front desk." And with that he went back into his bedroom.

"Let me pour everyone a cocktail," Neal said as he took the pitcher away from Dylan.

They all sat back shocked by what had just happened and waited for the waiter to serve them their martini.

"Wow! When he gets mad I guess it's not good to cross him," Olivia remarked.

"He just cares about all of us and everyone reaches a boiling point. I'm sorry you had to be the brunt of most of that," Ginger said looking at Jesse.

"I do not know if you will believe me or not. Maybe no one will believe me, unless the actual killer is caught, but I will tell you all once again. I did not kill Harper."

Just as he said that, Flynn also hearing him came walking back into the room.

"I need a drink," he said as he started to sit down next to Ginger. Before he finished sitting Neal was next to him with a glass in hand.

"Well, that was pretty awkward but at least it's over with. I couldn't have taken another three days with those two women. Jesse, I don't know if you killed your wife or not. But to accuse someone of that with no evidence is inexcusable to me. And if they said it once, it wouldn't be very long before they would keep up those snide remarks towards you around everyone. I think we all came here to have an enjoyable time together; not to have to put up with petty negative comments from a couple of gluttonous women."

It wasn't long before they heard Riley and Tess huffing and puffing down the stairs. Riley was holding an empty carry-on bag. She went into the kitchen and filled the bag with cans of soda and beer. She had another bag inside the carry-on that she had removed before putting the cans inside. She filled the second bag with chips, pretzels, and some other snacks. She and Tess then left the cottage, slamming the door behind them.

"I am so glad that is over," Ginger remarked. "But they're going to be upset when they discover lunch doesn't come with their rooms."

"I know only breakfast and dinner is usually included in the room cost. Because of that and the way those two eat, I added the lunch buffet to be included with the price of their room. They were told all meals came with this cottage, and I wasn't going to have them raise a stink if they didn't get their lunch as promised."

"Personally I think it was extremely generous of you to get each of them their own rooms in addition to including lunch. You didn't need to do that," Dylan said.

"I can afford it and I just wanted to get rid of them. Now let's get back to more pleasant conversations."

"Jesse, are you coming to dinner with us?"

"I don't think so, Ginger. Maybe I'm being paranoid but I'm not comfortable sitting there with a lot of people who are speculating whether or not I killed my wife."

Immediately Neal jumped in, "Let me take care of you, Jesse. I have a copy of tonight's menu. Why don't you tell me what you want, and I will go pick it up for you and bring it over when the restaurant opens."

"That would be great. Thank you, Neal. I appreciate that. I would enjoy sitting here having dinner and not hearing the television blasting."

Not wanting to talk about the murders in front of him, the four of them began telling Jesse about their horse and buggy ride and what they had seen on their adventure. The time passed quickly as they chatted. Neal left to get Jesse's order and at 6:30 p.m. the four of them said goodnight to the man and walked over to the hotel to go to the Cupola Bar.

CHAPTER 32

Once again they took glasses of wine with them as they walked over to the hotel. Ginger mentioned how she and Flynn thought it might be a good idea to question some of their friends who had been around the year of and the year after when the disappearance of Bree and George had occurred.

"We thought perhaps someone might remember some small detail that had been forgotten. We both think it's worth a try."

"What? You two are becoming amateur sleuths now?" Olivia asked jokingly.

"It could be our new mission in life. Now that I am getting used to finding dead people, we can travel the world finding bodies and solving their murders."

"Don't you think the local police are better equipped to solve crimes?"

"Yes, but we could bring a fresh eye or new perspective that they had not thought of previously."

"I hope you are joking about that, Ginger."

Smiling at Flynn, she entered the elevator to go up to the bar.

When they entered the lounge, they saw a small group of people surrounding a woman who was quietly crying.

"I wonder what that's about." Olivia asked Ginger as they climbed the stairs to the second level. Julie had told them that would be where they could find her. The room was very lively and noisy as they made their way over to an empty table Julie had saved for them. She and her husband, Chuck, were sitting at a table with another couple. She introduced the four of them to the new twosome. Their names were Ruth and David.

"You bring your own wine?" Ruth asked.

Ginger explained how their drinks were free since they were staying at the Mateo Cottage.

Then Julie interrupted her friend. "Tomorrow we get to tour the cottage I was telling you about a little while ago. The Welcome Reception will be held there since our friends here are hosting the affair."

"Everyone has been talking about that place. It will be exciting to go over there and get a look inside. And the weather is supposed to be fantastic again tomorrow. We really have had exceptional weather conditions this week."

"Are you two men interested in joining us for a round of golf tomorrow afternoon?" Dylan asked.

"That sounds great. We tried to get a tee time and they were all booked up," Chuck replied.

"That's why we are going in the afternoon. That was the only time available."

"What about Jesse?" Ginger asked.

"We asked him this afternoon when we called to get on the schedule. But he said he didn't want to go because he would keep thinking about what happened when he went there the last time with us."

"What happened?" David asked.

Dylan then explained to the other couple about Harper dying.

"We heard about that," Ruth told them.

"Then you won't believe what happened next, Ruth," Julie told her friend. "Two days later, Ginger and Flynn found those two bodies in the trunk at the stable."

"Really? That was you two? Have they said whether or not it is Bree and George?"

"No, they haven't but we think it must be," Ginger replied. "And, we were wondering, since we were only here two summers, if anyone who was here longer had heard anything else that following year about what happened to the two of them? Also, there is some woman in the downstairs bar, crying. I wonder what that's about."

"We'll check on those concerns for you," Ruth said.

"Are you two ladies coming to the afternoon tea tomorrow?"

"Once again you caught us off guard, Julie. What tea?"

"We had a note from the reunion committee under our door this afternoon, Ginger. You'll probably have yours when you get back to the cottage."

"That sounds like a lot of fun. Don't you agree, Olivia?"

"Yes. And that gives us something entertaining to do while the men are golfing. It will also give us a chance to get to know some of the others a little better before the cocktail party."

"And knowing the way they think those ladies will want to hear all about your exploits this week. It will also be a good occasion to check with them and see if anyone remembers anything from back when we worked here."

"Here comes Kathy and Tom, just in time for the sunset. You remember them from the other night, right?"

"We do." The four nodded as they said hello to the couple who had just joined them.

"I hope you don't mind but I took the liberty of reserving us a table for ten since I knew we would all be meeting up here."

"That sounds great," Ginger told her friend.

As soon as the sun set the majority of the people left the bar and headed to the dining room. They had a wonderful dinner and after they ate, proceeded to the

Terrace Room for dancing. It was very crowded since so many of the reunion people were now checked into the hotel. They found some tables and chairs and when the orchestra started playing everyone got up to dance. No one left until the last song was played.

When the orchestra stopped for the evening the two couples left the hotel holding hands.

"You know, I could get used to this way of life very easily," Ginger remarked as they walked back to the cottage.

Arriving at the house they said good night to each other and went into their rooms. As Julie had predicted, they saw the note about the afternoon tea the next afternoon, followed by the Welcome Reception at the Mateo Cottage.

"I confirmed the numbers yesterday and they are predicting somewhere around seventy-five to eighty people for the reception. I am sure everyone will come since they'll want to get a look at the cottage. Actually the hotel staff was happy we were hosting it. They believe it will be good advertisement and they feel some of the people may book this place after they see it."

"I know I'm happy that we rented this house. And it should be an even more awesome experience the last three days with those two women gone from here."

"I have some other news I forgot to mention. They want to come about 3:00 p.m. and set up, including extra tables and chairs outside. They are also sending over some additional maids to give the cottage an extra sprucing up."

"Well that makes sense, Ginger."

"Yes. And they don't want us in the way so they have set up some spa time so all five of us can get our hair done, or whatever, while they are doing the preparations. I'll let them know Riley and Tess are no longer living here. We don't owe those women anything extra. We also need to let the men know tomorrow about the spa."

"Once again it seems like we will be extremely busy tomorrow. I'm glad we have some free time in the morning to just do nothing."

CHAPTER 33

The next morning everyone met at 8:15 a.m. to walk to breakfast. Hearing their news, Jesse told them he was not interested in going to the spa.

"I plan to go back to the butterfly conservatory in the afternoon. If you don't mind I'll go to dinner in the hotel this evening and then come back to my room. I don't know any of these people and do not have anything in common with any of them. And, as I said previously, they just want to see me so they can say they met the man who murdered Harper," he finished contemptuously.

"We just need you to be comfortable with any decision you make. We also want you to know you can join us at any time."

"Thank you. I appreciate that, Ginger. And, Flynn, I can't thank you enough for getting rid of those two bullies. I am so overwhelmed by the loss of my wife and not having them blaring the TV or meddling with their sarcastic remarks is a blessing."

"You're welcome, Jesse. And I also want to tell you, as Ginger just did, that you are welcome to be with us any time you want to be."

With that the five of them walked over to breakfast.

They were just finishing up and Flynn was asking what their morning plans were when the Chief walked up to their table.

"Good morning, folks. I wondered if you would have time to talk to me today."

"Right now?" Flynn asked.

"Not this exact minute but when you finish your breakfast."

"We will be done in a few minutes. Why don't you go over to the cottage and wait for us."

"Thanks, Flynn. I'll do that."

"Do you want to speak to me, too?" Jesse asked him.

"No, I don't need to talk to you at this time. I just wanted to chat with the others about the bodies Ginger found."

With relief, Jesse got up from the table and said his good-byes. When he arrived back at his room he brushed his teeth and then went and sat in the alcove. He opened his windows just as the two couples were returning from breakfast. The chief was sitting at a picnic table below Jesse, as the others joined him. From his vantage point he could see and hear everything that was being said.

"Any news about Harper?" Flynn questioned him.

"No. I have nothing else to report since the preliminary results came in. At this point we're doing background checks and questioning anyone who was around her those last two days."

With a sigh Jesse knew he had a reprieve.

"Do the bodies belong to Bree and George? Ginger inquired.

"Yes. We know that much. I don't know if you all know about DNA testing. I realize the doctor has knowledge about it."

They all looked at him as he continued. "In a way we might get lucky about this cold case. DNA testing did not really get going until the late 1980s. So the killer didn't realize he was leaving his DNA at the crime scene, since no one knew about DNA at that time. Anyway we found some that didn't belong to the two bodies you discovered. We think it might belong to the murderer."

He then continued, "Since we don't have everyone's DNA on file, the problem is we can't find a match at this time. However, we had Bree's dental records and using genetic genealogy tests we could conclude it was Bree and George."

"Those kind of tests," Dylan explained to the others, "determine the genetic relationship between individuals. So by taking samples from Bree and Georges' families they were able to conclude they were related and identify them that way."

"The doctor is correct," the Chief said. "Luckily, years ago when the importance of DNA was first introduced, both families gave the police samples. They wanted to make sure we could make identifications if any bodies were ever found."

Then he continued, "Since the remains you discovered were sealed off from the environment and heat or wetness were missing, the DNA remained. You all heard the stories of wooly mammoths thousands of years old with DNA still intact. Freezing can slow the rate of damage to DNA and so can dry places. In this case the bodies were wrapped in a heavy plastic, probably so no one would be able to smell them. But because of those conditions, with the dry environment as well as the long winters on the Island, the medical personnel were able to extract DNA from the bones."

Knowing they understood what he was telling them, the Chief resumed. "We were able to determine whose DNA belonged to which subject. And we found additional DNA that has to be from the murderer. We have questioned some of the people who worked here at that time and learned you dated Bree briefly, Dylan."

A little flustered, Dylan nodded his head in affirmative at that statement. We would like to get a DNA sample from all of you, but especially you, Dylan. This is completely voluntary but it would help us to rule all four of you out."

Sitting upstairs listening in, Jesse was thinking thank goodness they had not asked him for a sample. He never liked to do anything he didn't have to do but at the same time he knew he would look suspicious acting in that manner.

"I don't mind giving you a sample, Chief," Dylan told the man.

"We don't either," the others said in unison.

"Thank you. I appreciate it."

"When will this happen? We all have plans this afternoon."

"I checked with the doctor and he is in the hotel and available this morning. So I'll call him and he'll stop by in a few minutes and collect the samples. All they do is take a swab from inside your mouth. It won't take long at all."

At that point, Chief Logan picked up the phone and dialed the doctor. Disconnecting the call he told them the doctor would be there shortly.

"Thank you again," he told the group as he started walking back down the street.

CHAPTER 34

As they sat talking about the new developments the Chief had told them about, they saw the doctor coming their way carrying a small black bag.

"He looks just like a doctor in the olden days coming for a house visit," Olivia mused.

The rest of them chuckled at her observation.

"I just want to get this over with," Ginger observed. "I was hoping to have a little time reading and rocking on the porch this morning before our afternoon activities."

Since the air felt so refreshing, they all decided they would do that. After the doctor had taken the samples they had gone back to the bedrooms for their reading materials. Then they headed over to the porch. Jesse watched them leave from his window perch. Maybe I'll go get in the hot tub while there isn't anyone else around here he thought to himself. As he settled into the hot bubbling water, he had no idea someone was watching him from behind a large tree.

The rest of them had decided against doing anything special for lunch. The men were planning on taking a bag of snacks to the golf course. And, the women had the afternoon tea at 1:30p.m., followed by a massage and their hair appointments at the spa.

The rest of the morning passed quickly and it wasn't long before they all went their separate ways.

There were about fifty people at the afternoon tea. Some of the men had opted out, like Dylan and Flynn had. But everyone who was there mingled, especially with the ones they remembered working with years ago. They were all looking forward to the evening's cocktail party and a chance to see what the Mateo Cottage looked like. Several remarked they had seen it online and were considering staying there.

Both Ginger and Olivia let them know how much they were enjoying their stay at the place. Others commented on how much they would enjoy the perks like the cocktails and appetizers every night; as well as having your own personal chef. One lady remarked, "You don't always feel like dressing up and going to the dining room every evening. It would be wonderful to know you could get an outstanding meal without leaving your place."

As they finished talking, Kathy, one of the ladies who had been at the Cupola Bar came up to Ginger. "There was so much going on when we were together those two evenings but I was hoping to get a chance alone with you. I know we weren't close but I remember you and Olivia from when we were young."

"Yes. I remember you also. I believe you were getting a degree in social work."

"I was. That was the 'in' thing back then. That and guidance counselors."

"Olivia told me she almost got her Masters as a guidance counselor but they were flooding the field back then and so she stuck with history."

"That definitely was the case. And a lot of bad teachers went that direction so they didn't have to work very hard. It was an easy way out while still having the benefits of teaching—like summers off. I knew one man who was a guidance counselor and couldn't even handle a roomful of study hall kids, but since he was also a coach, they gave him tenure and kept him on.

"I'm not sure how we got onto this subject."

"As I was saying, I remember the four of you. At the time I thought you were all so perfect for each other. I presumed you would get married and live happily ever after. Needless to say, I was very naïve in those days."

"Weren't we all," Ginger said with a chuckle.

"Anyway I decided to go into psychology. My masters' thesis was on long-term relationships, especially related to finding your spouse in your early years. Obviously the world changed a lot from back in those times and many marriages didn't make it. But I was incredibly shocked to discover not only didn't you two couples marry each other, but all four of you had marriages that ended in divorce or tragedy. And it is also interesting that none of you remarried. I have to tell you I thought your romances were perfect and that you belonged with each other forever."

"I still don't know why you are telling me this."

"To make a long story short, I went on to get a doctorate in psychology. I have been doing a long-term study about relationships after ten, twenty, and now over thirty years. It has taught me a lot and given me an understanding of romance in the 'boomer' generation."

"So what have you learned?"

"I have discovered that many of us have been going through divorce, loneliness, the death of a loved one or complications from illness. It's amazing when I hear so many people, both men and women, say 'I thought I was the only one going through that.' But despite the negatives, second romances are definitely on the upswing, especially among older people. We are living longer and I believe many are looking for companionship to combat loneliness. Sometimes they get married and sometimes they don't. Some could lose pensions or just want some alone time rather than marrying again."

"Well, that's encouraging. Did you know we were thinking of rekindling our relationships?"

"Yes, I heard that. I don't want to take up too much of your time right now but I was hoping you would talk to Olivia and the two men for me. I would love to include the four of you in my study. It's inspiring and heartening to know you may get back together again."

She then resumed, "I would meet with you once a year and you would fill out a brief survey every six months and email it back to me. I have written a couple of books on the subject and I'm now working on an update to my last one. I'm sure you have noticed that all the romance stories on television and in the movies are about twenty, thirty or forty year olds. But there are many, many stories of people in their fifties, sixties, seventies and beyond who are also enjoying romance and companionship. I want the public to realize, as the lyrics to the song suggest, no matter what your age, 'love is sometimes wasted on the young.'"

"That seems like a pretty interesting study. I think we might be interested in participating in your research. Why don't you give me your email and we'll get back to you in the near future."

"I would really appreciate that. And, thank you for taking the time to visit with me. I know you want to mingle with some of the others who are here," Kathy said as she handed Ginger her card.

As soon as Kathy left, Olivia came over to Ginger.

"You look like you were having an intense discussion with Kathy."

"I was and I think you might find it interesting. I still want to socialize with some of the others who are here, but I'll tell you all about our conversation while we are getting our hair done."

At that instant Ginger looked up and saw Riley and Tess come into the room. When Riley spotted the two of them, she turned her back and grabbing her arm she dragged Tess off with her.

"Good riddance," Olivia remarked when she saw what had just occurred.

The party was still going strong at 3:15 p.m. when Ginger and Olivia said their goodbyes. They knew it would end soon since people would want to get ready for the evening. They had both really enjoyed themselves especially with getting the chance to catch up with several people they had not seen or heard from in years.

They made their way to the spa and had their massages. Then while they were getting their hair done, Ginger told her friend what her chat with Kathy had been about.

"That really sounds interesting, Ginger. Maybe these new relationships of ours won't work out but I don't mind being part of Kathy's study. I don't think the men will either."

By the time they finished up it was 5:30 p.m. and they headed back to the cottage to get ready for the evening. They ran into Flynn and Dylan exiting the hotel at the same time as they did and the women listened to golf tales on their way "home."

CHAPTER 35

The evening turned into just as lively an affair as the tea party had been. At first everyone wanted a tour of the cottage so Ginger and Olivia took turns showing the place off. Eventually everyone spilled into the outside; probably because that's where the food and drinks were being served by Neal and three other waiters.

The cocktails were flowing and at first Ginger thought that had to be costing the hotel quite a bit of money that wouldn't have been covered by their reunion fee. But then she realized by having the party at the cottage they could probably write it off as a business expense.

The only thing that marred the evening was Tess and Riley's arrival. Riley was jamming as many appetizers as possible into her mouth while regaling everyone around her with stories of Harper's demise. Then she started talking about the two bodies that were found as if she had discovered them herself.

At one point, Olivia noticed Neal staring at Riley and once again reminded herself to talk to Ginger about him. She got the feeling he didn't belong but desperately wanted to.

The party continued long after dark. Since the appetizers were constantly replenished and the temperature remained pleasant, only a few couples left to go to dinner.

Ginger was going from one group to the other having a wonderful time. But she needed to use the bathroom, and on her way back outside found herself standing alone.

Seeing Tess with a cocktail in hand, headed her way, Ginger cringed. She started to go in the opposite direction when she heard, "Wait, Ginger. I need to talk to you."

Looking around Riley was nowhere in sight and she breathed a sigh of relief.

"What do you want?" she asked the woman.

"Please don't be mad at me for speaking to you. I know Riley can say some pretty nasty things and I don't blame you for being upset with us."

"Why do you stay around her? Even though you agree with her most of the time, I can tell you aren't cruel like she is."

"There are times when it is hard for me to be near her but I owe her."

"In what way?"

"I didn't divorce my first husband like we told you. He died from cancer. We were very poor at that time and the hospital bills were horrendous. Riley gave me money for some experimental drug they gave him. He lived another two years because of that drug. Jerry was the only man I ever really loved. And after he died, she helped me pick up the pieces of my life. She wasn't mean back then like she is now."

"I am so sorry, Tess."

"Thank you. Lately, however, she seems to be getting worse and worse. She has gotten so vicious and I just don't understand why. She has plenty of money and you would think that would make her happy. And every time I try to stay away from her for a little while she always reminds me I'm indebted to her. She's a very lonely person and she expects me to be her constant companion."

Continuing she then added, "Also, I don't want to forget to tell you. When you get a chance I would be very grateful if you would let Flynn know how much I appreciate my own room in the hotel. I think it's the only thing that's keeping me sane while staying here. Riley doesn't seem to mind spending hours in front of the television. So my own room has really given me a break to do whatever I want. I don't have to spend every waking second with her now that we have our own rooms."

"I will let him know what you said."

"Thank you. But that's not the real reason I wanted to talk to you. I think I might know who killed Bree and

George. And, I believe Harper's death is also tied in to theirs."

"Why do you say that? Who do you think did it, Tess?"

"I don't want to say anything yet. I need to find out a couple of other things before I say anything more. I just wanted to warn you to be very careful. Don't trust anyone you don't know well. I think you will be shocked, but not surprised, if my suspicions are correct."

"Can't you tell me anything else?"

"No. I am afraid I have already said too much," she said as she glanced around. "I will talk to you again in the morning. I should know a lot more by then."

Ginger looked behind her to see if anyone else was in hearing range. As she turned back, Tess had disappeared. Where did she go she wondered? Ginger was unaware that Jesse was sitting in his alcove above them listening to everything she and Tess had said to each other.

Thinking it probably wasn't as serious as Tess had imagined, Ginger turned around and went back to the party. It wasn't long before she had totally forgotten the entire incident.

At 9:30 p.m. everyone drifted back to the hotel. The orchestra was beginning to play and they hoped dancing would work off some of the calories they had consumed from their earlier eating and drinking.

Tomorrow everyone was on their own for breakfast. They didn't want people to have to get up at a certain time to go eat. And, once again the historian would give a special lecture about the hotel in days past. Then there was an exclusive picnic lunch being planned by the pool with the afternoon free for socializing or other activities. In the evening a special dinner would be held in one of the private conference rooms.

It promised to be an enjoyable day.

CHAPTER 36

Once again the four of them headed off to breakfast at their usual time. Jesse had not answered his door so they assumed he had already gone to eat. When they entered the hotel a flurry of activity was going on.

As they walked into the parlor, Riley came running over to Ginger and said, "This is all your fault. You told her to stay away from me. I will never forgive you if something has happened to her."

Just then the Chief walked in the front door of the hotel.

"What is going on?" Ginger asked the man.

"Tess has disappeared. Riley can't find her friend. But I don't know why we are looking for her in the hotel. She's probably at the cottage somewhere."

"We had a disagreement with them the other night. Flynn got the two of them their own rooms here in this building."

"Well that explains that," the man said.

Meanwhile Riley kept yelling at Ginger as she was wringing her hands, "This is all your fault. This is all your fault."

As one of the policemen forcibly removed her to another part of the parlor, Flynn leaned over to Ginger and said, "I think the lady doth protest too much."

Smiling at him, she turned back and said, "I still don't understand why you're here, Chief Logan. Tess is probably out walking somewhere. She talked to me last night about how Riley was getting on her nerves."

"I think you better tell me everything she said to you last night."

The four friends then followed the Chief to a deserted corner of the parlor, away from everyone else. Ginger told him exactly what Tess had said to her.

"Tess seemed almost paranoid last night. She told me she thought Harper's death was connected to Bree and George's. She said to be careful and not trust anyone I didn't know well. She kept saying she wasn't sure if her suspicions were correct but she would know more by morning. She then told me if she was right, we would be surprised but not shocked. I asked her several questions but she kept telling me she would talk to me in the morning and refused to say anything more. Then I turned for a moment and when I looked back she was gone."

"Why didn't you tell us last night about your talk with her?" Olivia asked her.

"Quite frankly I forgot all about it. Everyone was having such a good time and I just felt if she really knew anything she would have told me. I know Riley upset her a lot and she was so happy to be in her own room and having a break from the woman. I can't believe something happened to her. I'm sure she is just off someplace enjoying the quiet."

"I'm not so sure about that," the Chief replied. "Besides the inheritance, we can't find anything else to link Jesse to Harper's death. We checked on his first wife's death and it's true he inherited a lot of money then, too. But the police don't consider the death suspicious, contrary to what was said. If he did kill Harper, he is the most consummate actor in the world. And we have just found out that Riley is a big gardener. Because of her size, she doesn't do the physical work anymore but she would definitely know about hemlock and how to use it."

"Obviously we didn't know about Riley and her gardening but I was thinking the same thing about Jesse," Flynn told the man. "If he is acting, he deserves an Academy Award."

"Even though we don't know why, it is very possible those three deaths could be linked. That would be another reason not to suspect Jesse. I just pray, whomever the killer is, we don't find a fourth body."

Everyone was shocked by what the policeman had just said.

"You can't be serious," Ginger said, turning white as the implication sank in. "Oh, my gosh! I should have taken Tess more seriously. And I should have insisted she tell me what she thought she knew."

"And, if you had done that, we might be looking for you right now, too. Something very sinister is going on here and I am going to get to the bottom of it. Meanwhile we have to try and find Tess. I have my men scouring the grounds. If something did happen to her, I don't think the killer took her too far."

Just then they heard another ruckus coming from outside the hotel.

Now what, the man thought to himself as he saw one of his deputies coming into the parlor, obviously looking for him.

"Chief, we have a problem down by the Secret Garden."

Nodding at the four of them, the Chief turned to go with his officer. "Stay back," he yelled at the people crowding the door to get outside to see what was happening. "Jason," he motioned to his officer who was guarding Riley. "Keep these people back. Don't let them come down to the grassy area."

As Jason was holding the crowd back, Riley pushed him away and began to follow the Chief. That better not be Tess down there in trouble she murmured to herself. I will kill Ginger if it is. I know this is all somehow her fault. There is something wrong about the way she keeps finding dead bodies.

Both Flynn and Dylan were worried about Ginger. They could see that Riley was past being hysterical. She seemed to have lost all normal reasoning and they worried about what she might do in her condition.

"Keep an eye on Ginger," Dylan told his friend. "I'm going down to see if the Chief needs any help. I know the doctor went over to the mainland this morning to pick up test results so he could probably use my assistance."

With a nod from the officer who knew he was a doctor, Dylan followed behind Riley towards where the Chief had disappeared.

CHAPTER 37

When Dylan arrived at the entrance of the Secret Garden, he saw the Chief and his deputy wrestling with Riley.

"I want to see what is going on. I want to see…" the woman was screaming. Meanwhile a golf cart was headed in their direction. When it arrived the two policemen got her into it and handcuffed her to the seat so she couldn't get out.

"Stay right there and don't try and move or say anything else. If you aren't quiet, I will have the gardener take you down to my jail and lock you up."

Whimpering she sat there quietly crying, but at least she had stopped the terrible screaming.

"Chief, I know the doctor is on the mainland and I wondered if I could help you in anyway?"

"Yes, that would be great, Dylan. My man has found a body in those trees."

Although the face was turned away from them as they got closer they knew immediately it was Tess. The corpse was extremely heavy and wearing a skirt and blouse.

Handing Dylan a pair of gloves, the Chief said, "Do you mind checking and seeing if you can determine if she is really dead and what she died from."

Dylan stepped over to the body and put his fingers on her neck. "She's definitely dead. There is no pulse, she is cold, and rigor mortis has set in. My guess is she has been dead about ten or eleven hours." Then he rolled the body over and after looking at her, he said, "Obviously I don't know for sure because she still has her clothes on, but there are bruises on her neck and it looks to me like she was strangled."

Then he picked up her hands and looked at them. "It doesn't look like she scratched her attacker, although he or she may have been wearing long sleeves. I don't see any skin under her fingernails."

"Thank you, doctor. That helps. Do you mind staying here a little longer to assist me?"

"No problem. Give me a second. I want to call my friends and tell them to go to breakfast without me. I know they are probably sitting in the parlor waiting for my return."

He checked his phone and realized he didn't have Olivia's number programmed in. He told himself to be sure and do that next time he saw her. Meanwhile he called Flynn. He told his friend the body did belong to Tess and he was still needed to help the police.

"Go to breakfast without me. I am going to be tied up here for a while. And, please watch out for Ginger. They have Riley handcuffed to a golf cart right now because she was hysterical. I am afraid what she might do when she gets loose. For some reason she keeps blaming Ginger for this. Even if she is the murderer, in her state of mind, she could easily think Ginger caused her to do it. Right now we are busy with the removal of the body. However, I will talk to the Chief when I get a chance about Ginger's safety before he lets Riley go free."

"Don't worry. I'll take care of Ginger. We'll miss you at breakfast. If you're free, which is probably doubtful, we will be going to the history lecture after we eat. Then we'll go back to the cottage. Hopefully you will catch up with us before the picnic starts."

"I'm sure I will be back by the time the picnic starts at the latest. We plan to take the body over to the other landing for transporting over to the mainland. And then the Chief asked me to fill out some preliminary reports which will help the medical examiner with his write ups. So it's extremely doubtful I will be at the lecture."

As he disconnected his phone, he turned towards Ginger and Olivia and said, "Let's go eat. The restaurant will be closing soon."

"What did Dylan say?" Olivia asked. "Why didn't he call my cell?"

"He just realized he doesn't have your number programmed into his phone or he would have called you. As soon as we get our food I'll tell you what he said."

They decided to order off the menu, rather than eating off the buffet, since they wanted to eat light. It was now after 9:00 a.m. and they knew they would have a big picnic lunch in just a few hours. All three of them decided on cereal, toast and fruit.

As soon as they placed their order, Flynn looking at Ginger said, "It was Tess. According to Dylan, she's been dead probably since about 10:00 p.m. last night. He told me he would tell us more when he gets back. He needed to help with transporting the body and filling out some reports. He isn't certain how long it will take him but he believes he'll be back in time for the picnic lunch."

"I feel so horrible. I should have done something last night. I should have insisted she tell me who she suspected."

"You can't think that way. Like the Chief said you might have been killed, too, if the murderer thought you knew something. But I'm afraid I have to 'dog' you until this is settled. Dylan is really worried about what Riley might try to do to you if she is set free."

"Why is he worried about me?"

"Riley went ballistic when she knew Tess was dead and they had to handcuff her to a golf cart. For some reason, in her unstable mind, she blames you. Whether someone else killed Tess or she did it, Dylan feels she will find a way to believe it was your fault."

"But that's crazy," Olivia remarked.

"I know, but he's worried about Ginger, so think of me as your bodyguard until everything gets settled."

"I don't believe I need a bodyguard."

"Neither did Bree, George or Tess and look what happened to them."

"Oh," said Ginger. She really didn't have an answer to that.

CHAPTER 38

When they entered the room where the lecture would be given, the three of them were immediately surrounded. They heard voices coming at them from several different directions.

"What happened?"

"Is someone dead?"

"Was it murder?"

"Where's Dylan?"

"Hold it," Flynn told the group as he ushered the two women towards seats near the front of the room. As they went to sit down they saw an unfamiliar woman crying.

"There sure is a lot of crying going on around here. I wonder what that's about, Olivia."

"I'm not sure Ginger but I will ask Kathy or Julie if they know who she is."

People moved back as he moved through the throng and found seats for the three of them. Then the historian told the assembly, "Everyone sit down. Let's have Flynn get up and answer your questions or I will never be able to start my lecture."

At that moment Flynn stood up and told the assembly the basic facts he was aware of. "It appears Tess was killed some time last night. I guess the doctor was not on the island so Dylan went to assist the police. I don't know anything beyond that. Dylan said he would tell us more when he gets back here. At this time they are not aware if this is tied into Bree and George's disappearance or possibly even Harper's death. We will just have to wait and see." Then he sat back down.

"I believe there isn't much more to be said about what happened," the historian added. "I plan to start my lecture now but if any of you would rather not listen you are free to leave the room."

No one got up to leave so the man started talking about the hotel in the 1950s and some of the famous guests who had stayed there. Before they knew it they were transported back to those days and what had happened to Tess was quickly forgotten for the moment.

When the lecture was over the room emptied quickly.

As they were about to exit the room, they heard, "Thank you for telling everyone what you knew Flynn. It would have been chaos and no one would have listened to me if they were busy speculating over the morning events."

"I'm glad I was able to help. Your talks are very interesting as you can tell. As soon as they had the facts, at least as we knew them to date, everyone settled down and listened to you. Will you be joining us for the picnic lunch this afternoon?"

"No, I have another engagement this afternoon off the Island. I won't be able to come to your banquet tonight either."

"That is too bad. I know we would have enjoyed your company." Flynn said to the man as Ginger, Olivia and he turned to leave the room.

As they headed back to the cottage, Ginger mentioned, "I didn't see Jesse at the lecture and he didn't go to breakfast with us either. I hope he is all right."

"I'm sure he is fine," Olivia replied. "I think I would also feel uncomfortable around a lot of people, especially since he doesn't know anyone but us. And, I know he thinks they suspect him of killing Harper."

When they got back to the cottage they found Jesse rummaging around the kitchen fixing a sandwich.

"Hi everyone," he said. "I took a walk early this morning and all I had was a bowl of cereal real early so I was getting very hungry."

"Aren't you going to the picnic this afternoon?" Ginger inquired.

"No. As I told you I don't know any of those people. Since I don't have Harper to be with, I'm not interested in talking to any of them. I will probably go get some soup at one of the other restaurants later."

"You missed out on all of the action this morning."

"Really? What happened, Olivia?"

"Tess was murdered. It happened sometime last night. They found her body in the Secret Garden this morning."

Turning white and grabbing on to the counter to keep from falling he said, "Surely they made a mistake. It was Tess, not Riley?"

"Yes. It was definitely Tess," Ginger told him.

"But she was half way decent towards me. I saw her turn the television down several times when she knew Riley wasn't looking. Why would someone kill her?"

"It's speculation at this point. We think she might have known something about what happened to Bree and George."

"Well, I suppose the police will come and question all of us again. I don't know why they would think I had anything to do with all this. I wasn't anywhere near this Island all those years ago when they disappeared. All I want to do is go home."

"I know what you mean, Jesse. Things are getting pretty intense around here," Olivia continued.

"I realize all of you are staying until Monday morning but I was hoping the police would let me go home tomorrow. I really have no reason to remain here. But I suppose with this new murder they won't let anyone leave the Island."

"We'll just have to wait and see what they tell us."

At that moment they all looked up as they saw Dylan come through the door.

Just like what had happened in the lecture room, the four of them surrounded him, peppering him with questions.

"So what happened?"

"Where is Riley?"

"Did you get everything done the Chief needed you to do?"

"Stop a minute," he said. "Let me get a drink and then we can sit down and I'll tell you what I know."

CHAPTER 39

After he got a glass of lemonade, Dylan sat down and told them what he could. "I really can't say a lot. The Chief doesn't want all the facts out since it might help him to catch the killer if certain details aren't revealed. But I can tell you she was strangled. It took a lot of strength and she was a big woman. So the killer had to have been in a rage when he murdered her."

Giving him a piece of paper with her phone number on it, Olivia said, "You have to be hungry. You never had breakfast."

"They had some snacks at the police station I ate so I am okay for now. It is almost time for the picnic so I'll wait until then to eat."

"But can you at least tell us what happened to Riley? And do they definitely think it's a man?"

"They took her to the medical center. Normally they wouldn't have needed me because there are three doctors on the Island. But since this is the slow time, two of them are on vacation. I guess they go up to Canada fishing every year in September. They like to go now because most of the vacationers are gone and the cold hasn't really settled in yet."

Then he added, "I think they believe it is a man because of the strength and force it took to kill someone that large. She had been drinking so she was probably more vulnerable. I think it has to be a man or someone very large like Riley."

"You said they took her to a medical center. So is there a hospital here on the Island?"

"No, Ginger. You have to go to St. Ignace to get to the hospital. The doctor didn't think she needed a hospital and I didn't either. He gave her a strong sedative so she should sleep a long time. They hired a nurse to stay with her throughout the night." He didn't tell them she had been handcuffed to the bed.

"I never liked her, especially after I learned what she did to Harper, but I do feel sorry for what she is going through. In her own way she seemed to care about Tess."

"Yes, you could be right, Ginger. But there is still a question of whether or not she was the one who committed all the murders."

"Why would you say that Dylan? That is horrifying."

"I can't go into details at this time but in a way I'm glad she is being watched. I didn't trust her not to hurt you, Ginger."

"That seems to be the perfect place for her," Jesse remarked. "The best thing that has happened this whole trip is when you threw those two women out of here, Flynn. I'm sorry someone killed Tess but I certainly don't miss those two here at the cottage."

"I guess none of us do, Jesse. But being killed that way is a tragedy. It was not an easy way to die."

Then Olivia told him, "Be ready for a mob to descend on you when we go to the picnic. They had a lot of questions when we first went to the lecture this morning."

"Well, I will answer as much as I'm able but the first thing I'm going to do is have lunch when I get there."

"And what is the second thing?" Olivia asked him with a mischievous smile.

"Why play croquet and try to beat Flynn, of course."

Everyone laughed when he told them that.

It was soon time to go to the picnic so they said goodbye to Jesse and went on their way down the hill. There were already about fifty people gathered around the pool and the aroma of bratwurst and hamburgers being grilled was wafting through the air.

Dylan's mouth began to water and his stomach growled when he smelled the food. "I'm definitely ready for lunch," he remarked.

As predicted he was surrounded by the group when he walked in.

"Give a man a break," he told all of them. "I have had no breakfast and I'm starving. Let me get some food and after I sit down I will answer any questions I can."

Everyone watched as he took both a bratwurst and a hamburger and then piled his plate with potato salad, macaroni salad and several pieces of watermelon.

He found a picnic table that had been set up and he and Olivia sat down while everyone crowded around him. He ate his hamburger and some potato salad and was ready to eat his bratwurst. But he knew there would be no peace until he answered their questions.

"Look," he told them. "I know Flynn told you Tess was murdered last night. They have sent her body over to the mainland to be autopsied. There is not a lot more the police want me to tell you except I can say she was strangled."

When he told them that, there was an audible gasp from the group.

One of the women was overheard saying, "I wonder if we are safe here? Maybe we should leave the Island before we all get killed."

"I think you're okay," Dylan said to the group at large. At this point the police believe she may have been killed because of something she knew related to Bree and George's disappearance. And that is all I can tell you right now."

CHAPTER 40

Everyone began to disperse after Dylan's last comment. Ginger and Flynn joined them after everyone left.

"Thank goodness that's over," Olivia said to him. "Now we can enjoy ourselves."

"I hope you are ready for another round of cutthroat croquet. I signed us up when I got my lunch. They'll call us when it's our turn."

"I don't think we have a choice, do we?" Ginger said.

"I wouldn't force you but I am looking forward to beating you all again."

"You never know," she told him with a playful expression on her face. "Oh, look. There's Neal. I wonder why he's here helping out. I just assumed he would be at the stables."

"Why do you care?"

"I was thinking I would ask him if he noticed anything funny about Tess these last few days."

"You need to be careful Ginger. I don't want anything to happen to you because you asked the wrong person the wrong question."

"Well, surely you don't think Neal is involved?"

"No, I wouldn't think so. I can't imagine what kind of motive he would have. But the killer could be somewhere around and might have overheard you talking to Tess last night. Maybe fearing to be discovered is the reason someone killed her. I don't want you to be next. "

"I will be careful. I just want to ask him a couple of questions. Look, Dylan, there is some man waving at you from over there. I think he's trying to get your attention."

Gazing in the direction Ginger was pointing, he said, "For heaven's sake. That is my friend Andy. I haven't seen him in years. I'm going to go over and say hello to him. I will see you all when our names are called for croquet.

"You be careful, Ginger," Flynn said to her as she also got up to leave to talk to Neal.

"I guess it's just you and me," Olivia told him.

After Dylan left for the other side of the pool, Ginger went over to where Neal was standing near the buffet table.

"Hi, Neal. How are you?"

"I'm fine Ginger. How is your day going?"

"It's going well but naturally I am a little depressed. Did you hear the news about Tess?"

"Yes, obviously everyone is talking about it. There has been only one unsolved murder on this Island since

Bree and George disappeared. I guess I should amend that and say since they were killed. And now there have been two more just a few days apart. No one knows what to think."

"I'm curious why you're here working this afternoon. Shouldn't you be at the stables?"

"Normally I would be there. Helping out as your waiter at the cottage was just something extra I was doing. I pretty much spend all my time at the stables."

"That's what I thought."

"They called me to assist with this picnic. It was pretty quiet where I work, and with so many people here at the party they needed extra help. A couple of the regular waiters are out today since they are not feeling well so they asked if I would mind helping with the picnic. I like to be of help when I can so I said, 'yes'."

"Well that makes sense. You're a man of many talents." she said smiling at him.

"Thanks, Ginger. You have always been so nice to me."

"Do you mind answering a couple of other questions for me?"

"I can't imagine what you would want to know that I would be able to help with."

"I'm just wondering about Tess."

"I don't think there is a thing I can tell you about that woman."

"I am curious if you noticed anything about her when she was still living at the cottage? I know you took drinks upstairs to the two of them before leaving in the evenings."

"It's strange you should ask that. I couldn't understand why she wanted to be friends with Riley. That woman was always putting Tess down. She took the best seating in the media room and never shared it. Why Tess put up with her nasty behavior is beyond me. She was such an unpleasant woman to be around. And I would overhear her talk about the vicious things she did to people, including what they did to Harper years ago. Honestly, I don't know why someone didn't kill her instead of Tess."

"It's horrible to say that but I know what you mean. Did you know the police are looking seriously at Riley as a suspect?"

"No. Really? It's hard to imagine she would do that. But the woman does have a very malicious streak. I even overheard her talking about Bree. She insinuated that she slept around with anyone. I only knew Bree slightly but I don't believe that she was having sex with a lot of guys as Riley suggested. She did not seem to be like that at all. And if she had been sleeping around, the rest of us would have seen evidence of her behavior. I know Riley is a liar. I heard her say some things that were definitely not true. Personally I would not believe a single thing she says."

"I agree with you, Neal."

"Do you know where she is now? I thought she would be here at the picnic acting like a know it all."

"They have her at the clinic under heavy sedation. I think she has lost all sense of reality. She keeps blaming me for Tess getting killed."

"That's just crazy. I hope the police don't think you had anything to do with it."

"I don't believe they do. Flynn was helping them this morning, and I think he would have told me if the police thought I was involved somehow."

"Well that's good. I know you would never do anything like that."

"One more question. I don't mean to bother you but…"

"You need to ask fast, Ginger. My supervisor has been giving me looks and I don't want to get in trouble."

"I saw you helping out at the cocktail party. I had a very weird conversation with Tess last night while the party was going on. I know she suspected someone but she wouldn't tell me who. She said she would tell me in the morning but, of course, she was killed before she could say anything to me. Did you notice anything suspicious during the social? Did you see her talking to anyone?"

"I would really like to help you Ginger but I didn't notice anything. I was pretty busy since I was in charge of the drinks. There was supposed to be another bartender but he had another obligation so I had to handle fixing the cocktails alone. Truthfully I don't think I saw her at all last night. I better go now I think my superior is heading this way."

Ginger looked up and saw a man approaching them.

"I don't want to get you in any trouble, Neal. Thanks again for taking the time to answer my questions. I know you are a great asset to this hotel, especially jumping in where needed."

"Thank you, Ginger, for saying that. I really appreciate it. But a word of advice. Be careful who you question. I don't want you to get hurt because you asked the wrong person a question. Leave the interrogations to the police."

"I will, Neal. That is exactly what Flynn told me, too." And, turning and seeing Olivia, she walked over to her friend.

"It looked like you were deep in conversation with him. Did you learn anything interesting?"

"I was just asking him about Tess and especially if he saw anything last night."

"What did he tell you?"

"Not a whole lot. But it was strange. He said he didn't see Tess last night but he was the only bartender and I remember when she came over to talk to me she had a drink in her hand."

"Honestly, if you were a bartender to seventy some people, would you remember everyone who came for a drink? Besides maybe someone else ordered the drink for her."

Then she added, "But I have been meaning to talk to you about him. A couple of times I saw him looking very strangely at Riley and Tess during our evening social. I know several times they acted like he was beneath them. Maybe it's nothing but I kept wanting to say something about it to you."

"I guess you're right. I probably wouldn't have remembered everybody if I was as busy as he was last night. And even though he might have acted strange, I can't believe the man was involved in these murders. He has always been so pleasant around us. He just doesn't seem the type to fly into a rage as the killer seems to."

"I know all we're doing is speculating with no way to back it up. Come on. Let's go find the men. I saw Dylan talking to his friend over on the other side of the pool. He said it was someone he knew years ago but it is weird that I don't remember him, too."

CHAPTER 41

As soon as Ginger left to talk to Neal, Dylan left and walked over to the other side of the pool where his friend Andy was standing.

"Andy, how are you?"

"Dylan, I don't believe it. It has been years since I've seen you. What have you been doing? Did you become a doctor? Did you ever get back with that woman you broke up with? All you did was talk about her the two years I knew you."

"So many questions at once. I'm not sure where to begin."

"Start at the beginning."

"I did become a doctor, specializing in oncology. I didn't see Olivia again after we broke up. But ironically we met here at the reunion this week, and I think there may be a chance for us this time around. I believe we both had to grow up before we found our way back to each other. But I'm beginning to imagine living with someone again. I think if I don't dream of the possibilities of a future with someone again, I will lose the excitement of what a relationship might hold and bury myself in my research."

Then he continued, "I don't know if that makes sense." He told his friend about marrying his nurse and what she had been like and finally giving up his practice to go into cancer research.

"Well, it sounds like you're finding your way hopefully to a brighter tomorrow."

"One can only hope. I don't want my past to define the present. It took me a while to get over Olivia but I finally understood why she did what she did. And it was odd because when I came to terms with it, I felt so much better. And if things don't work out with us this time, I really believe I can accept that."

"I wish I had my act together as you seem to."

"You know we are over fifty now. I think it's about time, don't you agree?"

"Absolutely. Although I have to say I had a wonderful marriage. She was the love of my life. I know some people are not lucky enough to find true love as I did. When I say it out loud it sounds kind of sappy. But it's the way I feel."

"You said had?"

"Yes. Abby died two years ago of breast cancer. You know you can have all the money in the world but it doesn't guarantee happiness or good health."

"So what are you doing now? Are you still working?"

"No, I'm retired. "

"That's interesting. If something happens between Olivia and me, I think I will semi-retire. She has retired and wants to continue traveling like she has in the past. And, I have to tell you that sounds very appealing."

"Do it, my friend. Time slips by so quickly and if you have someone you love to spend your life with, don't take it for granted."

"So let's get back to you."

"Well, I got my degree in Business Administration and then kicked around going from job to job for the next ten years. I was making good money but it just seemed like something was missing. You remember how I loved to play computer games?"

"Yes. Every spare minute you had. When the computer field opened up I went back and got my Master's. I learned to program and found it fascinating. Then in my spare time instead of playing games, I began designing them."

"That's incredible. I had no idea you did that."

He then told Dylan about starting his own company and how it had taken off. "Everything looked so bright. Those were really fun years. And that is also when I met Abby. She was working with the city police department. But at that time they didn't give very challenging work to policewomen. She was bored and not making enough money to live. So she had to find work to supplement her salary."

"It wasn't easy for women back in those days, that's for sure."

"You're right and she was brilliant. I met her when she was working at a fundraiser I was attending. There was an incident and she stepped in and handled it brilliantly. I found myself asking her out for coffee. I was careful when dating back then. I was just getting started and I didn't want to marry someone who thought I was going to be rich and then they could divorce me and be set up for life with my money."

"That's pretty cynical."

"I know it is but I saw it happen to a lot of men I knew when I first started working."

"I know you're right. It happened to me. And, I'm not sure if you knew that lady who just died. She and her friend supposedly divorced several times just to have men take care of them the rest of their lives by getting big settlements and alimony. But it's not necessarily just women." He then told Andy about Jesse and how he was suspected of killing his wife for the life insurance money.

"That's exactly why I wanted to be careful if I found someone I loved and wanted to marry. But I could tell from the start that Abby was not like that. We clicked immediately. It was almost love at first sight and if anyone had said that was possible before I met her, I wouldn't have believed them."

"You really have a wonderful love story."

"And, it gets better. I was looking to set up a security office for my business and we talked about it. She had such great ideas I convinced her to resign from the police department and come work for me. She did and the rest is history as they say. We had twenty wonderful years together. I woke up every morning thanking God for finding her."

He wiped a tear from his eye as he continued, "We had decided to sell the company and set up a foundation. We had just bought a yacht when she was diagnosed. I spent the next two years constantly by her side. I didn't want to lose her but the disease ravaged her body and she could no longer fight. She made me promise to go on with my life but it has been very difficult at times. So as I said, don't take your time for granted, especially if things work out for you and Olivia."

"I think that's very wise advice."

"Now let's think about more pleasant things." As Andy had been talking, Flynn had come over to them and Dylan introduced him. Flynn was thinking maybe he should listen to Andy's advice, too, as far as he and Ginger were concerned.

Dylan told his friend how Flynn had a similar career to his. "You both ended up in the computer field and it is amazing because it didn't really exist when we were in college."

"I have a book you might like," Flynn said to Andy and with that he left to go back to the cottage to get it. Just after that Andy noticed two women headed their way.

Turning, Dylan saw them, too, and waved them over.

CHAPTER 42

As they walked towards the other side of the pool they saw Dylan waving at them. They started over towards where he and Flynn were standing with another man. Just before he departed, Flynn motioned Neal over and spoke to him briefly.

By the time they got to Dylan, Flynn was nowhere to be seen. Coming up to where the two men were standing, they saw a man as tall as Dylan. He had short blond hair with white running through it. When he took off his sunglasses they noticed his eyes were grey. Then they heard, "Ginger and Olivia, I would like to introduce you to my friend, Andy. And, Andy, this is my friend, Olivia and Flynn's friend, Ginger," as he pointed at each woman.

"Nice to meet you," the women said to the man.

"And, I am also glad to meet the two of you."

"Is Flynn here?" Ginger asked while looking around for him.

"No. He went back to the cottage to get something."

Then he continued, "Andy was one of my best friends back in the day. We worked together as carriage drivers here at the hotel. You won't remember him Olivia because he worked on the Island the last two years I was here after you left."

Nodding as Dylan cleared up that mystery, he continued, "Andy's father worked here when he was in college and since he had been around horses all his life that's how he ended up working at the hotel. He also loved playing video games, such as they were back then. I would go out at night with Flynn but Andy preferred to play his games with a couple of friends so Flynn never knew him either."

Laughing, Andy told them, "When I think of the hours I spent playing Pac Man and some other games, especially how archaic they are today, it truly boggles my mind."

"I remember my brother spending hours playing those games, too," Ginger told the group.

"Well, it paid off for me. I got my BA in Business Administration but after Windows 95 started I went back and got a Masters' Degree in Programming. Everything about computers was in its infancy at that time. But I still loved computer games and I started designing my own. Eventually I started my own company which was bought out about ten years ago by an even bigger company."

"To say he made a fortune is an understatement," Dylan added.

"I guess you're right about that," he said in a self-conscious manner.

"Andy has always been modest. He has set up a philanthropic foundation that today helps support several charities."

"I always considered myself lucky for being at the right place at the right time. I like being able to give back especially since I was so fortunate."

"Anyway, Andy cruised up here on his boat and is anchored at the marina. He is staying in one of the suites at the hotel but he has invited us all to go for a ride around the Island tomorrow afternoon. He is not planning on leaving until Monday, as are we."

"That sounds like fun," Olivia told her friends. "We biked around the Island and now we will be able to get the perspective from the water.

"I'm glad you want to join me. And when we come back there is a restaurant downtown that serves the best whitefish I have ever eaten. I would love it if you were my guests for dinner."

"What about dinner?" they heard Flynn say as he came walking up to the group with a book in hand.

"We're going for a ride on Andy's yacht around the Island tomorrow afternoon and then he's treating us to dinner."

"I think we will all like that," Flynn replied as he handed the book to Andy.

As the others looked at him, he said "I just finished this book that Dylan gave me. I thought Andy would enjoy reading it. It is about famous serial killers who were gamers."

"What, are we going to have to put your name back on the suspect list?" Olivia asked Dylan jokingly. "After all you did date Bree at one time."

"Well, that's interesting," Andy said.

"Speaking of killers," Flynn interrupted, "the Chief called while you were talking to Neal. He wants to talk to all of us again. I invited him over for appetizers and cocktails at 5:00 p.m. And I asked Neal if he could bring the food at that time because we were having company."

"So that's why I saw you talking to Neal."

"Yes. Nothing sinister about it, and I wasn't checking up on you, Ginger."

"I don't want you to think that I thought you were checking up on me. It just seemed a little strange. You were saying something to him right after I had been quizzing him. But I totally agree I would much rather be questioned during our cocktail time. Is Andy coming, too?"

"Yes. Dylan also invited Andy. Besides designing games, he also set up his own security company. They needed protection and took precautions at his business so others would not steal what was being created. Because of his background, I checked and the Chief welcomed him to join us. Besides, I don't believe the Chief wants to interrogate us. I think he wants our opinions on some matters."

"What about Jesse?" Olivia asked.

He should be happy that the Chief is coming over. I think it is very possible that he will let Jesse go home tomorrow. After all, this investigation may take some time and he knows where Jesse lives if he needs to follow up with him on anything."

"Does that mean Jesse will get the insurance money right away?"

"No, Ginger, it does not. There will not be any payout until the case is resolved. After all, if someone else with no ties to Jesse committed the murder, he would be in line for the double indemnity clause," Andy added.

"Wow!" Olivia replied. He would really be in the money, so to speak, if that happens."

They mingled a little longer by the pool and even got a croquet game in, which once again, Flynn won. Then they strolled back to the cottage for a little quiet time before the evening activities began.

CHAPTER 43

It was just before 5:00 p.m. when the women came out to the living room and found Flynn already mixing a pitcher of martinis while Dylan was setting out glasses. The two women were wearing floor length evening gowns. Olivia had chosen a beautiful soft peach and Ginger's was emerald which looked beautiful with her red hair. The men were wearing tuxes and black ties.

"You two women look gorgeous," Flynn remarked.

"You two look very snazzy, too," Ginger replied. And then with a smile she added. "I see you still take your bartending duties very seriously."

Just at that moment they saw Neal coming in. He had rolled a cart over filled with all kinds of appetizers, including cheeses and crackers.

"Let me help you get those trays in here," Dylan told him. "Riley would really be upset to be missing all these appetizers if she saw them."

"You can say that again," Olivia added.

As Neal prepared the food the Chief and Andy came walking in the door at the same time. Dylan went over and greeted the men while introducing them to each other. Andy also had on a tux with black tie. Meanwhile

Jesse came down the stairs and looked out of place in his casual clothes. It only took a minute for him to eye the policeman and he had all he could do to not retreat back up to his room.

"What is he doing here?" he whispered to Ginger.

"I'm not sure but Flynn says you may be able to go home tomorrow." Jesse sat in a chair as far from the Chief as possible. Meanwhile Dylan was serving everyone drinks while Neal brought a tray around with the canapes.

"What would you like to drink?" Flynn asked the policeman.

"I will have what everyone else is having. I haven't had a martini in forever."

"And, I haven't had so much food and alcohol in forever," Olivia chimed in.

After Dylan had poured everyone a drink, Flynn went back behind the bar and made another pitcher of martinis.

When Ginger looked at him, he smiled at her saying, "We don't want to run out while we're talking."

She just rolled her eyes at him, replying. "If I drink a second one, I'll have to give up the wine with my dinner."

Soon everyone settled into seats and started chatting about the reunion. Neal went to clean up in the kitchen and the Chief began talking. "Thank you for inviting me to this shindig. It seems I haven't had a moment to relax since we found Harper. It feels so good to sit here and have a drink with all of you. And, I want to tell you I especially appreciated all your help this morning Dylan."

"I was happy to do it. And, don't worry. I know you'll solve these crimes, Chief."

"The problem is I have to come up with an answer sooner rather than later. Mackinac Island is the biggest tourist attraction in the state. We can't have business start falling off during our important fall foliage time because people think they could be murdered if they come here."

"Surely the public won't think that."

"I think they already do, Olivia. When I was answering questions at lunch some woman voiced that exact opinion."

"But that's crazy. Don't they realize these murders are all tied up with the disappearance of Bree and George thirty-five years ago?"

"We think that but, not only do we not know for sure, the public definitely doesn't know that fact. They are beginning to believe there is some serial killer running around the Island."

Just then Ginger's cell rang. Looking to see who was calling, she told them, "Excuse me. I have to take this," and she left the room.

When she returned she said, "That was Julie. She met a woman at the picnic this afternoon who said she and her boyfriend were best friends with Bree and George the year they disappeared. She wants to talk to me at the banquet tonight."

"Be careful, Ginger. The killer might be listening in. I don't want what happened to Tess to happen to you, too," Flynn said.

"I agree," the Chief reiterated. "But at the same time you might learn something useful that the woman wouldn't tell the police. I would really appreciate you letting me know anything new you discover."

"I will definitely do that, Chief. If there is only some way we can actually find out what occurred to those two. I just knew deep inside something had happened to Bree when she disappeared. For a long time I kept hoping I would hear that she had made it in show business. But then as the years went by I forgot all about her."

"You can't beat yourself up over that. We all just moved on and led our lives the way we were meant to at the time. For all you knew, Bree might have failed in show business. And, being too embarrassed to tell her family, she and George might have settled down somewhere to live out their lives."

"I never considered that, Flynn. Thank you. That thought makes me feel a lot better."

"Let's get back to the reason for my visit."

They all looked towards the Chief.

"First of all, I have made a lot of inquiries to a lot of different people. Jesse..."

The man almost jumped out of his chair as he looked towards Chief Logan. "Yes?"

"I checked on your first wife's death and there was nothing suspicious about it when it happened. I have also talked to some people who knew both you and Harper. Everyone says the two of you seemed devoted to each other. I'm sure you know there will be no insurance payoff until either we find Harper's killer or you are totally ruled out. And, since you weren't here when Bree and George were killed, I decided you can go home tomorrow if you want; although I think Monday would be better."

"Really? I can leave? Why should I stay until Monday?"

"Yes, you can really leave. I know where to find you if I need to and I don't believe you will take off for parts unknown with the insurance payment up in the air. I just think it would be easier if you left Monday because at some point you are going to have to meet with the authorities and make arrangements for Harper's body to get back to Wisconsin."

"Yes, I think you're right. I don't want to have to make a second trip up here. I will do as you suggest. Is it okay if I leave now? I was planning on getting some sushi for dinner and settle in with a good book I just started."

"Yes, that's fine with me."

"Good night, everyone," he said with a sigh as he left to go get his dinner.

Neal was going around refreshing everyone's drinks when Jesse departed. He stopped and said to the group, "If you don't mind I'm going to take off now, too. They wanted my help with setting up for the banquet since they are short on staff with the sick men. I plan to come back here sometime while you are out and clean everything up. So don't worry about glasses and plates. I will take care of them when I return. Besides you are all dressed up and I don't want you to get your clothes soiled."

"That sounds perfect. Thanks, Neal," Ginger said to him. "We'll probably see you in the banquet room.

As he departed the Chief continued, "That brings me to the second reason I wanted to come visit with you here. We have a very strong suspicion that Riley is the killer."

"Really," they all said in unison.

"We can hold her in custody for seventy two hours, and if by chance she is not the killer I'll release her Monday morning. I'm still worried about her trying to hurt Ginger or even someone else. The sedative the doctor gave her didn't knock her out as long as he thought it would. He was probably not allowing for her excess weight. She was unusually calm when she woke up and that worried us all.

I did have time to make a few calls and I have enough circumstantial evidence to hold her."

"Has she asked for a lawyer?" Andy asked.

"No. And that's why I plan to hold her. With her mental frame of mind and since it is the weekend I thought it would be better to keep an eye on her until Monday. We are detaining her at the Medical Center so she's comfortable." He didn't tell them she had originally been handcuffed to the bed but they had now removed the cuffs. "We have her locked in a room and there's a nurse and one of my deputies standing guard outside her door in case she needs something. And we brought her food. So she should be safe for the present and so should everyone else."

"But can you tell us why you suspect her?" Ginger asked.

"Let's just say we may have some DNA, and she never made secret her intense hatred of Harper. We're still looking into this but I also found it interesting that some of the people she knew told us she is an avid gardener."

"You're kidding. Somehow I don't picture her on her knees pulling out weeds," Olivia remarked.

"You're right about that. Obviously she doesn't get down and dirty, so to speak, but she has a gardener she hired and she supervises everything he does. So if she did poison Harper, she would certainly know how to use and handle hemlock.

"I really thought she liked Tess, in her own way," Dylan said. "Why would she kill her friend?"

"Tess did imply she knew who the killer was. Looking back she seemed frightened when she was talking to me. I believe she was going to tell me her suspicions in the morning. And she kept looking around when she was talking to me. I had an impression she was worried someone was listening. It's obvious if Riley thought Tess knew she was the killer, she would have murdered her to keep her silent."

"I hate to think you're right, Ginger," Olivia told her friend.

Looking at his watch, Flynn told the others, "I hate to break up our little gathering. It's fun to speculate about the murders but it's almost time for the banquet."

"Thank you for having me," the Chief said as he stood up. "Just keep me in the loop if you come up with anything interesting."

They all said goodbye to him, and despite what Neal had said, they took their glasses and plates to the sink and followed the Chief out the door.

CHAPTER 44

As they were walking along the sidewalk to the hotel for dinner, Andy commented on how much he liked the cottage.

"Although having a suite is gorgeous, I like the privacy the cottage provides. And the nightly social is definitely a bonus. You can have as little or as much company as you want."

"And there were a couple of times we had no desire to go to the hotel dining room for dinner so having your own personal chef fix your meal is also a plus," Dylan told his friend.

"If the weather is bad, walking outside to get to the hotel wouldn't be very pleasant but at the same time you don't walk any farther to the dining room than if you are in a suite.

"And I noticed there is a coat closet in the cottage near the kitchen area with a container filled with lots of umbrellas. They seem to think of everything for the comfort of their guests."

Arriving at the door into the hotel they walked down the hallway and into the parlor. The room was filled with guests but since the dining room didn't open until 6:30

p.m., which was in another half hour, only reunion people filled the space.

"Now I know why we're having dinner so early. If the other guests were in line to eat, since our private room is right next to the dining room, this hallway would have been packed."

Everyone was dressed up and it was fun to see all the different gowns the women were wearing. Even though they had not been specifically told, all the men were in black tie.

The doors to the private room, which was called the Cottage Restaurant, must have opened because the crowd began surging forward. As they were waiting to go in Ginger saw Julie walking towards them with another lady in tow.

"Ginger, I want to introduce you to Belinda. She and her husband Harry were best friends with Bree and George. They went out together everywhere that summer before the disappearance. They would like to speak to you after dinner if that is okay."

"Nice to meet you, Belinda. This is my friend, Flynn. Why don't the four of us get together here in the parlor after dinner? They usually serve demitasse and that would be the perfect time to talk before the dancing starts. Everyone else will probably crowd up to the Cupola Bar so we will have more privacy down here."

"That would be awesome. Harry was George's best friend and I don't think a day has gone by in all these years he doesn't think about him. He always had a feeling something horrible had happened to George but no one would ever believe him."

"As soon as dinner is over why don't we come back out here? We can meet in that section over there," Ginger said as she pointed to a corner in the room.

"Perfect. We'll meet you and Flynn there," she answered as she moved forward to catch up with her companions.

"Olivia, I don't mean to exclude you and Dylan. But Julie said they were reluctant to talk to too many other people. They don't want to somehow get targeted by the murderer."

"With what has been going on that makes perfect sense. Besides Ruth mentioned another couple who might know something. So Dylan and I will try and see if we can talk to them after dinner. Then we can compare notes."

"Great idea," she nodded to her friend.

They finally entered the banquet room and were once again amazed at how pretty it was. The bottom half of the walls were white paneling and the top half had wallpaper in different hues of green with splashes of white. The floor was tiled in white and gold that gave a marble effect. The tables had white tablecloths with gold chair coverings and sat eight. On top of each table was a light gold vase with white flowers and green leaves. And hanging from the ceiling were lights with white lampshades. The room was stunning when you walked in and looked very fresh and spotless.

It turned into an awesome dinner party. They were served a five-course dinner and even though it lasted almost two hours, the conversation was lively and the time flew by. Andy was seated next to a widow, and although he was not interested in the woman in a social sense, he enjoyed being paired up with her while they ate.

After dinner some of the group had been chosen to give short presentations about the time they spent on the island. The sections had been divided into four year periods since many of them had spent all their college summers on the Island. The talks covered all the years represented by those who had come to the reunion.

When the banquet was finished Andy's dinner partner went off to be with some of her friends. So he asked Olivia and Dylan if he could join them. "My only real friend was you Dylan and I would rather hang out with the four of you if you don't mind having me."

"The more the merrier," Dylan told him.

During their meal, Olivia had spotted the woman Ruth had told her about. And, so she had gone over and asked if she and her husband would meet up with them in the Cupola Bar after the banquet was over. Getting an affirmative reply she went back and told the two men.

"I don't know how long we will be talking to Belinda and Harry but if we don't meet up with you in the bar, we'll get back together for the dancing."

"That'll be great. And, whoever gets there first can get a table for all of us."

And, so after dinner was over they got up and left the room, going their separate ways.

CHAPTER 45

Ginger and Flynn reached the parlor before the other couple. When Belinda arrived she introduced her spouse, Harry, to them.

"I have to tell you my husband was really worried about talking to anyone with all these murders happening. And he definitely didn't want to say anything to the police. But since you have been involved with all of these crimes, he thought you might be the right folks to speak to."

"I think you'll be interested in what my wife has to say but first I just want you to know that George was my best friend. We lived next door to each other and played together before we even went to kindergarten. We both had sisters so we were like brothers to each other. I know you worked at the stables together, Flynn. Did you know George?"

"Not really. There were quite a few carriage drivers and I spent most of my time with the horses and vets. I don't even know if I could put a face to his name."

Then looking at the couple Ginger said, "I'm so glad you decided to talk to us. I'm not sure what we can do with your information. But I thought the world of Bree and I never got over the feeling something was terribly amiss with her disappearance. She was in the room next door but that first summer she would bum around with us all the time. I don't think she particularly cared for Riley and Tess."

"That's for sure," Belinda said. "Harry and I double dated with them your second summer here and that is why you didn't see her as much."

"I knew she was dating someone but Riley used to insinuate that she was seeing a lot of guys."

"That is totally untrue. She and George met about two weeks before the first summer ended. And they wrote to each other throughout that next college year. When they came back to the Island they were inseparable. But she did tell me there was someone else always following her and trying to get her to go out. She kept telling him she had a boyfriend but he was very persistent."

"Who was he?"

"I don't know, Ginger. She would never divulge his name but I know she and George had a couple of fights about it because he wanted the guy to stay away from her. She was worried what George would do to him if he found out who he was. So she never disclosed his name to George."

"That's pretty interesting. No one ever mentioned she had a stalker."

"I have to tell you I never heard a good thing about Riley. She was jealous of all of you according to what Bree told me. Because she thought Harper was so incredibly beautiful she was always doing mean things to her."

"I know Harper told us she short sheeted her bed."

"Trust me she did more than that to her. And she never had a kind word to say about you and Olivia either. But the reason you never heard about a stalker is because Riley constantly spread rumors about Bree sleeping around. Of course, it wasn't true. Bree and George were deeply in love. But people believe what they hear and those allegations took on a life of their own."

"It seems that woman has spent her life putting everyone down. No wonder she is such a miserable person. You spend your life spewing negative, you become negative and friendless yourself."

"That's for sure," Harry concurred. "Anyway to make a long story short George never said a word to me about running away with Bree. And we were so close I know he would have told me. On top of that, I know Bree had a horrible home life so I could understand her running away and never contacting anyone again. But George would never have done that. He loved his family and he definitely would have sent me a letter or phoned or somehow contacted me."

Even after all the years both Ginger and Flynn could hear the pain in his voice. They knew what he was telling them was absolutely true. "I tried, believe me I tried, to convince George's parents to get a private detective to look into the matter. But they were so grief stricken they didn't want to admit George might be hurt or even dead. So they went along with the running away story and convinced themselves he didn't contact them because Bree was so insistent."

"I wonder what they think now."

George's dad had a heart attacked and died about ten years ago. He was heartbroken over George vanishing. And his mother never got over the loss either. She has been in and out of mental facilities for the last twenty years. It is ironic how a couple's disappearance can affect so many lives. His sister is alive and has a family. I know she'll be happy to have closure. She always believed me that something happened to him."

"I am so glad you told us this. I'm still not sure whether Flynn or I can do anything but we'll try our best to find some kind of resolution for these murders. Belinda, I saw a woman crying in the Cupola Bar the other night and then again at the lecture. Was that you?"

"Yes. I couldn't believe that we might actually find out something about what happened to Bree and George. I was devastated to think they were found and possibly murdered and that is why I was crying. But now that I have had time to think about it, like George's sister, I finally feel relief that we at least now know they are dead, and not just hiding somewhere."

Meanwhile, as they were talking to Belinda and her husband, Olivia, Dylan, and Andy had met up with the other couple whom Ruth had told Olivia about. They had decided to sit and talk on the first floor of the Cupola Bar since it was very noisy and rowdy on the second floor.

When the five of them compared notes later, they learned that Stan and Alice had also been friends with Bree and George. They didn't want to talk too openly about their relationship with the murdered couple in case the murderer overheard and came after them. They also were aware that someone who had been on the island at that time was stalking Bree. They believed that man, whoever he was, had killed her as well as George. They had alerted the authorities at the time of the disappearance. But the police seemed to think since they were just kids, they didn't need to take their suspicions seriously.

"It was just a different time back then when adults thought kids didn't know anything," Stan told the three of them as they were sitting in the bar.

Thanking them for their time while agreeing with Stan's assessment, they departed the bar and proceeded to the Terrace Room to find their friends.

Ginger and Flynn had arrived first and the orchestra was busy tuning up. They were sitting at a table with five chairs. They told each other what they had learned. Then the orchestra started playing. Andy went over to talk to some people he knew and soon was dancing with someone. The four of them also got up to go to the dance floor.

As they were dancing Flynn said, "It's kind of strange how scared those couples are about talking to anyone, including the police, about the murders. I don't care what you say, Ginger. I'm going to stick close to you as long as we are on the Island."

"That's fine. Actually I think I would enjoy that."

"Good, because it's going to happen." Then murmuring in her ear he said, I don't want anything to happen to you. I have a feeling we might make it this time around. Since we already knew each other previously, I believe we will be able to appreciate each other better now. Times have changed and I don't want you to think I would leave you like I did the last time. I have faith that we can have an equal partnership and just have fun being together. I know we have lived alone for years and I don't want you to think that I will try to smother you. What I really want is to spend as much quality time together as possible. However, I will always make sure to give you any space you need."

Feeling a knot start to form in her stomach she looked up at him and their lips met. They didn't even remember staying on the dance floor until the orchestra quit.

CHAPTER 46

They had agreed to meet Andy for breakfast and had just sat down in the dining room when Ginger's phone rang. Turning it on, she said, "Oh, hi, Chief Logan. What can I do for you?"

The others looked at her with questions on their faces as she continued listening to him.

"Okay. Give me an hour. And Flynn will be with me. See you then. Goodbye."

"What was that all about?"

"The Chief wants to meet with us after breakfast. It is the strangest thing. He says Riley insists on talking to me."

"I don't think that is a good idea, Ginger."

"I don't either but he says she will not let it go, and he'll have a deputy stationed right outside the door to keep us safe. And you will be right there with me, too. So I think we should go see what she has to say."

"After the new things we learned about her last night, I don't know whether we should believe a word that woman tells us."

"You're probably right, Flynn. But the Chief seemed so distressed by the situation I think we should go.

Besides it will give us a chance to tell him what we learned last night.

"I know you're right, Ginger. But I don't like it."

"Let's not think about it right now. We'll have a nice breakfast with our friends and then this afternoon we have our boat ride to look forward to," she said as she smiled at Andy.

And, so they all focused on breakfast as they chatted about different things.

"You know," Dylan commented. "This is like when we were working on the Island. We have been here a week and I have no idea what is happening in the outside world."

"You're right," Andy replied. "And it's a good feeling. I often go through this when I am out overnights on my boat. It forces you to slow down and relax. Although I don't know how you four can be very relaxed constantly finding dead bodies."

"It's not a problem," Olivia told him. "Ginger is the only one who finds the bodies."

"Thanks. I appreciate your support," Ginger said to her friend, amused.

"As long as you will be downtown why don't you meet us at the marina when you're finished? That would be a lot easier than coming back and forth from the hotel to the boat."

Then looking at Dylan and Olivia, Andy said, "Why don't we meet out on the porch in an hour and a half and walk downtown together."

"That sounds perfect," Dylan answered him.

"I need to stop back at the cottage and get a coat and some things since we aren't coming back here before the boat ride."

"Yes, I need to get some things, too, Ginger."

With that, everyone left the dining room and went their separate ways. Olivia and Dylan decided to take a walk over to the stables. They both liked the idea of some exercise since they would be sitting on a boat all afternoon.

After they retrieved their belongings, Ginger and Flynn walked downtown to the police station. As soon as they saw the Chief they could tell he was stressed and they were glad they might be able to help him. It was obvious he was not used to bad things happening in his little corner of the world.

Ginger filled him in on what they had learned the night before.

"I'm so grateful for your information. I read all the reports from back in those days but there was not a single mention of Bree being stalked. That might be the key to solving these murders. Obviously, from what you heard about George's parents, I got nowhere asking questions of that family. George's sister was about three years younger and really didn't remember a whole lot about that time except that her brother went missing."

Then he continued, "Bree's parents wanted nothing to do with her back then, and even less now. This might blow a hole in my theory that Riley was the killer. The problem is there is evidence against her but most of it is circumstantial. Realistically I probably don't have enough to charge her when the seventy-two hours is up."

"Maybe something will develop. If the same person killed everyone then that means he has murdered two people this week alone. He could be escalating. You know someone mentioned there was an unsolved murder that happened a long time ago on the Island."

"Yes. It was sixty years ago. A woman named Mrs. Frances Harper was taking a three and a half- mile walk from her hotel to a cabin where her relatives were staying in the summer of 1960. She was only forty-nine years old and was raped, robbed and murdered by being strangled with her underwear. They suspected she sat down on a log to rest and the killer came up from behind her."

Then he continued, "There was a large search with blood hounds and divers and it took several days before they found the body. There was a serial killer they suspected named Hugh Bion Morse. Even though four hundred people were questioned and twenty two state police worked the case, it was never solved. But why are you asking about that crime?"

"I don't know. Someone mentioned it and I thought I would ask you if you had heard about it."

"Well, that has no relevance to these crimes. So, if you don't mind, let's go over to the Medical Center and see Riley."

"As I told you, the information I have on her is mostly circumstantial. I detained her more because I worried that in her mental state she might try to hurt you, Ginger, or possibly someone else. But I didn't want to put her in one of my jail cells. They are more for holding someone for a few hours, not days. She is much more comfortable at the Medical Center and we can still watch her closely."

CHAPTER 47

When they reached the building where Riley was being held they walked in and went down the hall to what looked like an examination room. Unlike normal medical rooms with a table this one had a bed and a chair. There was also a sink and toilet in a small area inside the room with a door for privacy.

Outside in the hallway by the examination room door a nurse and police officer were sitting at a small table. The door to the room had a window in the upper part so they could look in to check on her.

Chief Logan walked in to speak to Riley. When he came out he said, "She wants to speak to Ginger alone."

"That's not going to happen," Flynn said forcefully. "I go in with Ginger or she doesn't go in at all."

Returning into the room he soon came back out and motioned for the two of them to go inside. When they entered, he closed the door behind them. The officer then stood up and watched through the window. He couldn't hear what they were saying but he could see in case Riley got violent.

When they went into the room Riley was sitting in the chair looking totally disheveled. Flynn and Ginger sat down on the bed across from her.

"Why did you want to see me?"

Ignoring Flynn, she said, "Ginger, I know you don't like me and I guess it's understandable. I haven't been a very nice person most of my life. Sitting in here the last twenty-four hours, I have had time to reflect on my life. I can't believe Tess put up with me as long as she did. I know I have been mean all my life. I have never told anyone this but my father left my mother when I was seven years old. She was so upset about it she used to beat me and tell me how ugly I was. I know it's not an excuse but I realize now I have acted the way I have because of that treatment. I always believed everyone else was prettier and smarter than me and I always thought it wasn't fair."

"I'm sorry you went through that as a child. It certainly explains why you do the things you do."

"Even though I have done wretched things to people I would never physically hurt anyone; much less kill them. I know the Chief said there was DNA evidence on Tess that belonged to me but I helped fix her hair before the party and she was wearing one of my blouses and skirts. And I'm sure you have heard by now that I used to spread rumors about Bree sleeping around. I mainly did it because I knew she loved George and I was jealous of her. But are you aware she had a stalker? I saw someone in the bushes outside our dorm rooms one night but I couldn't see his face."

"Why didn't you say something when she disappeared? And, what about Harper?"

"I really thought she had run away with George. And, Harper was so beautiful, like Bree, and very successful. I did hate her and for the reasons I told you before. But I didn't poison her. Also I love to garden but look at me. I can't physically do that work. I have hired a man to do the physical labor for me."

Taking a deep breath, she continued, "I have lots of flowers and rose bushes and also some vegetables. But I don't even know what hemlock looks like. And as far as Tess, besides the fact I would never hurt her, look at me! If I had tried to strangle her the two of us would probably have been rolling around on the ground with all the weight we both had. She could have ended up strangling me."

Both Ginger and Flynn turned their heads to hide a chuckle just thinking about that scenario.

"But why did you want to talk to me?"

"Despite what has happened between us, and at that point she looked directly at Flynn, I know you are a fair person. And I saw you talking a lot to the Chief so I hoped you could convince him to let me go."

"Just so you are aware, I think most of the evidence the Chief has is circumstantial. I don't think he plans to charge you, at least not at this time. He was mostly worried about your mental state, and that's why he decided to hold you. He could have thrown you in one of his cells but he put you here in the Medical Center where he knew you would be more comfortable. Since it was the weekend and you were sedated at first, he planned to let you call an attorney first thing tomorrow morning. I'm sure you will be let go then."

"Thank you, Ginger, and also you, Flynn for coming in to see me. I really appreciate it. I have already decided if I get out of this mess intact I'm going into therapy to help me deal with my issues. I have plenty of money to live on and maybe I can start doing some good with it after all the bad I have done to people all my life."

After her last statement the two of them stood up to leave. Flynn reached into his wallet and pulled out a card. "We will be leaving tomorrow but if you need any help with anything my cell and email are on the card."

"Thank you, Flynn. I don't deserve your kindness."

Telling the Chief the gist of what Riley had told them. They said their goodbyes and began walking towards the marina.

"Why did you tell her the evidence against her was mostly circumstantial?"

"I don't think she is guilty and you don't either or you wouldn't have given her your card."

"That makes sense. And, you know me too well. You're right. I think she has done a lot of nasty things in her life but I don't believe she murdered anyone.

CHAPTER 48

As Ginger and Flynn were talking to Riley, Olivia and Dylan were taking a leisurely stroll around the grounds. Holding hands as they walked, Dylan said, "We leave for home tomorrow. Even with the murders I can't believe how fast this week has flown by. It has been a few days since we first talked about us. Now that you have had time to think things over, do you have any thoughts on getting back together with me?"

"Yes. I have decided I would like to try dating you again. I don't know how busy you are during the week but we could definitely get together on the weekends."

"I would really like to cut back on my job a little. I love what I do but I have worked so hard and so long that I feel life is passing me by. Just being here this week I realized I like to travel and get away to new places. And, I know how much you love traveling. Maybe we could plan a trip somewhere and possibly Ginger and Flynn might like to come along with us. But, first, why don't we try going out to dinner one day during the week? I could work half days on Wednesday and we could do little day trips around our area and then have dinner."

"That sounds like fun. Since I have the time I could research where we could visit, with input from you, of course."

"How would you begin?"

"You can tell me the names of some areas you would like to know more about and then I'll go on Trip Advisor. They have great ideas of things to do and also restaurant choices."

"That sounds great. You could even send me what you come up with so I can give you some feedback. I don't even mind looking some things up so you are not stuck with all the work. Then we could go out on Saturdays to museums or plays or activities like that and breakfast on Sundays. To be honest, I have done nothing like that in years and living in the Chicago area there is so much to see and do."

"You're right about that. And even though I have traveled the world, I haven't been to very many places here in the United States. It would be great to see some of the historical sites that I have taught my students about and that I've never visited."

"And I wouldn't be surprised if Ginger and Flynn wouldn't want to join us on some of our adventures."

Not paying attention to where they had been going, they found themselves by the hotel's stables. Seeing Neal working with the horses they waved and called hello but he didn't acknowledge them.

"That was sure strange," Dylan said.

"Yes. But did you notice it seemed like he was talking to himself."

"I thought maybe he was singing as he was brushing the horses."

"I didn't think about that but it is probably a more logical conclusion that he was singing."

"We better start heading back. I need to get a sweater before we go on the boat."

"Good idea. I need to get some things, too. And, I told Ginger I would call the kitchen and tell them we don't need appetizers tonight."

Turning around still holding hands they started towards the cottage.

When they got to the house they found Jesse standing there with his bags packed.

"I thought you were waiting until tomorrow to leave," Olivia stated.

"I was just going to leave a note for everyone. Despite losing Harper, I appreciate how good you have all been to me, especially including me in your activities."

"I know the circumstances have been horrendous for you but we have enjoyed meeting you," she replied.

"Are you driving all the way home today? Didn't you say it was a long drive?"

"No, I'm not going home. I need to meet with the medical examiner and take care of the details of Harper's body. But my car is in St. Ignace and I thought I would go get it and then cross the bridge to the Mackinac City side. That is where the authorities I need to consult with are located. I just thought it would be easier to get a hotel room there tonight. Then, in the morning, as soon as I get everything settled, I can drive home."

"That sounds like a good idea. If you have to take the ferry to get your car in the morning and then go to Mackinac City you will probably save a lot of time going today rather than waiting until tomorrow to leave."

"We are on the way to get Andy and go to the marina for a boat ride," Dylan told him. "Why don't you walk with us downtown? That way you will have some company on your way to the ferry."

"That would be nice. I would like walking with all of you."

When they got near the hotel, Andy saw them coming from his vantage point on the porch, and he came down the steps to meet them.

"Hi, Jesse. Are you coming on the boat ride with us?"

"No, I need to go to the mainland and my car is in St. Ignace so I am taking the ferry to get it."

"Nonsense. We are just going to cruise on the lake. We'll take you to St. Ignace first. I don't mind dropping you off there at all."

"You're sure I'm not putting you out?"

"Not at all. We'll enjoy your company."

They continued to stroll to the downtown. As they got close to the marina, they saw Ginger and Flynn sitting on a bench waiting for them.

CHAPTER 49

"Hi, Jesse. We did not expect to see you here," Ginger told him. "This is a nice surprise."

"I decided to leave today. If I stay overnight in Mackinac City, I can see the medical personnel first thing in the morning and then head home."

"We'll miss you tonight but I understand you wanting to tie everything up and get back to Wisconsin."

"Thanks, Ginger. Everyone has been so nice to me, especially you. Andy says he can drop me in St. Ignace where my car is parked. I just hope I won't put you all out."

"We don't have any specific plans so, as I told you, it is not a problem to take you there. But let me show you my boat. I live a pretty simple life now that I am retired but I always wanted a yacht and I have to confess I really splurged on this one."

As he walked them over to his boat Flynn said, "Wow, splurged is an understatement."

"Abby and I had this built to our specifications by Westport, a leading yacht builder. She had so much fun picking out the colors and decorating and we spent a lot of time on the boat. We often slept over before she got too sick to spend any more nights on here. After she died, I hid away on the boat going from one place to another for six months."

The yacht was a tri-level with a raised pilothouse and staterooms in the lower level. They entered on the middle level and passed the open deck which had a lot of seating on their way to the inside. When they walked in they all gasped. The salon was very spacious and dramatically open. There were couches and chairs lined along the wall area with large windows on both sides and a bar at the end of the room.

"This is awesome," Ginger said. "It's so huge."

"It was the perfect size for Abby and me. It's actually the smallest boat in length the company makes. While this is one hundred and twelve feet, they make yachts to one hundred and seventy two feet. But this was exactly what we wanted. It has four staterooms below that sleep eight. There's also room for the Captain and four additional crew members although usually I only have one or two extra crew. I could tell you all about the cruising speed, displacement, and the engines but you're probably not interested in all the technical aspects."

"I can see why you spent six months cruising. I think I could spend the rest of my life on here."

"I'm seriously considering that, Ginger. I have a condo in Chicago where I live, especially when I have foundation work to do, but I find myself spending more and more of my spare time on this vessel."

"Do you always have a Captain and crew?"

"No, Olivia, I don't unless I am going on longer trips or have company on board. I like to spend time with my guests as I'll do this afternoon with all of you. That's when the Captain comes in handy. Besides, I was thinking of going up into Lake Superior tomorrow, and I would definitely not take this boat up there alone. That can be a very unforgiving lake when storms come up, especially out of nowhere. Now let me show you around."

From the salon they entered a formal dining area with a table and chairs for eight people. There was a state of the art kitchen with an island in the middle and a counter to the side with bar stools for a more casual place to eat. When they went upstairs to the wheel house, there were computer screens and instruments along a control panel. A large leather chair with armrests was placed right in the center of the monitors. And there was a man seated in it. Andy introduced them to the Captain. He then gave the man instructions to take the boat to the St. Ignace ferry landing so Jesse could be dropped off.

"If you don't mind climbing back down, we can go to the bottom level and look at the staterooms. As they entered the Master Suite they saw a raised queen-sized bed and a couch to the side of it. The room seemed massive considering you were on a boat. They then peeked into the other rooms as they felt the yacht moving. After seeing the other bedrooms, they went back up the stairs to the salon.

"I guess we're on our way," Olivia said with a smile.

Since it was still a little too early to have cocktails, a man with a tray began handing out glasses of lemonade or ice tea.

"This is Jonathan," Andy told them. "He's the only crew I brought on this adventure."

Since it was a half hour ride over to St. Ignace to drop Jesse off, Ginger and Flynn told the others about what had happened during their talk with Riley.

"I know it doesn't excuse her meanness but I feel a little sorry for that woman."

"That's what we felt, too. Flynn even gave her his card in case she needs someone to give her advice."

It wasn't long before they pulled up to the ferry dock to drop Jesse. The Captain had radioed the ferry company for permission to tie up at one of their docks briefly. Since one of the regular ferries was on a run, they let them tie up to that pier.

The men shook his hand and the women gave him a hug as they all went outside to wave goodbye to him.

"Call us if you need anything," Flynn yelled at him as they watched him wheel his luggage over to his car.

Flynn had given him one of his cards the previous day, just like he had done for Riley today.

It was sad to watch him wheel his suitcase over to the car. He looked so dejected and his shoulders were slumped.

"Just think," Ginger said to the group. "The last time he was here, Harper was with him. Now he has that long lonely drive all by himself. And, when he gets home his house will seem so empty to him. I wonder if we'll ever see him again."

CHAPTER 50

As the shore receded, the temperature got cooler so they went back into the salon.

"He's another person I feel sad for," Olivia remarked. "Unless they find the murderer, Jesse will always be under suspicion for killing Harper. I would absolutely hate to live with that doubt hanging over my head."

"That's for sure." Andy observed. "But now let's continue on our journey. I always do research into the areas I am traveling to and since we are underway let me tell you a little about St. Ignace."

He then continued, "As I'm sure you all know, the town is in the Upper Peninsula of Michigan. It has a population around twenty-five hundred, with roughly one third being Native Americans. They are part of the Bands of Chippewa and Ottawa Indians and naturally there is a casino right outside of town. There are actually several casinos here in the Upper Peninsula."

"I didn't realize there were so many Indians living here," Ginger remarked.

"They have been here for hundreds of years and some of them have lived for thousands of years along the shoreline of Lake Superior. Historians also believe the Vikings came through here on their way to Minnesota way before Christopher Columbus."

"I know about the Vikings," Olivia added. "Eric the Red sailed to Iceland in 982. He landed in Greenland and founded a colony there. They think his son, Leif Erickson, arrived in Minnesota about 1000 and called it Vinland. Evidence was later found that Paul Knutson went to the prairies of western Minnesota in 1362 searching for Erickson's Vinland. Both those voyages were way before Columbus sailed."

"The history around here is amazing," Andy continued as he smiled a thank you at her. "What makes the past so interesting here is that they have been able to prove so much of it. St. Ignace, which we are now leaving, is the second oldest city in Michigan and was founded by the Jesuits. The French explorer Father Jacques Marquette established a mission here in 1671 and named it after St. Ignatius Loyola who founded the Jesuit order."

"Andy, can I jump in again?" Olivia asked. When he nodded, she said, "As a former history teacher, I used to tell my students back in those days 'the rivers were the roads.' There were a lot of missionaries all over North America at that time. In 1673 two years after founding this mission, Marquette joined with Joliet to find the Mississippi River. They were successful going all the way down to Arkansas. I remember reading that up until the early 19th century, this was a very important fur-trading center."

"That's right. Thanks, Olivia. Now if everyone will look to the left, you will see the entrance to the St. Marys River, although often you will see it spelled without the 's' on Mary. It's just under seventy-five miles from the mouth of the River in Whitefish Bay where Lake Superior is located down to Lake Huron where we now are. The river is the international border between the United States and Ontario, Canada. There is a twenty-three foot waterfall by Sault Ste. Marie and that is why they built the Soo Locks."

"I know the big freighters go through the locks but will you use them to get to Lake Superior?"

"No, Dylan. In 1895 the United States wouldn't let the Canadians use the Locks so they built their own. The current Canadian Lock is now used for recreational boats."

"So you will be using that Lock when you go into Lake Superior."

"Yes. Even though I have been to many places on my boat I have never been to that lake. The pictures always show forests, hiking trails, great beaches, and lighthouses built before the Civil War on the south shore of the lake."

Then he continued, "The Soo Locks opened in 1855 and at the mouth of the river is Whitefish Bay. You can view a lot of canoeists and kayakers there in the summer when the waters are calm. The rest of the year, after the Locks were built, many shipwrecks happened near the mouth of the river. You probably all remember the song 'The Wreck of the Edmund Fitzgerald,' which occurred during 'the gales of November.' That boat went down not too far from the mouth of the river."

"I know the locks are closed from January through March," Olivia added, "since so much ice forms in that area. But Lake Superior never fully freezes over since it is about 1,300 feet deep. It is also the largest freshwater lake in the world. But winter storms are vicious."

"I remember that song," Dylan replied. Then he added, "Where are we going next?"

"We are going to circle around Mackinac Island first going east, then south and finally coming back up the west side. The hotel and bridge are on the north side. Remember, the Island is only eight miles in circumference. Just south of Mackinac Island is another island called Bois Blanc Island, although the natives call it Boblo Island. From the eastern side of that island you can still see Mackinac Island and the bridge."

They continued listening to him as he continued, "We can see Boblo Island now coming into view. It's much bigger than Mackinac at twelve miles by six miles. However, there aren't a lot of amenities on the Island, even though it is rather large. All you can find is a combination restaurant and general store, a tavern, two chapels, a post office, airport and a one-room school."

"Oh, look, there is a lighthouse."

"Yes, Olivia, that's called the Bois Blanc Lighthouse. The structure is two stories high with light brick and an attached thirty-eight foot square tower jutting out the front. It was built in 1867 and is the third lighthouse at that location."

"Are there any places to stay on the Island?"

"You can camp, Olivia, and there is a house called Wood Cottage. I don't know anything about that place. But there is another accommodation that is well known. It is called Insel Haus, German for 'Island House', and is a Bed and Breakfast that serves both breakfast and lunch. The place sits on two hundred acres and has three unique suites and five other bedrooms all with outstanding views. They can accommodate up to twenty guests. There are many antiques throughout the house, a three thousand volume library, and several fireplaces. I think it would be a fun place for a retreat or even a small wedding."

"I never knew I was going to learn so much today," Flynn commented. "This has really been fun, Andy. Thank you for inviting us."

"It has been my pleasure. I love sharing my boat and adventures with others. And, just so you all know, I realize you are missing your appetizers tonight so Jonathan is going to fix some for us now. Also, I promised you dinner when we got back. However, I called the restaurant and they could not guarantee us a table as soon as we returned. They have the best whitefish I have ever had, as I told you previously, and they are always packed. Because of that I hope you don't mind that I am getting the food as take out. The Captain will call the restaurant just before we dock and Jonathan will go get our dinner and we'll eat here in the dining room. The view will be just as good as at the restaurant and actually it won't be as noisy."

They did not get back to the pier until almost 6:30 p.m. and having eaten all the appetizers Jonathan had prepared they were happy dinner was going to be later. They had a very enjoyable meal and everyone told Andy they didn't want to leave his boat.

They walked back to the hotel as a group about 9:00 p.m. and Ginger remarked how peaceful and quiet the day had been, especially since they had not brought their cell phones along thinking they would not have service.

They could hear something going on down by the Secret Garden area and wondered what that was all about. It was getting dark so they couldn't really see but there were some flashlights bobbing around.

"Probably some animals, maybe coyotes, got in there and they are trying to chase them out," Dylan observed. "I know that was a problem years ago when we worked here."

Saying goodbye to Andy at the hotel entrance, they continued on to the Cottage, reflecting on how quiet the place would be with the rooms not occupied upstairs.

They had all agreed to meet up with Andy for breakfast before leaving for their homes.

CHAPTER 51

The house was dark when they entered and Ginger immediately noticed the red light flashing on their telephone.

"Who in the world is calling us now," she said out loud to the others.

Turning the answering machine on the Chief could be heard on the other end of the line.

"Dylan... Flynn... or Ginger is anybody there? I've been trying to call you and no one answers. Did you lose your cell phones? Someone please call me back as soon as you get my message."

"Going into their rooms, they picked up their cells and saw there were messages from the Chief on those, too.

"I'll call him back and put the phone on speaker so we can all hear," Flynn told them.

Dialing the number the Chief picked up immediately.

"This is Flynn, Chief Logan. You called us?"

"Flynn are all four of you together? Where have you been? Are all of you alright?"

"We're all here. We went for the day on Andy's boat. None of us took our cells because we didn't think we would have service out on the lake. Why are you calling? Is something wrong?"

"What about Jesse? Is he with you?"

"No. Actually, we took him over to St. Ignace on the boat and dropped him off at the ferry landing where he had left his car. That was early this afternoon. He's staying at some motel in Mackinac City tonight. But why are you so worked up?"

"Riley has disappeared. We can't find her anywhere. She seemed fine and I let her know I would release her in the morning with the provision she stay on the Island another couple of days. She seemed okay with that. Then I let the nurse go home because I didn't feel she would be needed any longer."

"Do you think she left the island?" Dylan asked.

"I don't know what to believe. My deputy went to get her some dinner. He said she was looking forward to the food and told him she was hungry. But when he came back she was gone. And he swore to me her door was locked when he left."

"I take it you checked the hotel to see if she went back to her room," Flynn enquired.

"That was the first thing I did. And I checked with the ferry and no one answering her description boarded either boat. Can you check your cottage just in case she went back there?"

Nodding Olivia went upstairs and was back down in no time.

"No one is upstairs in any of the rooms."

"Did you hear that, Chief?"

"Yes. I guess I was just hoping. I have a terrible feeling in my gut about this and I am running out of options."

"Were those your men with flashlights we saw down by the Secret Garden area when we got back just now?" Ginger asked.

"Yes. I was worried if someone did hurt her, they might have left her body there like Tess'. But so far they radioed they have found nothing. We'll look again in the morning when we have light but I am not optimistic."

"I'm sorry we weren't able to help you. It does seem weird she would leave when food was coming," Flynn told him.

"Well, I can't do anything else at this point except wait for daybreak. I was wondering if you could all stay over another day or two. I don't know what kind of obligations you all have. But I did speak to the hotel manager and there's no one staying at the cottage until Thursday. He said you could all stay for free until Wednesday."

"That's sure nice of him," Flynn told him. "Let me talk with the others and I'll let you know in the morning. Thank you for checking on that, Chief. I know we would all like to help you anyway we can."

"The manager was happy to have you stay if I thought it would help. As I told you before, this reflects very negatively on the tourism of this Island. If I don't solve this mystery quickly, vacancies at this busy time, will quickly increase."

As they all sat down, Flynn went behind the bar and found a bottle of wine. Opening the bottle and pouring some into four glasses, Dylan passed them out.

"What do you ladies think?"

"I don't know about Ginger but since I am retired I have nothing pressing this next week. I need to call my neighbor, who is watching my house, and let her know so she doesn't worry when I don't come back there tomorrow night."

"I also have nothing important going on until the end of the week. I will need to call my daughter since she has been looking after my condo. I don't want her to be concerned if I don't come home either."

"I'm also free but what about you, Dylan? Do you have to get back to work?"

"Since I am doing research, I don't necessarily have to account to anyone on a daily basis. I'll plan to call the lab right away in the morning and let them know I'm going to be out another couple of days. I'm sure it won't be a problem especially since we don't have anything pressing going on at the moment."

With that settled they sat back and sipped their wine.

"I'll let the Chief know first thing in the morning that we'll all be staying. And, I will also call the desk and let them know we are extending our visit. Is that okay with everyone?" Flynn asked the others.

"That's fine by me," Olivia answered as the others nodded. "Remember we have breakfast with Andy in the morning. I wonder if he'll want to stay on with us. He seems pretty 'footloose and fancy free,'" she observed.

"I'll call him and ask," Dylan told the others.

They remained a little longer enjoying their wine but eventually they all got up and went to their rooms.

CHAPTER 52

Everyone was awake early the next morning. The men came out of their room at 7:00 a.m. and Ginger already had the coffee made. They sat enjoying their drinks as Flynn made the calls. When he talked to the Chief he asked Flynn if they could all join the search party at 10:00 a.m. He told him, they would be happy to do that.

When he was finished with his calls, he told everyone about joining the search party. After that, Dylan called Andy. Knowing he was an early riser, he wasn't surprised when his friend immediately answered the phone.

Dylan told him about Riley and their conversation with the Chief the previous night. Letting him know they were extending their vacation by a couple of days, Andy eagerly agreed to stay with them.

"We're going to breakfast at 8:00 a.m. because the Chief wants us to help with the search this morning. Why don't you check out of the hotel and move over to the cottage. The rooms are all cleaned upstairs. I know you would be very pleased with the accommodation Jesse and Harper had. There's a large bed and an alcove sitting area overlooking the lake. I know we would love to have your company and those two bedrooms are just sitting vacant."

"Thank you, Dylan. I would love moving in with the four of you. And that will give me a chance to experience the cottage in case I decide to rent it some time. I'll plan to pack my things and meet you at 8:00 a.m. for breakfast."

After Dylan put the phone down, Flynn called the hotel back and asked to speak to the manager. He told the man about Andy moving in with them.

"That's no problem," the manager told him. "You paid for the cottage for eight people and since you lost four, there will be no additional charge for adding one, especially since you paid extra for those two rooms in the hotel. I'm just hoping the Chief can tie everything up very quickly. This situation is definitely not good for business."

"Well, that's all settled," Flynn told them as he put the phone down. I'm going to have another cup of coffee and then it'll be time to go to breakfast.

As they walked over to the hotel they could hear a lot of commotion coming from the front of the hotel. They realized it was probably the Chief's men rechecking the Secret Garden and other areas around the building.

When they met Andy by the dining room he said, "I'm really sorry for the reason we are staying over but I am also happy that it's happening. It will give us more time to spend together."

As they sat eating their food, Ginger asked, "Do you think Riley is dead? I hate to say this but I'm almost becoming immune to these happenings."

"That's a typical reaction," Dylan told her. At first, finding someone dead, you are terribly shocked. But if it keeps happening then you start being unaffected by the situation since it becomes more common place. I know that sounds awful but you become almost immune to the tragedy surrounding you. I hate to say you get used to it, but in a way that's what happens."

"I said a prayer last night that Riley isn't dead. I know it doesn't look good for her but I really believed what she said yesterday."

"What did she say, Ginger?"

"She told us she wanted to go into therapy and hoped since she had quite a bit of money she could start doing good with it to make up for all the bad she has done all her life, Olivia."

Flynn, who had left the room briefly came back in and sitting down said, "As soon as we finish let's go get Andy settled into his room. Since it's a little chilly outside, I think we need a jacket before we walk downtown to the police station. I know the Chief said we should come at 10:00 a.m. but I don't think it will matter if we go sooner. I'm not really in the mood to sit around here doing nothing when we could be helping out. And, I just talked to some men outside and they told me the Chief is putting together a search party and sending it to the British Landing area."

"Where is that, Flynn? Didn't we go by there on our horse and buggy ride?"

"Yes. It is on Lake Shore Drive about two miles northwest of the downtown and harbor. You might remember one of the rules said you couldn't pull the horse and buggy over when you leave the stables until you got to British Landing."

"But why in the world would he look over there for Riley?"

"It was because of you, Ginger."

"Me?"

"Yes. You asked him about that murder long ago. I know it was sixty years ago so obviously, whoever the killer is, most likely is not from those days. But if the killer knew about that murder he might have decided to replicate it. If that's the case then he would have taken her to that area. I know it sounds like a stretch but since the Chief is running out of ideas, he had a hunch to try there."

"I think when I was reading about that murder, it said the killer concealed the corpse under a pile of vegetation just beyond a stone-pillared gate."

"Yes. That's correct, Ginger. And, that's why the Chief wants a search party to go there and look through the brush. When we go back to the cottage put on jeans and wear long sleeves. You also need shoes and socks—no sandals. We don't want to get hurt searching through all that underbrush."

"I'm finished eating and ready to leave if everyone else is," Ginger told the others.

Nodding their heads, they stood up from the table and headed to the cottage to get jackets and change their clothes. As they made their way down to the police station, they saw several men searching through the trees that bordered the hotel.

CHAPTER 53

The search party was getting organized when they arrived at the police station. There were two carts pulled by horses that were taking everyone involved over to the British Landing area. They all got into a cart that already had three people in it. The other wagon was carrying six individuals.

They introduced themselves to the other three persons in their cart. When they arrived in the area they were paired off and given specific search areas. At first, they had no luck and were discouraged that the Chief's hunch was not correct. They had been searching almost an hour and noticing a log on the ground a little ways back from the road, Ginger wanting to rest a bit, went to sit on it. As she cleared some of the scrub from around the fallen tree, she spotted a foot.

"Dylan, come here quick," she yelled.

Standing back she pointed to the foot as Dylan came running over. Realizing someone was lying on the ground, he said, "Stand back everyone," as the others started crowding in.

The figure was a heavy set woman wearing a skirt. Bending down, he looked closer and realized immediately the body belonged to Riley. He saw underwear wrapped around her neck and carefully put his fingers there to feel for a pulse. He spun around and said, "I don't know how it happened but I feel a slight pulse. Let's get her back to town as quick as we can."

Meanwhile Flynn called the Chief to let him know they had found Riley and were bringing her back to the Medical Center. He told him to make sure the doctor was ready. They had to keep the cart on the road but they brought it as close as possible to where Riley was laying.

It took four men to lift her up and put her in the wagon. Olivia, Ginger and Dylan stayed on the cart with her while the others got in the other wagon to go back into town. It seemed to take forever as Olivia and Ginger each held one of her hands on the journey back.

The women were not aware of her condition. They thought Riley was unconscious but she was actually in a coma. The cart she was in continued to the Medical Center while the other one dropped everyone off in front of the police station.

Chief Logan was standing by the Medical Center with the doctor when they arrived. "I see you are still finding bodies," he commented to Ginger. "But this time it will hopefully be a good thing."

Flynn and Andy, as well as the same four men who had carried her out of the brush, came running over from the police station. The doctor had brought a stretcher out to the street. They carefully moved her onto it and took her inside. This time she was put in a room that had an examination table. Then the men left to go back to their businesses.

The doctor immediately put her on oxygen. Dylan also went into the examination room while the others sat outside in the small lobby. It was about a half hour later when he came back out to where they were seated.

"I don't know if she is going to make it or not. If she does she will be extremely lucky. Since she's in a coma we don't want to move her to the hospital at this time. The doctor put her on oxygen and we were able to examine her after the nurse removed her clothes.

"It's obvious she tried to fight off her attacker. The killer tried to strangle her with her underwear. I think he thought she was dead when he left her out there. However, he didn't realize when he was strangling her, she managed to put three of her fingers under the cloth. So instead of dying right away like he thought she had, in reality she had only passed out. I am sure it didn't help that she was outside all night but being under the brush probably helped keep her a little warm. Although, both the trauma and the outside conditions caused her to slip into a coma."

"Wow, she really went through a lot."

"Yes, Ginger she did. We don't have any way to check for brain damage at this time but the doctor's biggest concern is that she doesn't get pneumonia. He has her sedated and, there will be a nurse sitting with her constantly to monitor any changes. However, there's no way she'll wake up for a long time so we may as well go back to the hotel."

As they walked back up the hill they stopped at The Gate House Restaurant and picked up soup and sandwiches for lunch. The day was much cooler than the previous days so they decided they didn't want to eat outside.

"I wonder how Jesse made out this morning. I suppose he's on his way home by now. I would bet he would be surprised to know that we're all still here.

"He might actually be happy about it, Ginger. With someone attacking Riley there's even more reason to believe that Harper's death was somehow tied in with all these other murders. I become more convinced by the minute that he didn't have anything to do with his wife's death."

"I think you're right, Flynn. And, I don't know if you read about the murder on the Island a long time ago but that woman was also strangled with her underwear. Either that is ironic or we have a deranged killer trying to duplicate the past."

They began laying out the lunch on the dining room table when Andy asked, "What are the plans for this afternoon?"

"I know you men have been coming up with all the ideas of what we should do. Don't get me wrong. I have enjoyed everything. But I have an idea. I don't know if it will make a difference. But I was thinking it might be worthwhile, with everything that has happened, to spend a little time sitting here at the table. We should start from the beginning and brainstorm what all these murders have in common."

"That's a great idea, Ginger. And then we could go play some more croquet."

Ginger rolled her eyes at what Flynn said. Meanwhile Dylan jumped in and told them they also needed to play the rubber match of their duckpin bowling games.

"What is duckpin bowling?" Andy asked.

Groaning, the two women both said at the same time, "A Sport!"

CHAPTER 54

As soon as they finished eating, Ginger handed out small notepads and pens she had found in the writing desk. Before they started, Olivia and Dylan refilled everyone's ice tea or lemonade before sitting down at the table with the others.

"I don't know if you want to use these but you can make notes if you so desire. Let's start with what we know."

"Do we know anything, Ginger?" Olivia asked.

"Yes, we know quite a few things and I believe we can make some assumptions from those facts. First of all, several people have told us that Bree had a stalker. I think we can conclude it was someone about our ages and working on the Island at that time."

"I agree," Andy joined in. "I know I didn't know you or those kids who died at that time since it happened the year before I came. But that first year I started working here, I heard a lot of speculation about their disappearance. And, maybe I can be a little more objective than some of you since I never knew either of them. It makes sense to me, if we truly have a deranged killer involved in these murders, he was stalking Bree and she probably rejected him. He then flew into a rage and killed her."

"That does make sense," Flynn remarked. "Then following your thinking, George just happened on the murder and the killer murdered him, too."

"I think that is logical to presume especially since they were buried together."

"I agree with you men but why was Harper killed and why now?"

"Maybe he was worried she saw something long ago, but not being sure, he decided not do anything about it at that time. Remember the murders happened two weeks before we left the Island, and after Bree disappeared, we all stuck close to each other until it was time to leave. And, none of us girls came back the following summer. I know at the time everyone thought Bree and George had run away but I never felt that was true," Ginger added.

"I'm sure we would all have pushed the authorities harder if we had known those things their friends told us the other night. I know I would have gone to the police asking lots of questions and demanding answers."

"You're right, Olivia. Especially after what Harry said. He and George were best friends and he was right. There was no way George would have run away without either leaving, or at the very least, sending some kind of note to him even if it had been a couple of weeks later."

Then Flynn responded. "I don't believe Harper knew anything or she would have said something at least to the two of you. And, if she had known anything or talked to anyone about the disappearance, I believe the killer would somehow have heard about it. And then he would have certainly tracked her down and killed her sooner. But maybe he was afraid when she returned something might trigger her memory of what had happened back then."

"I guess we'll never know for sure the answer to that particular scenario until or if they catch the killer." Andy said.

"I'm a lot more hopeful now that he might be caught."

"Why do you say, Ginger?" Flynn asked.

"Don't you think it's obvious he is escalating? He killed Bree and George thirty-five years ago. But in the last week he has killed two people, if we assume he murdered Harper, and has tried to strangle Riley. From what Tess told me, I know she suspected someone. If she confronted that person, then he had to kill her to keep her quiet. I get that. But why Riley? She knew nothing. For a while she believed I had something to do with it."

"Maybe he didn't like her and decided to get rid of her since he was getting away with all the other murders," Olivia replied.

They had no idea there was a man listening to them outside their window. But when he heard a noise he looked up and saw two maids walking towards them. He decided he better leave so as not to get caught. Besides he had heard the gist of their thinking and knew he had to come up with a plan.

As he left the bushes where he was hiding, Ginger continued her train of thought. "Yes, Olivia. And that's why I say he is escalating. He didn't know about DNA when he killed Bree and George. And I don't believe the Chief has released the information that some had been found at that long ago crime scene."

Looking around the table at the others, she continued, "So when they find someone they suspect, a DNA test might seal his doom. But everyone keeps asking questions and I imagine he's not thinking very clearly because he's afraid of being found out. So he's extremely unstable right now and that is when people start making mistakes."

"I am curious, Dylan. If you can't say anything, I will understand. But do you know if Riley was raped?"

"We did a cursory check and there was no sign of sexual assault. Why? Is that important?"

"The reason I brought it up is because of the fact of Riley being strangled with her underwear. That is what happened to that woman sixty years ago. And he left her in the same area as Riley was found. But the difference is the other woman was sexually assaulted and you're telling us Riley wasn't."

"There are two answers to that. He is not into sex when he kills and could have easily been turned off by her size."

"What is the other, Dylan?"

"The second reason is connected to the first. Since everyone knows about DNA now, even if he did want to have sex with her, he might have been afraid to leave any DNA behind. I have a feeling, Ginger, as you presumed, he's killing without thinking things through very well, and he might not have had protection with him. Somehow he knew she was in the Medical Center. And, if he had been watching the building, it's obvious he took the opportunity to grab her when the deputy went to get her dinner."

"We should probably let the Chief know what conclusions we have come up with," Ginger told the others.

"I'll tell him," Dylan told them as they started to get up from the table. "I promised the doctor I would look in on Riley this afternoon in case there is anything I can do to help. I'll plan to stop by the police station and let the Chief know what we have discussed. Why don't the four of you go play croquet? A little exercise is just what the doctor orders."

Thinking that was a very good idea, they got their sweaters and headed down to the pool area.

"Be careful, Andy," Olivia laughingly told him. "Flynn can be vicious about winning when it comes to this game."

The four friends played two games with Flynn winning the first and surprisingly Ginger taking the second. When they were finished, they went back to the cottage to read for the remainder of the afternoon. They all commented on how nice it was to sit inside and enjoy the day without the television blasting.

Meanwhile Dylan stopped at the police station and let the Chief know what they had come up with while discussing the case after lunch. From there he continued on to the Medical Center. When he arrived he went to the room where Riley was being kept. Luckily the examination table was equipped with side bars to keep her from falling off; although in the condition she was in, there wasn't much of a chance that would happen.

The doctor was standing beside her with another man. He noticed Riley was hooked up to an IV and there was a blood pressure cuff on her arm so obviously they were checking her vitals quite often. As the doctor turned, he saw Dylan and greeted him.

"Hi, Dylan. Let me introduce you to my friend Abbott. He is a retired neurologist and has a cottage on the

Island. He usually comes here from June until the end of September every year. I called and asked him if he would mind consulting with me about our patient."

"Nice to meet you, Dr. Abbott," Dylan said to the man. They didn't shake hands since the doctor had gloves on and was obviously checking on Riley.

"As you know, Dylan, it's important to get a test score from the Glasgow Coma Scale within twenty four hours of the injury when a patient is in a coma. I have been testing Riley's eye, verbal and motor responses to come up with a score and I have had some positive results. Normally a score of three or four means the patient is likely to die or stay in a vegetative state. But on the other end of the spectrum a score between 11 and 15 means they are likely to make a good recovery."

"I have not dealt with those issues in my practice but I do remember the scale from medical school."

"Research shows that a comatose patient's outcome relates very closely to their score on this test. While not great, Riley's score is an eleven, which I view as an optimistic sign."

"Well, that's terrific considering what she's been through."

"Yes, it is. You realize recovery is gradual with patients becoming more and more aware over time. Most comas don't last more than two to four weeks. When she wakes up she'll only be alert for a few minutes the first day. But gradually she will stay awake longer and longer periods."

"Do you think she'll remember what happened when she wakes up?"

"That's hard to say. We have no idea how long oxygen was cut off to her brain while he was strangling her. But she needs to be in the hospital rather than here with such limited access to medical care. I think it's best to try and move her tonight."

"Do you think she can survive the move?"

Doctor Paul has done everything he can for her. She is on an IV and he is giving her diuretics to limit any secondary damage to her brain. You know that should reduce fluid in her tissues and help reduce the pressure inside her brain. I know it's not practical or wise to leave her on this exam table."

"How are you going to move her?"

"I have some men coming to help get her into the emergence vehicle. Then we will take her to the airport. A medevac helicopter will fly her over to Traverse City. There is a larger hospital in that town and they can get her stabilized. Eventually she will probably be moved to the University Hospital in Lansing. They have a really good Trauma Department."

"Hopefully she'll make it okay. She wasn't the nicest person in the world but nobody deserves to have to go through this. Thank you to both of you for all your help and taking such good care of her," Dylan said as he said good bye to the two men.

Walking back to the hotel he realized how lucky Riley was. Her prognosis was more on the positive rather than the negative side. Besides that he knew she was being taken care of as well as could be expected considering the gravity of her condition.

CHAPTER 55

When Dylan got back there was no one about. He realized everyone was most likely getting ready for cocktails and dinner. Looking at his watch he saw that it was past 4:30 p.m. I wonder where this day has gone he thought to himself. The hours just seem to fly by while we're here. Going into his room he could hear Flynn in the shower.

As if by magic at 5:00 p.m., everyone came out of their rooms and congregated in the living room. As usual Flynn began making the martinis while Dylan got the glasses ready. Andy was just coming down the stairs and he said, "Thank you for letting me move in with all of you. This has been so much fun being with everyone today despite the morning activities."

They all smiled as he said that and then turned when they heard a noise at the door. As they looked they saw Neal coming in with a tray of hors d'oeuvres.

"I can't believe it. Are you all still here? I thought it was weird they wanted me to bring this tray over here since this is not normally my job. I thought you were all leaving this morning."

Flynn spoke first. "Hi, Neal. I hope you have had a good day. To answer your questions, the Chief asked us to stay a couple more days so we made arrangements with the hotel to extend our stay. But, quite frankly, we didn't think we would be having appetizers anymore."

"If you stay in the cottage more than one night, the appetizers are automatically brought over to you. And, that explains why they wanted me to deliver them. So have you done anything interesting today?"

"Well, as you might know they were looking for Riley so we joined the search party."

"Yes. All the stable hands were talking about it. That was really nice of you, especially considering how horrible she treated everyone. But it's a shame she was killed."

"She's not dead, Neal."

"What? Not dead? But I thought they said they found her beside a road somewhere."

"Yes, they did. It was actually Ginger who found her and it was in some brush."

"Really? You sure have found a lot of bodies lately, Ginger."

"Don't remind me, Neal," she said with a sigh.

"You mean to tell me she wasn't dead when you found her, Ginger?"

"No," Dylan cut in. "She still had a very weak pulse so we took her to the Medical Center where they worked on her."

"Is that where she is now?"

"Maybe."

They all looked at him with surprise at his answer.

"I never got a chance to tell any of you when I got back here. Riley is in a coma and they don't know the extent of her injuries. However, there is a neurologist who lives on the Island in the summer and he tested her. The results are fairly decent and he thinks she'll make a positive recovery."

"That is terrific. Do they think she will be able to identify her attacker?"

"They're not sure about that, Neal. It will take a while before she wakes up and then it'll be very slowly at first."

"Hopefully she will remember and can tell the authorities. I wonder if they need help taking care of her. I could take a turn sitting a couple of hours a night. I am guessing they will have round-the-clock care."

"That is very nice of you to offer, Neal. However, they aren't keeping her here. They just don't have the proper facilities to give her good medical care. She's going by medevac to a bigger hospital than what is available in this area. That's why when you asked me if I knew where she was, I said 'maybe.' I don't know if they have moved her from the Medical Center yet. If they haven't, I know it won't be too much longer."

"Thank goodness she will get good care. I know she was very mean to people but no one deserves to be strangled like that."

"How did you know she was strangled, Neal?" Ginger asked.

"As usual, everyone in the stables was talking about it this afternoon. I know one of the men who had helped with the search party and I think he was the one who mentioned it to me. Naturally, I just assumed she was dead. But it is still amazing they found her so quickly."

"Do you remember hearing about the murder on the Island that happened sixty years ago?" Olivia asked him.

"Vaguely. But what has that got to do with anything?"

"The Chief had his men looking everywhere, and when they couldn't find her, he decided to send the search party out to where that other murder took place. And that's where we found her."

"It's sure lucky they looked there, Ginger. Anyway is there anything else you need right now?"

"No," Ginger replied. "You can take the rest of the night off, Neal. We'll put all the dishes in the dishwasher and refrigerate what we don't eat. Thanks for bringing the food over. Have a good night, Neal."

"Thanks, Ginger. I hope all of you have a nice evening. Will you still be here tomorrow?"

"Yes, we will. See you then."

With that, he picked up the empty tray and left.

"Now that he's gone, what are our thoughts on dinner tonight?" Flynn asked the group.

"I don't know about anyone else but now that we have had these appetizers I don't think I will be real hungry. Maybe we should try that sushi place Jesse went to the other night."

"That's a great idea, Ginger. Sushi sounds perfect for dinner. And then we can go back and finish our Duck Pin Bowling Contest," Dylan said with a smirk.

CHAPTER 56

Since they decided not to go to the hotel dining room, after they finished their cocktails, they went back into their rooms and changed into more casual clothes. Then they walked down the hill to the Sushi Grand. The restaurant was connected to the Gate House and since the area inside was so small they were actually seated by the Gate House Bar.

The service was great and the waiter was very friendly. The décor was cute and fit the atmosphere. It turned into a great sushi experience with fresh food made to order. As soon as they sat down they brought hot, steamy towels to refresh their hands. Since they had appetizers at the cottage they all ate lightly.

Flynn ordered the Shrimp Tempura Roll while Dylan went for the Avocado Bomb. He was not sure what ingredients were used but he told everyone it was outstanding. He also noted how artisticly the sushi was presented. Olivia opted for the Miso soup with mushrooms and a salad but she took a bite of Dylan's Avocado Bomb and declared it wonderful.

"If I ever come back here, I will definitely order that next time. It was awesome," she told them.

Meanwhile Ginger requested noodle soup and salad. She also asked for the spicy tuna that she shared with Olivia. Not wanting to be outdone by the others, Andy chose the spicy firecracker roll.

"The hotter the better," he told them as everyone laughed.

Knowing they couldn't leave without dessert they split the gooey pecan ball. The pecans surrounded a sphere of ice cream with sauce on the outside, and it was definitely gooey. When they asked for five spoons the waiter laughed and said, "Good choice."

"I don't know about the rest of you but I have had more sugar this week than in the last five years," Ginger remarked.

"That's what diets are for," Olivia answered back. "And I'm sure we'll all be on one when we get home."

Flynn knew the bowling was back at the Woods Restaurant, which was a thirty-minute, one and half mile walk towards the state park.

"I knew it would be getting dark after dinner, and as much as we could have used the uphill climb, I thought it would be better to get a carriage to take us there. I called the number on the card our driver gave us the other night and he is going to come down here and pick us up and take us to the Woods. With five of us walking on the street, I didn't want someone to get run over by a horse because they weren't visible," he said, chuckling.

"That's probably a good idea," Dylan added.

While they were eating dessert Flynn had called for the carriage. When they finished with their meal, they waited outside and soon saw one coming. At first they weren't sure if it was the one they had ordered since it was all enclosed but Dylan recognized the driver.

"You brought a different conveyance tonight. This looks like a stagecoach," he told the driver.

"Yes, the other gentleman said there were five of you when he called so I brought the bigger coach."

"That's perfect. Thanks for thinking of that."

The men helped the women up into the carriage and then they stepped in.

"Not only is this a much better choice with five of us," Ginger observed, "But it's colder tonight so I'm glad it's enclosed."

It took about twenty minutes for the ride to the Woods. On the way, they were talking and laughing about who would be the winner of the duck pin bowling competition. When they arrived, since it was Monday night, there was no one else playing. The men told Andy how they had won the first game and the women the second.   He explained the place had closed before they could compete in the rubber game of the match.

As they started playing, it was a pretty even match for most of the game. But when they got to the last frames the women took a slight lead and ended up beating the men.

"You definitely won't let us live that down," Flynn told them.

"You're right about that," Ginger replied back to him.   "I like this game especially since it's a lot different from regular bowling."

After that they played two more games before the place closed. But the last two games they did not play as teams; it was every man for himself. This worked perfect since there were five of them and that way no one felt left out.

Andy was content to sit and watch them finish their match before playing. Being an avid gamer, whether real or on the computer, he watched as they played and got a feel for how it worked differently from normal bowling. Because of that, he ended up high scorer for the night.

Flynn went to call the carriage driver on his cell only to discover he was already waiting for them. Since it was closing time the man realized they would be ready to leave.

As they started moving Ginger said, "I remember the last time we went bowling was the day I found Bree and George's bodies. It seems so long ago considering all that has happened since then."

Agreeing with her, it was totally quiet the rest of the way back to the cottage with everyone lost in their own thoughts.

CHAPTER 57

The next morning the sun was shining brightly as the five of them walked over to breakfast at their usual time. This would be their last full day on the Island. They originally were going to take another bike ride to the interior of the Island. They had also discussed playing tennis but when Andy suggested taking another boat ride for the day, they all agreed that would be a lot more fun.

"Who needs exercise when we can spend the day on the water? I can't believe this is our tenth day here and the weather has been so amazing. It's sure not a given when you are this far up north in September," Ginger commented.

"Yes. And it has been very nice that you haven't found any more bodies," Olivia added.

After breakfast they went back to the cottage and got things they needed for the day out on the water. Walking back into town Flynn told everyone, "I can't walk through the downtown this morning without getting my sugar fix."

"What are you talking about?" Andy asked him.

Flynn explained to him about all the Island fudge shops and how it was their patriotic duty to sample their way through town."

"If you put it that way we better do it."

"Oh, my gosh. How can you possibly eat fudge when we just ate breakfast?"

"You're right, Olivia. I could not do all that sugar justice after the big meal I just ate. And that's why I brought these along." He put his hand in his jacket pocket and withdrew five sandwich bags. "I found these in the drawer of our kitchen. We can put the samples in these and then can nibble throughout the day."

"That was a good idea but I am serving you all lunch on the boat. I didn't want anyone to starve."

With that everyone was laughing as they walked into the first fudge shop. Naturally they all took a sample. Since they were placed on a small piece of tissue paper, they went back outside and put the little piece in their baggy. They continued going into all the shops with fudge until they reached the end of the street by the marina.

"It's a good thing the men only did one side of the street," Ginger said to Olivia.

"Don't worry. We will probably hit those other stores on the way home," Dylan told them as he laughed.

It was a little after 10:30 a.m. when they climbed aboard Andy's boat. The Captain already had the engines running when they settled into the salon.

"Where are we going today?" Olivia questioned him.

"First stop, I guess I should say, slow down, will be the bridge."

"Our ferry gave us an explanation on the way across on our first day," Ginger told him.

"We had one, too," Dylan added.

"I figured you already knew about the bridge. But since we circled the Island last time I thought we could cruise along the shoreline of the Upper Peninsula going west from St. Ignace. It will just be a different perspective."

"That sounds like a great idea," Olivia told him. "That's the way Jesse and Harper came on their way up here."

At that point they put their jackets on and went to sit outside. Although the windows in the salon were big, there was nothing like having a wholly opened view.

It was not long before they very slowly went under the bridge. "It's an awesome sight to behold when you're driving across the bridge but you really get a feel of how massive it is when you cruise underneath it," Dylan commented.

As they came out from underneath the bridge, Andy started talking again. "This will be a perfect day for navigating the waters up here. With such a dazzling sun the lake looks like sparkling little diamonds. I love looking at the water when it shines like this. We aren't too far off shore, and you can see the beautiful sandy beaches with the dunes behind them."

"I wonder if these beaches up here ever get very many people who use them." Olivia asked him.

"In the summer, especially on weekends, the beaches will have quite a few people, especially families. But nothing like you see farther south. From St. Ignace to Ironwood, Michigan is over three hundred miles and there are only six towns between those two cities. That means every town is roughly fifty miles apart with nothing but the Hiawatha National Forest in between. One time I drove through the U P and I would clock my mileage between towns."

"Why did you do that?"

"Because, Olivia, with no billboards and nothing but trees after going ten miles, it felt like you had driven thirty, and you wondered if you would ever get to the next town."

"I know Jesse complained about that as he drove through here on his way to the Island.

"It is hard to understand until you actually drive it, I guess. But now we are headed to Naubinway. It is the northernmost community on the Lake Michigan shoreline and the largest commercial fishing port on the Great Lakes in the U P. You all know they refer to this area as the U P, which stands for Upper Peninsula."

"Yes, when we worked here years ago, they always called the land above the 'mitt' of Michigan the U P," Olivia agreed.

"Naubinway was founded in 1873 and most of the current residents are descendants of the French Voyageurs and the Indians. It is only forty-two miles from St. Ignace and is one of the best natural harbors on the northern shore of Lake Michigan. Visitors to the town can purchase fish that has been caught locally directly off the dock. It doesn't get any fresher than that."

"I would love to stop and pick some up if I am ever in this area again."

"Actually we're going to stop today and buy some. Jonathan will be making fish for our lunch."

"That certainly sounds yummy," Ginger told everyone.

"He is an amazing cook and I don't think you will be disappointed. But to get back to my history lesson.

Because of the natural harbor, this was a perfect port for the lumber ships when the lumber boom was going on. But the lumber died out in the late 1800s so the settlers that stayed became fisherman."

Then he continued, "Don't expect to find any yachts in port today, except mine. They only have commercial fishing boats. Although Lake Michigan can get rough with fierce storms, they are nothing like you find on Lake Superior. But the boats here are enclosed for protection from high seas, wind and cold. And that is the end of my lecture."

"Thank you, Andy. As a former social studies teacher I love your history lessons."

Andy smiled at Olivia as the boat started moving closer to shore.

It wasn't too long until they tied up to the dock. Everyone left the boat since they were interested in watching what was going on and they all wanted to get out and walk on dry land again. Andy and Jonathan went to three different boats and the others could see them talking to the captains. Finally at the third boat, they nodded their heads and soon returned to the yacht with Jonathan carrying a large package.

"Looks like lunch has arrived," Dylan observed as they all climbed back aboard.

Before going to the kitchen to cook their meal the deckhand came around with ice tea and lemonade for everyone. The boat was untied and soon left the dock. They watched the shore recede as they smelled fish cooking.

It was an incredible lunch as Andy had promised. After they ate everyone went back out to the outside deck and enjoyed the ride back to the Island.

CHAPTER 58

Skipping the other fudge shops on the return, everyone was chatting happily as they walked up the hill from the marina.

"That was another wonderful day," Olivia told the others. "We have been so lucky with the weather and being out in the boat most of the day was really enjoyable. I'm sure glad Dylan ran into you, Andy."

"It's been fun for me, too. I have kept to myself, for the most part, for so long now that I forget how pleasurable it can be when you have friends around. I can't thank you all enough for including me in with your group."

They had already decided that they would spend their last night dressing up and going to the dining room for dinner and then to the Terrace Room for dancing. "We might as well take advantage of the hotel's amenities since we're leaving in the morning," Flynn observed.

"And just in time. There's a front coming through late tonight, and it is supposed to rain all day tomorrow. It will be a good day for driving home," Ginger added.

"We have been lucky. The cold front is supposed to last a few days. I told my Captain this afternoon I want to return to Chicago tomorrow. There is no point in traveling up to Lake Superior when it will be cold and wet for the next several days."

When they arrived at the cottage it was almost 4:00 p.m. so everyone went into their rooms to freshen up for dinner. While Olivia was showering the phone rang and Ginger went to answer it.

"Hi, Ginger. I hope I'm not bothering you."

"No, everyone is cleaning up for the evening, Neal."

"The reason I am phoning you is the Chief found some evidence related to Tess's murder in the stable here at the hotel. He wondered if you could come over for a few minutes and check it out."

"Right now?"

"Yes, he thought you might be able to identify the items."

"I guess I can come right now. Olivia is in the shower and I'm just waiting my turn."

Putting the phone back in the receiver she left a note for Olivia telling her the Chief wanted to see her at the stables. She told her friend she wouldn't be gone too long, and then she put the message on Olivia's nightstand. Finally, grabbing a sweater she left for the stables. As she walked on the road towards her destination Andy happened to be looking out his window.

That's odd he thought to himself. I wonder where Ginger is off to. I would think she would be getting ready for dinner. I will have to ask Flynn about it as soon as I finish showering. I didn't think he wanted her going anywhere alone.

It wasn't too much longer after that Olivia came out of the bathroom. The window in the room was slightly opened and she didn't notice the note because a breeze had blown the message onto the floor when she opened the bathroom door. Not seeing Ginger, she took her time putting on her makeup and getting dressed.

When she finished she realized it was getting late and knew Ginger needed to shower. She went to find out if her friend was sitting in the living room. Not seeing her there, she became apprehensive. Quickly going up the stairs, she looked in the unoccupied bedroom and media room. But both rooms were empty.

Walking back down the stairs she became even more uneasy that something might be wrong. She immediately went over to the men's room and knocked on the door.

Flynn, still in a bathrobe, answered the door. She could hear the shower running and assumed Dylan was in the bathroom.

"I can't find Ginger. Did she say anything to you about going somewhere?

"No. How long has it been since you saw here? I took a shower and I got out about twenty minutes ago. It seemed strange but I thought she was sitting in the living room for some reason. But I just checked and I can't find her anywhere. I even looked upstairs."

"Just a minute. I have to put some clothes on." He closed the door as he went back into his room and quickly put on a pair of jeans and a sweater. Knocking on the bathroom door, he told Dylan that Ginger was missing.

Coming out of the bedroom he asked Olivia if she had checked with Andy. Shaking her head "no" he hurriedly ran up the stairs. Olivia could hear him knocking on the door to Andy's room. A couple of minutes later he came back down the stairs.

"Andy saw her walking down the street. He thought it was odd but she seemed fine.
Let's check your room again, Olivia. I can't believe she would take off and not say something to you."

Looking around the room they saw nothing. Then walking to the nightstand on the other side of the bed, Flynn saw a piece of paper on the floor. Picking it up, he read the note.

"This says she had to meet the Chief at the stables for some reason. I have his cell. I'm going to call him and find out what's going on. She knows I didn't want her to go anywhere without me."

"I'm sure she is fine if she is meeting with the Chief."

"I don't know, Olivia, I have a bad feeling about this," Flynn said as he picked up his cell to call.

CHAPTER 59

When Ginger arrived at the stables no one was around. Going into the barn where the horses were kept, she yelled out for the Chief and Neal. From behind one of the stall doors, Neal came walking towards her.

"What's going on, Neal? Where's the Chief? I don't have a lot of time. I need to get back and get ready for dinner."

"The Chief isn't here," he said as he raised a gun towards her. "Don't move, Ginger, or I'll shoot you."

"Shoot. What are you talking about?"

"Don't act like you don't know what is going on."

"But I don't know what is happening. Where are Tess's items?"

"The thing is, Ginger, I really like you. You are one of the few people who was ever nice to me and didn't put me down. I hate to have to kill you but you ask way too many questions, and it's just a matter of time until you figure everything out."

All of a sudden it hit her that Neal must be the killer. She immediately realized that she had to try and stall him. Olivia would find her note and tell Flynn. She had to try and stay alive long enough for them to rescue her. And that meant getting him to talk about what he had done and why he had killed so many people. She only hoped he would want to talk about it.

"Neal, you're the killer?"

"Now you finally understand."

"But you can't possibly get away with this. If they find me dead, everyone on the Island will be questioned."

"So? Who is going to suspect me?"

"They'll take DNA samples from everyone."

"They don't have my DNA anywhere."

"If you're the killer they do. They found it on Bree and George."

"You're lying. I doubt very much you're telling the truth." He couldn't believe they would have found his DNA on the bodies from so long ago. But he had taken precautions to keep the bodies tightly sealed to keep them from being discovered. So maybe they did have his DNA like she said. I should have buried those bodies long ago he was thinking. Well it's too late now.

"No, I'm not lying. The Chief held that fact back so the murderer wouldn't run away."

"Then I will just have to leave sooner than I planned."

"Where will you go? Everyone will be looking for you."

"I have a little cabin deep in the woods in the U P. It isn't listed in my name so they will never find me. I usually spend my winters there. I have enough supplies to keep me going for months."

"If you're going to kill me, could you at least humor me for just a few more minutes?"

"I don't have much time. I have to go get the appetizers and take them to the cottage. Everyone will be pacing the floor worried about you, and I will pretend I know nothing is wrong. Then I will take the 8:00 p.m. ferry and be gone before they even find you. But, what do you want to know?"

She realized he was not reasoning normally. He didn't need to kill her; just tie her up until he got away. But at this point he saw killing her as his only option.

"Will you at least satisfy my curiosity before you shoot me and tell me why you did all those murders?" She was thinking his ego would relish recounting all his actions to someone and she was correct.

"I don't suppose it would hurt. After all, it would be nice if someone could appreciate how smart I am. I was listening outside the window after your lunch and heard you all speculating about the murders. You were certainly on the right track. You only got a couple of things wrong.

First of all, I did not kill Bree first. I was shadowing her, if you call watching in some bushes while she was in her bedroom, stalking. I asked her a couple of different times to go out with me. I knew she was seeing George because he worked at the same stables with me, and he was always talking about her."

Then he continued, "George kept trying to figure out who was pursuing her but she wouldn't tell him. I know I have a bad temper but George also had one. I realized she was worried what he might do if he found out it was me. That day of the killings, I had just gotten back to the stable after asking her out again. She was so mean to me and said I was no good and just a 'townie' and even if she wasn't seeing George she still wouldn't go out with me."

He paused for a minute and had a look on his face as if remembering that long ago day. "George was in the stable when I arrived. I don't know if he could tell from my demeanor or not but I immediately got the feeling he suspected me. He started asking me questions about Bree. I kept telling him I was not interested in his girlfriend but he kept pressing me. I don't know if it was our shouting or what but one of the horses in a stall started bucking. The yelling probably spooked the animal. George turned around to calm the horse down. I saw a pitchfork by the wall and I grabbed it and shoved it in his back. He was dead in a couple of minutes."

"Then what did you do?" she asked horrified, at what he was telling her.

"Luckily there was no one else around. All the help was eating dinner. I knew if George disappeared, Bree would never let it go, so I had to do something about her. I went back to where she was staying and told her George had gotten hurt. I knew she would follow me. When we got back to the stable she saw George lying on the floor and went running to him. When she bent over I put the pitchfork in her back, too."

"Then you took the bodies up to the loft?"

"Yes. I knew there were some old foot lockers up there and we always kept heavy plastic around. I wrapped them together, so they could hold each other for eternity, and stuffed them in the trunk. And there they have rested in peace for thirty-five years until you had to stick your nose into things."

"You didn't feel any remorse for what you did?"

"No, not really. All my life my father put me down and told me I was no good. When Bree started in on me, I guess I just snapped. I was sick and tired of being told that I was worthless."

"Did you kill Harper, too?"

"Yes. I got kind of lucky when no one suspected me with her husband taking out that big life insurance policy."

"But why did you kill her?"

"If she had just stayed away from here she would still be alive today. The problem was I didn't want her to link me with the disappearance of Bree and George. I knew everyone would be talking about it during the reunion and I worried something could jog her memory."

"In what way?"

"When I went back to get Bree, I ran into Harper on the street. She saw George's blood all over my pants and she asked me about it. I told her a horse had gotten hurt and I had gotten blood on my pants and I was going home to change. I know she believed me at the time but I worried she might remember that took place and I didn't want her suspicious of me. I thought it was safer just to get rid of her. I love working with the plants and help the gardeners a lot. So I knew about hemlock. I put some in her wine I served you at dinner that evening."

Oh my god, he is a maniac, Ginger was thinking. I sure hope someone gets here soon. I can't believe Olivia hasn't found my note yet.

"So what about Tess? I know when I talked to her she was suspicious of someone."

"She sought me out when the cocktail party was ending. She started asking questions and I knew she was starting to suspect me. I told her I was working with the Chief and had nothing to do with Harper dying."

He then continued, "I told her we had found something related to Harper's death down in the Secret Garden and if she met me there I could prove I was innocent. She was so stupid, she believed me. When she got there, she told me she was sure I had killed Bree and George and she was going to tell everyone. She didn't think I had anything to do with Harper's death which was her downfall. I pushed her down and when she was struggling to get up I strangled her and rolled her into the bushes. And now it's time. I hope you have said your goodbyes."

"Wait," she told him as she thought she heard a noise outside the door. "What about Riley? I don't understand where she fits in."

"She didn't suspect me of anything. I just hated that woman. She was always putting me down and treating me like a servant. She was even worse than Tess. I knew she was in the Medical Center because you told me when I asked during cocktails that one night. So I watched the place. I saw the Chief let the nurse go home and knew there was just one officer in there. When he left to go pick up her dinner I went inside and unlocked the door. I had helped out when they were refurbishing the place awhile back and the doctor had shown me where he kept a spare key in his drawer."

Ginger definitely heard movement from the other side of the room. She realized Neal was so wrapped up telling his story he didn't hear anything.

"So how did you get her to go with you?"

"It wasn't hard. I told her the Chief decided to let her go back to the hotel and they had fixed her a five course meal and were setting it up in her room. She is so gluttonous I knew she would follow me anywhere. I had the cart outside and she got in. When I went down Lakeside Drive she questioned me but I told her I had to stop and get some wild mushrooms for the restaurant."

"So that's how you got her into the bushes."

"Yes. She is another stupid person."

"But why did you take her there?"

"You were correct about it being tied to that old murder."

"But you weren't even born then."

"I wasn't. But when I was little, my mom and dad fought constantly. My mother told me she suspected my father of being the killer. Finally, when I was eight, she left and didn't take me with her. My father emotionally and physically abused me for years after she left. He kept saying he didn't kill that woman but he had a brutal temper.

And, since I hated Riley so intensely, I thought it would be fun to recreate the murder since I had heard so much about it. I didn't think she would be found for days, if at all. I was shocked that not only did you find her but she was still alive. Okay, that's enough explaining. Your time is up."

"Neal, put the gun down right now."

Looking up he saw the Chief pointing a weapon at him. Flynn was also standing there and some policemen were next to him.

"You will never take me alive," he said as he shot the pistol towards Ginger and the Chief. Luckily Ginger had just turned to look back and the bullet grazed her arm. The Chief and his officers shot their guns at the same time. Neal fell and was dead before he hit the ground.

Flynn went running over to where Ginger was standing.

Taking her in his arms he said, "I don't know what I would have done if something had happened to you." And then he learned over and kissed her passionately.

Flynn, held his sweater around her arm to stop the bleeding, and one of the officers helped her to the emergency vehicle.

"I'll take her to the Medical Center and then come back for the body, Chief."

Nodding, the policeman was so relieved that the case was finally solved. Now my Island can return to normal he thought as he looked down at Neal's body.

CHAPTER 60

Everyone was waiting in the cottage when Flynn returned with Ginger. Her arm was in a sling and they all surrounded her asking questions.

"Are you okay?"

"What happened?"

"Was Neal really the killer?

"Did the police put him in custody?"

"Hold it, hold it. Give her a chance to sit down and breathe," Flynn told them. He was wearing a gown from the Medical Center since his sweater had been used as a tourniquet. He immediately left for his room to get another sweater to wear.

"Are those appetizers over there? I think I am a little hungry and it looks like I am going to miss the dining room tonight."

"Ginger, I was so worried about you, especially after reading your note," Olivia said.

"I'm so sorry. Neal just sounded so realistic when he said the Chief wanted to see me. If I thought it through, I might have called the Chief back to double check."

Then she continued, "But all I was thinking was I needed to hurry so I could get back and get cleaned up for dinner. Flynn told me you found my note on the floor. I should have put it in a different place. It makes me shudder to think what might have happened if you hadn't found my message."

"Even if we hadn't found it, we would have called the police station. Flynn was frantic as to where you had gone. But finding that note definitely helped us find you quickly. You're right, though. If we hadn't discovered your note on the floor, Neal might have killed you before Flynn and the police found you," Olivia replied shivering at the thought.

"So tell us what happened before you get too sleepy. They told us they gave you pain medication for your arm. Did they have to operate to get the bullet out?"

"No, Olivia. Luckily I turned to look at Flynn just when Neal shot the gun and the bullet only grazed my arm. But it does hurt like heck although the medication is starting to help."

"Well, I hope you have given up thoughts of a new career pursuing killers," Dylan said with a twinkle in his eyes.

"I'll have to think about that," she said sleepily.

"Before you go to sleep, please give us the highlights and then Dylan, Andy and I are going over to the hotel for dinner before they close."

So Ginger told them what Neal had told her about killing Bree and George. They were horrified he had done that and felt no remorse. They were also shocked that he had killed Harper because she 'might' remember something.

"At least Jesse will have his name cleared and it sounds like he'll come into a bundle of money," Olivia said.

"Yes, especially if you call two million dollars a bundle," Flynn added as he came back out from his room wearing a sweater.

"I thought it was only a million," Olivia said.

"No. Since Harper was murdered, and Jesse had nothing to do with it, the double indemnity rider will kick in. When we were talking one day after Harper's murder, I asked him if he had added that rider and he told me he had. He said Harper had insisted on it because they sometimes travelled to dangerous places around the world."

"He sure got lucky."

"Yes, but it's also rather heartbreaking. He really loved Harper and he told me he had found the woman of his dreams in her. Now he has a lot of money and no one to share his life with. I have a feeling he will feel very lonely for a long time."

"Okay, now tell us quickly about Riley and Tess so we can go to dinner," Olivia cut in.

So Ginger told them about Tess suspecting he had killed Bree and George, but not Harper, and how he had lured her to the Secret Garden to murder her. She also disclosed his tormented relationship with his father and how his hatred for Riley made him try and replicate that long ago crime.

"Thank goodness he failed with that killing," Olivia chimed in. "I just hope Riley can survive her trauma."

"I think we all do. Now I'm getting tired and Flynn just ordered room service because he doesn't want to leave me to go to dinner with all of you. So I'll see all of you in the morning."

With that, the three of them left for the hotel just as a waiter was delivering their food.

"Just leave it on the table," Flynn told the man.

Sitting on the couch next to Ginger, he took her in his arms and held her as tight as he could watching out for her injured arm.

"Aren't you going to eat your dinner?"

"There will be time for that when you fall asleep. Right now, I just want to hold you and never let go. I see no more murders in your future," he said kissing her gently on her lips.

Smiling to herself, she wondered. But as she laid her head on his shoulder, she quickly fell asleep.

EPILOGOUE

It was now the week before Thanksgiving and two months had passed since they had left the Island. Riley had been in the Traverse City Hospital for two weeks when she finally started waking up. They had moved her to the University Hospital in Lansing not long after that where she stayed another three weeks. Her prognosis was excellent when they released her. She still had a sore throat but the doctors felt that would become less severe as time passed.

She lived in a condo in downtown Chicago and had hired a nursing assistant to help her until she felt strong enough to live on her own. There were a few flakes of snow in the air as Ginger and Flynn headed to see her. When they arrived the nursing assistant left to run some errands while they were visiting with her.

Hugging her, Ginger said, "You've lost some weight, Riley."

"Being in a coma will do that to you but I'm also eating more healthy and trying to lose some more. Besides losing weight, there is a psychologist who lives in my building and I have been seeing her a couple of times a week as I promised you."

"That's terrific. Do you remember what happened to you?"

"I can recall leaving with Neal to go back to the hotel. I remember going on a cart to get some wild mushrooms but after that everything is a blank. I really hope you'll fill me in on everything else."

So Ginger told her about why he had committed the murders and the attempted murder on her.

Finally having a serene look on her face from finding out the answers she said, "Thank you, Ginger for clearing that up. It means a lot. I owe you my life. They told me if you had not found me when you did, I wouldn't have made it. And I see you have added something to your left hand."

Blushing as she looked down at the ring on her finger, and nodding in agreement she replied, "There was so much death we dealt with that week, I am so happy we were able to save you."

"I appreciate you coming to see me and I hope you two will keep in touch."

Saying good-bye, Ginger and Flynn commented on how they felt Riley was actually going to turn her life around.

"She has been given a second chance and it looks like she's not going to throw it away this time."

"I can hardly believe we have been given a second chance, too, Ginger. Winning your love has been so amazing. There are days it takes my breath away to know we're back together. And I can hardly believe our luck. We no longer have to worry about the future when we have been given this wonderful gift of the present."

"The only thing that mars the joy we're experiencing is the fact that Jesse committed suicide. It just shows you money can't buy happiness. I guess he did love Harper much more deeply than we all realized. At least he used the money to set up a foundation to give college scholarships to journalists in Harper's name before he took those pills."

Then she continued. "He was so full of life when he was around Harper and loved travelling. I knew he was very depressed when he sent me that letter about the foundation. But I had no idea he was thinking of killing himself."

"Yes, that was very distressing. I'm glad they found your name and number among his effects. I know you didn't have to take care of the funeral arrangements but I'm happy you did. But, now for some good news. I didn't get a chance to tell you but Andy called me. He wanted to know about our wedding. I told him we had not made any serious plans yet. He was really pleased because he had an idea."

"I hope he doesn't want to go back to Mackinac Island. Someday I will probably want to return there, because that is where we found each other again. But I'm not ready too soon."

"No, he thought your daughter and my son and Olivia and Dylan might like to go on his boat up to Bois Blanc Island. Remember the big island behind Mackinac Island? He was thinking that B & B, Insel Haus, with all the antiques and room for twenty people would make a great location for a wedding. He said there would be room for any other wedding guests who wanted to drive or fly up there to be with us for the occasion. He felt it might be a good idea to just rent the whole place for a few days. And, after our children and the other guests go home, he wanted Olivia, Dylan, and you and me to continue our journey on his boat up to Lake Superior."

"That does sounds like a great idea and going on the yacht would be a fun thing to do for our honeymoon. I don't need to go someplace alone with you. Having friends around to celebrate with would be enjoyable, too. Hopefully, we wouldn't run into any dead bodies on that adventure. You know I am always offering to plan things but somehow you men always end up doing it instead," she said laughing. "But don't get me wrong. I love your ideas."

"There also might be a sixth person with us. Andy told me he has reconnected with a woman he knew as a kid, when they were growing up. They both want to take their relationship real slow but he thinks it might develop into something meaningful. He said being with all of us in September made him realize he was lonely and needed a friend."

"That would be great. I like being around Andy a lot. It had to be hard for him always feeling like the odd man out with no partner when he was with us on the Island. Now, let's hurry or we'll be late for our get together with Dylan and Olivia. We have our after Christmas vacation to plan with them. I still like the idea of winter in Yellowstone."

As they walked to their car, he pulled her into his arms and said "I am so lucky. This is forever." And, then standing on the street as onlookers walked by, he kissed her passionately.

Made in the USA
Middletown, DE
19 September 2021

48493460R00215